STANFORD WONG

WITH HIS OWN

FLUNKS BIG-TIME

BY LISA YEE

SCHOLASTIC INC.

NEW YORK TORONTO LONDON AUCKLAND SYDNEY
MEXICO CITY NEW DELHI HONG KONG BUENOS AIRES

No part of this publication may be reproduced, stored in a retrieval system, or transmitted
in any form or by any means, electronic, mechanical, photocopying, recording, or otherwise,
without written permission of the publisher. For information regarding permission, write to
Scholastic Inc., Attention: Permissions Department, 557 Broadway, New York, NY 10012.

Text copyright © 2005 by Lisa Yee. All rights reserved. Published by Scholastic Inc.
SCHOLASTIC, APPLE PAPERBACKS, the LANTERN LOGO, and associated logos
are trademarks and/or registered trademarks of Scholastic Inc.

ISBN-13: 978-0-439-62248-6
ISBN-10: 0-439-62248-4

Arthur A. Levine Books hardcover edition designed by Elizabeth B. Parisi,
published by Arthur A. Levine Books, an imprint of Scholastic Inc., October 2005.

12 11 10 9   10 11 12/0

Printed in the U.S.A.   40

This edition first printing, April 2007

TO MY DAD, WHO LOVES TO PLAY BASKETBALL,
AND TO THE REST OF THE GUYS ON MY TEAM —
SCOTT, BENNY, ROGER, AND HENRY
—L.Y.

AT AGE ELEVEN, MY DAUGHTER, KATE, WAS CONVINCED THAT
ALL BOYS WERE STUPID AND SMELLY AND HAD NO REDEEMING
QUALITIES. I WROTE THIS BOOK TO SHOW HER
THE OTHER SIDE OF THE STORY.

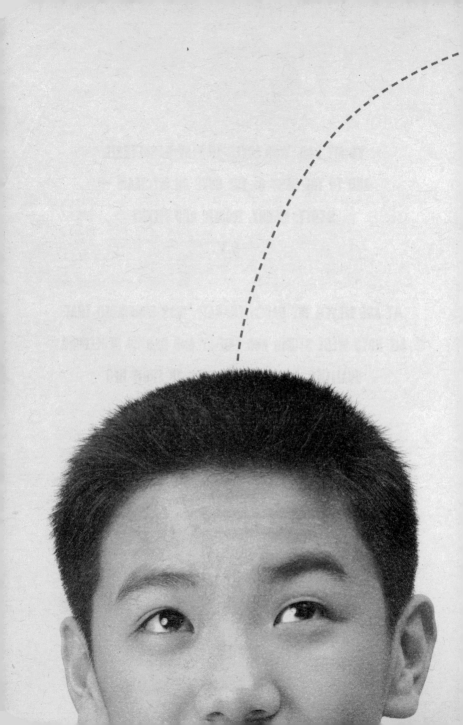

JUNE 7, 1:40 P.M.

Today's the last day of school, the only school day that I look forward to. I grab my basketball and head to Mr. Glick's class. Once I make it through that I'm *free* for the entire summer. Good-bye, school — *hello,* camp!!!

It takes a while to make it down the hallway.

"Stanford, way to go!"

"Congratulations, Stanford!"

"Have a great summer, Stanford!"

"Stanford, send me a postcard!"

I'm grinning and waving and *crash!*

"You okay?" I ask. *Star Trek* action figures lay scattered on the ground.

"I'm fine," the boy sputters.

We face each other. It's Marley. We both redden. I step on Captain Jean-Luc Picard as I back away. Marley raises his hand to me and parts his middle and ring fingers in the Vulcan salute. *Gotta get out of here.* I take off running.

I spot Stretch heading toward me and slow down. He doesn't say anything, but from the way he's drumming every locker I can tell he's happy school will be over soon. We take our seats in the back of the room and I brace myself for my final boring day of sixth-grade English.

As Mr. Glick blabbers on, my eyelids get heavy. Soon I'm seeing myself, Stanford Andrew Wong, as a starter on the Rancho Rosetta Middle School Basketball A-Team. I flash forward two weeks when I'll be on center court at Alan Scott's Basketball Camp in the San Gabriel Mountains, "Where basketball is not just a game, it's a way of life." I get chills every time I read the brochure.

During the last three days of camp, Alan Scott himself comes in to coach. He's this season's top NBA scorer. Everything about him is cool, from his spiked hair right down to his Alan Scott BK620 basketball shoes. At the end of camp he presents each basketball player with his own personally autographed pair of BK620s. I can't wait to get mine. I close my eyes and imagine me and the man shooting hoops. I can hear Alan Scott now: "Hey, Stanford, great layup!" Or, "Stanford, a one-handed reverse triple-loop crosscourt slam dunk? You're amazing!" Or, "Stanford Wong, snap out of it!!!"

Huh? What's that? Why is Mr. Glick glaring at me?

"Stanford Wong, snap out of it!" he booms. Does he have to be so loud? "Put the basketball down. I'd like you to stay after class. There's something important we need to discuss."

Uh-oh. He's holding my final book report and he doesn't look happy.

The bell rings. Mr. Glick makes his way toward me as kids stream in the opposite direction, pushing toward the door. Toward summer. Toward freedom.

Why am I still here?

The room clears out fast. My desk feels like an anchor wrapped around me. I am sinking. Mr. Glick slides the report toward me, facedown. I lift up the corner, then slowly turn it over. All I see is red, like the paper is bleeding.

"An F," Mr. Glick says. "Not a C, not a D — you got an F. Stanford, I expect you to show this to your parents. They need to sign it and get it back to me within three days."

I try to leave, but Mr. Glick is not finished with me yet. "Young man, wait one minute. This is not something you can shrug off. This is serious business. If you don't do something about your grade this summer, you won't make it to the seventh grade. Do you understand?"

Mr. Glick is staring at me. We are standing face-to-face. He's not that much taller than I am. I'll bet I could take him down.

"Stanford," Mr. Glick says, unblinking. "Do you understand?"

"An F." My voice is flat. "I get it."

I grab my book report and tear out of the room. I'm supposed to meet the Roadrunners at Burger Barn, but I run in the opposite direction. I run past the park and through the empty lot. I run over the bridge and toward the train tracks. I run as far away from school as I can and only stop when my lungs are about to explode. Panting, I drop to my knees and uncrumple my report. The paper looks blurry, yet one thing is clear — the big fat F scrawled on the page.

JUNE 9, 7:16 P.M.

These past couple of days I've been at the top of my game. All the Roadrunners say so. I hope they remember that when I'm dead, because in about two minutes my father's going to kill me. I can already see my tombstone:

STANFORD A. WONG
Loving Son
Great Basketball Player
Rotten Student

My parents are in the kitchen. Mom's rearranging the utensils as Dad talks about work. Here goes nothing. I rush in, hand my father my book report, and pivot around to make a fast exit.

"Stanford, come back here this instant!" Dad is gripping my paper. "An F? Stanford, you got an F? This is not acceptable!" I am frozen and on fire at the same time. "What's the matter with you? Do you want to explain to me why you got an F?"

I don't want to explain anything. I want out of here.

"I've put up with a lot from you, Stanford, but an F crosses the line."

I glance at my mom. She looks as upset as I am. I stare at the floor as my dad goes on and on and, ". . . now that you won't be going to basketball camp, you'll have the whole summer to raise your grade."

What???!!! I jerk my head up. "No fair! Coach had to pull strings to get me a spot. Only the top players go to Alan Scott's Basketball Camp."

"Flunking this class means you could flunk sixth grade."

"If I go to camp I'll be the best player Rancho Rosetta's ever seen."

"You need to study more."

"Basketball camp is the only thing I've ever wanted."

"If you had studied, this wouldn't have happened."

"I have to go to camp!" I insist.

"Stanford, listen to me: You are not going to basketball camp and that's final!"

"Mommm!" My mother knows how much this camp means to me. She's been to my games. She's heard the cheers. Mom just shakes her head.

As my dad continues to shout, my grandmother, Yin-Yin, peeks in from behind the door and then disappears. I look at Mom as she turns away from Dad. My mother hates it when my father yells. I've heard him tell her, "Raising my voice is the only way I can get that boy to pay attention to me."

He's wrong about that.

"I have to go to camp," I plead. "I'm on the A-Team. Everyone's counting on me!"

"Well, they can stop counting," Dad says. "I'm going to call your English teacher and get to the bottom of this."

5

My father leaves the room. My mother puts dinner in front of me. Fried chicken, my third-favorite food. I can't eat, so instead I try to listen to my dad yelling at Mr. Glick. All I hear is a lot of nothing. Maybe Dad's using his low voice on him. His low voice is even scarier than his yelling.

Wait! He's coming back and he looks pleased. I wonder if Mr. Glick changed his mind about flunking me. Or maybe Mr. Glick made a mistake and I didn't flunk after all.

"It's settled," my father says, smiling.

Suddenly I am starving. I pick up a drumstick and tear into it. "Well, I'm glad that's over," I tell him. "Thanks, Dad."

"Stanford." His voice is serious. "I talked Mr. Glick into taking you in his summer-school class. You'll start on Wednesday."

"Summer school?" I try not to choke on my chicken. "Summer school?"

"Mr. Glick said you hardly ever handed in your homework and that you never paid attention in class."

"And you believed him?"

"Yes."

My dad believes everything teachers tell him.

"Wha . . . what about basketball camp?"

"I told you. There isn't going to be any basketball camp. You're lucky Mr. Glick agreed to take you for summer school." Dad picks up a piece of chicken and salts it. "I hope it's not too late to get a refund from camp."

Then it hits me. No camp? School all summer long? Whoaaa . . . this is way, way too much to take in. "Mommmmm," I yell. *Mom!* My mother rushes to my side. "Dad says I have to go to summer school. He says there's not going to be any basketball camp."

She looks at Dad. He gives her a little nod. He's trying to hypnotize her! "Stanford, your father is right," she says. "I'm sorry, but school comes first. Maybe you can go to camp next year."

He did hypnotize her! They never see things the same way, and suddenly they're ganging up on me. I push my chair away from the table, grab my basketball, and run out, slamming the door behind me.

11:57 P.M.

I'm drenched. I am at the park playing hard, weaving in and out of the twenty guys guarding me from every angle. Only there's no one on the court but me. Water is pouring down my face, but it's not tears, it's just sweat. Athletes don't cry.

When I was little I used to cry a lot. I wasn't good at anything. I couldn't even spell my own name. I was always in the lowest reading group, and whenever we had partners on class projects I'd hear: "Aw, why do I have to be stuck with Stanford?"

Basketball saved me.

No matter what else was happening at recess, I was always drawn to the basketball court. Different groups of guys played all the time. Every morning I went to school praying I'd be invited to join them. Every afternoon I went home depressed.

Finally one day I took a giant gulp of air, then asked, "Can I play?"

The world stopped until Trevor, the best player on the playground, spoke up: "Sorry, loser, but you have to be good to play on this court." Laughing, the boys gave each other high fives and went back to their game.

I started running and swore never ever, ever, to go back.

But I couldn't stay away. It was as if basketball was in my blood. One week later, there I was, first watching from a distance, each day getting closer and closer. I watched how the guys shot the ball. I studied how they guarded each other. I memorized the moves.

At night my mom would quiz me, "How's school?"

"Fine," I'd mumble.

"Not so fine according to your grades," my father would say.

I couldn't win. Not at home. Not in class. Not on the court.

"Can I play?"

"No."

"Can I play?"

"No."

"Can I play?"

"Give up." Marley was standing next to me. "They're never going to let you in."

Marley and I were friends by default since we both sat at the reject table in the cafeteria. He was wearing his Mr. Spock shirt. Marley always wore Spock on Tuesdays and Scotty on Wednesdays. Just the week before I had buried all my *Star Trek* T-shirts in a bottom drawer along with my Trekkie trading cards and Klingon Battle Cruiser. The only thing I couldn't bear to hide was my 1988 *Next Generation* Galoob Phaser. I still have it.

"Do you want to come over after school?" Marley asked. "I'm still working on my model of the *Voyager*. Did you ever finish your Stargazer?"

Trevor glanced our way and snickered. I braced myself and then said in a loud voice, "*Star Trek*? Are you still playing with *Star Trek* stuff? That's only for geeks!"

Marley looked right at me. "What's going on, Stanford? Why are you acting like this?"

I turned away, unable to face him.

"This is mutiny, mister," he muttered, quoting episode twenty-five of the original series.

After that I wasn't welcome at the reject table. I wasn't welcome anywhere.

A few days later my grandmother asked me to come over to her house. "Stanford," she said as we ate *shu mai* in her kitchen, "I know you're having a hard time at school, but it doesn't have to be that way. Here." She held up a black leather cord with a bright green stone dangling from it. "This is for you. For good luck."

Yin-Yin explained that the stone was from the fabled Hengshang Mountain, one of China's Five Famous Mountains. A group of monks trekked there to fetch the jade, and the eldest monk carved it under the moonlight so that it would be infused with the magical rays. "Then," she said, "while I was visiting the Great Wall, the eldest monk personally presented the pendant to me."

I protested. What kind of boy wears a necklace? "Wear it for a week," Yin-Yin insisted. "After that, if it doesn't change your luck, you can do with it what you want."

The next day, I went out to the court again. There was a new group playing basketball.

"Can I play?" I asked, already turning around to leave.

To my surprise, a freckle-faced kid said, "Give him the ball. Let's see if he can even get it near the hoop. It'll be good for a laugh."

"Jeez, he's a waste of time," Trevor groaned. "He's just a dork."

Someone handed me the ball anyway. "Good luck," a boy with dark curly hair whispered.

Jaws dropped when I shot the basketball. It sailed through the hoop and I heard the most beautiful sound in the world: *whoosh*.

"Bet you can't do that again!"

At first everybody thought my free throws were a fluke, including me. But when it became clear that not only could I make free throws, I could dribble, I could block, I could score impossible shots, the other boys stopped ignoring me. Instead they started asking me to play basketball.

Then Digger invited me to join the Roadrunners with him, Stretch, Tico, and Gus. They were okay before me; they won with me. We took the Parks and Rec title three consecutive times. I was league MVP three times. I moved from the reject corner of the cafeteria to the popular table. I got taller and stronger.

Basketball's big in Rancho Rosetta. Even before I started middle school last year, people knew who I was. I was the leading scorer for my school's B-Team, breaking the league record. I got my picture in the newspaper. I was unstoppable. Everyone's forgotten that I used to be a nobody. Everyone but me and Marley.

My mother drives up to the park. She rolls down the car window. "Stanford, time to go home."

I make one last basket. An amazing jump shot. The kind of jump shot that made Alan Scott famous.

It is quiet in the car. The radio is on, but the volume is way down low so I can only hear murmurs. It sounds like people drowning. My mother doesn't seem to notice. She is just staring straight ahead. I was afraid she would be angry, but she's not. She seems tired. It's hard to figure her out. Sometimes I get in trouble for just being alive. But here, it's almost midnight and she doesn't even blink.

"Stanford," Mom says, "you owe it to Coach Martin to tell him you won't be going to basketball camp."

"Do I have to?"

She gives me that look.

As we near our house, I ask, "Do you hate me because I'm stupid?"

Through the living room window I can see my dad pacing. Mom doesn't answer. Instead, she keeps driving until we're on the next block. Carefully she parallel parks the car but leaves the engine running. "Honey, I don't hate you, and you're not stupid. Grades aren't everything."

"Dad thinks so," I mutter.

She sighs. "Yes, well, they are important to him. But as long as you are doing your best, I'll be happy." Mom pauses. "Stanford, did you do your best in Mr. Glick's class?"

I think about it. I think about the books I didn't read. I think about the homework I didn't turn in. I think about how I skipped class to play basketball. . . .

My mother is waiting for my reply. I take a deep breath. "Yes," I tell her. "I did my best."

"Is that true?"

"Yes," I mumble.

"All right then," she says. Mom doesn't look at me. Instead, she puts on her blinker and eases the car back onto the road.

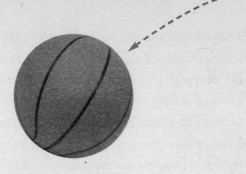

JUNE 11, 10:07 A.M.

Summer classes don't start until tomorrow, so why are lots of teachers at school today? Don't they have a life? If I didn't have to be at school, I'd be as far away from it as I could. I'd be at the North Pole. I'd be on Mars. I'd be at basketball camp.

Coach Martin is in the gym. My throat tightens. It was Coach who told my parents about Alan Scott's camp in the first place. He even came to our house to convince them. While my father sized him up, my mother passed him a plate of fancy cookies, the kind she saves for company. Coach is a big guy, but he looked small in our living room. I could tell he felt awkward around my parents. I feel that way sometimes.

"The program would really benefit a great player like Stanford," Coach said as he perched on the edge of the couch. "A basketball camp of this caliber will give him an edge to his game."

Two days later, I got the good news. I was going to camp! If Coach hadn't come to the house, if he hadn't thought it was important, there's no way my parents would have let me go. He delivered for me.

Now Coach Martin is counting volleyballs. Even though

there are no kids around, he's wearing his whistle. Without even looking up, Coach asks, "Stanford, are you here to talk to me?"

Do all teachers have eyes in the back of their heads?

I come out from behind the bleachers. Coach walks over and we sit down and face the empty court. Just last week at closing assembly, he announced the A-Team lineup for next year. Coach Martin leaned into the microphone and said, "It's rare to have a seventh grader on the A-Team, but our final player has proven himself. How can we lose with Stanford Wong on the team?"

As I touched my good-luck charm in thanks, a roar went up in the gym. Stretch started punching me in the arm as Gus and Tico leaped up and began chanting, "Stan-ford! Stan-ford!" Trevor shook my hand and said, "Welcome aboard the A-Team."

Now there's a volleyball rolling around the free-throw line. It looks out of place.

"I failed English," I mumble.

"I know," he says.

"You know?" *How does he know this?* "I'm going to summer school," I tell him. I must not cry. I'd be such a sissy if I cried. I stare straight ahead and don't blink. My words run together: "I'm not going to basketball camp."

There, I've said it. I wonder if he's going to get mad at me. Coach doesn't say anything. I hate it when grown-ups are silent. It means that whatever they are going to say next is bad.

Finally he speaks. "I know how important the team is to you, Stanford. You have a natural talent, something special that I don't see very often. But Stanford, school comes first." *What, was he talking to my mom?* "It's important that you do well in summer school." Coach pauses. "I hate to have to tell you this, but if you fail, you're off the team."

If you fail, you're off the team.

"What about the B-Team?" I plead. "Can I still be on the B-Team?"

He shakes his head.

"Can I at least be on the C-Team?"

"Listen, Stanford, you don't belong on the C-Team or the B-Team. You've earned your spot as an A-Team player. We need you and I want to see you out on the court when we kick off the school year with the Hee-Haw Game. But you have to have the grades. Stanford, if you don't pass your summer school class you won't move up to the seventh grade, and that's instant disqualification for any school sport."

"I know," I mutter. I don't want to hear any more.

As I leave, Coach Martin scoops up the wayward volleyball and puts it with the others. "Stanford, wait!" he yells after me. I turn around. "Call me if you ever need someone to talk to."

Coach Martin gives me his phone number.

I write it on my shoe.

12:22 P.M.

If you fail, you're off the team.
    If you fail, you're off the team.
    If you fail, you're off the team.
    Coach only said it once, but it sounded like a thousand times, a million times. A zillion times.

If you fail, you're off the team.

I can't fail that stupid English class. If I fail that, I fail the sixth grade and I'm off the A-Team. And if I'm off the team, I might as well be dead. Dead and buried. Six feet under with worms eating my eyeballs.

"Fries with that?"

"Huh? Oh. Yeah, sure. Fries."

"Next!" the Burger Barn lady yells.

"She should be nicer to you," a voice says.

I turn around and see two guys who were in my P.E. class. "Tell her you're going to take Rancho Rosetta to the championship!" Joey exclaims.

"Yeah," says the other boy. "Now that Stanford Wong's on the A-Team we've got the title locked up!"

I thank them and then consider hurling myself off a cliff. Great. If I don't pass English, I'm going to let the whole school down.

Last year, I ate five Barnstormers on a dare. I threw up the last one, so Gus claims that it was really only four. Today I can barely finish my first hamburger.

I'm supposed to meet the Roadrunners at the park at 1:30. Except for me, of course, all the Roadrunners will be B-Team starters next year, even Tico. "We're going to be the number-one most popular seventh-grade group at school," according to Digger. Already kids offer to let me cut in line in the cafeteria, and if someone's sitting at the Roadrunners table and sees us coming, they get up and leave. I remember when I used to do that for the popular kids.

A lot of girls look at us and a lot of guys look up to us. I think the real reason we're popular is because we all play basketball and because Stretch could pass for a model or a movie star. Besides, the really popular guys are the football players.

Well, it's not going to matter anymore anyway. Once I tell the Roadrunners I'm a failure, it'll be back to the reject table for me.

2:10 P.M.

Digger and Stretch are practicing passing the ball to each other. They miss every time. Both are wearing paper bags over their heads.

On the other end of the court Gus is shouting, "You are so wrong! Snots are hard, boogers are soft!"

"Excuuuuse me," Tico protests. "But boogers are hard and snots are soft. Look it up!"

Tico and Gus have been having the same argument for years.

Stretch and Digger give up passing the ball after Digger gets hit in the face.

"Where have you been?" Digger asks, holding his nose. "You're late!"

"He's not that late," Tico pipes up.

It's brave of Tico to stick up for me. Even though he has lots of freckles and funny red hair, Digger can make himself look pretty scary. I'll never forget when I was eight and shooting hoops by myself after school. Some big kid came by and tried to take my ball.

Out of nowhere, Digger appeared and frightened the kid away by screaming like a maniac and threatening to get him kicked out of school for stealing. When I tried to thank Digger, he said,

"You owe me one. Don't ever forget that." Then Digger said the words that changed my life.

"Say, you're pretty good at basketball. Do you want to join my team?"

We've been friends ever since. He's the reason I'm a Roadrunner. He's the reason any of us are. Digger's dad is Don Ronster of Ronster's Monster RV World. He sponsored our Parks and Rec team and named it the Roadrunners because at the end of all of his television commercials, a cartoon roadrunner gets flattened by a giant recreational vehicle.

"Hey, guys, I have something to tell you," I say.

"Whassup?" Gus asks. He drops a beetle in Tico's hair, but Tico doesn't notice.

I take a deep breath and blurt out, "I'm not going to camp."

There is total silence.

Gus looks like he's been slapped in the face. "Stanford, you've got to go. You'd be nuts not to."

"Then I guess I'm nuts," I mutter.

"Why aren't you going?" Tico asks. He starts swatting himself in the head.

Do I tell them I am a total loser and failed English and might even flunk the sixth grade? Do I tell them that I might not even be on the basketball team, *any* basketball team? Not even the girls' basketball team! *Loser, loser, loser,* there might as well be a big sign over my head that says LOSER.

The guys are waiting for me to say something. I open my mouth and start slowly. "My dad says I can't go to camp because —"

"I knew it!" Digger cuts in. "Your dad doesn't want you to

have any fun, does he? Is it your grades? Remember last year when my dad grounded me for a month because of one stupid D?"

"Was it Glick?" Tico wonders. "I heard that one time he flunked an entire class."

"You didn't flunk, did you?" Gus sounds shocked.

"Noooo. . . ." They're all staring at me. Before I know it, I blurt out, "I got an A."

"Really?" Gus says. "Glick gave you an A? That's awesome."

"Yeah." Tico whistles. "I got a B from Glick and thought that was a miracle."

Stretch gives me a funny look. I turn away.

Gus grows serious. "Then it's got to be the money. Everyone knows that Alan Scott's Basketball Camp's like the most expensive one in the universe."

Tico slaps me so hard on the back that I almost fall down. "Don't worry, Stanford. We'll have our own camp, and we'll only charge half of what you were going to pay the pros." He lowers his voice. "Attention, Stanford Wong, Roadrunners camp will commence first thing tomorrow morning."

"Oh, right," Digger scoffs. "We'll just work our entire summer around the all-important Stanford Wong. We'll all get up early so that Boy Wonder can get his practice in."

"I can't play in the morning," Gus grumbles. "I've got a summer job mowing lawns."

"I can't either," I say. "I have a summer job too." The guys turn from Gus to me. I start to panic. "My dad says —"

Digger cuts me off. "Oh man, not your dad again? What does he want from you now?"

"He wants me to work for him," I begin. "My dad really

needs me to help him out at the office. He says he wants to see more of me this summer."

"Does his office have good snacks?" asks Tico. "At my mom's work they always have a lot of good stuff there. One time I went to visit her and they had three kinds of cake in the break room."

Digger gets close. His breath smells like licorice. "I can't believe your dad would pull you out of Alan Scott's camp and make you work. That's a bummer. So besides being good at basketball, I guess we've got idiot dads in common."

I wince. My dad's not an idiot. Even though Digger's always dissing his dad, Mr. Ronster is good to us. He has all our Roadrunners Parks and Rec trophies and photos on display in a special case in his showroom. We don't play for Parks and Rec anymore, but he still springs for Roadrunners T-shirts and takes us to at least one Laker game every season. We all pile into one of his RVs, and Mr. Ronster always invites me to sit up front with him.

Digger's dad went to every one of our B-Team games last year and cheered so loud whenever I made a basket that he always lost his voice. He says he's my "number-one fan."

My dad's never even been to one of my games.

I break away from the guys and head for the hoop. Stretch picks up my signal and passes me the ball. Energized, I leap into the air as my arms reach up and my hands release the basketball — it floats across the court and then *whoosh!*, clean through the basket. I'm flying high until Digger shouts, "Stanford, you were out-of-bounds," and I come crashing back down.

6:05 P.M.

I'm not sure if he's trying to be funny or mean or what, but my father has posted my book report on the refrigerator. He made a copy of it before signing it and returning it to Mr. Glick. Now every time I get something to eat, I have to look at the big fat F and it makes me lose my appetite. Hey, now there's an idea: the Stanford Is Stupid Diet. With my grades, it has the potential to make millions of dollars. Maybe I won't have to go to college!

HOLES BOOKREPORT
BY STANFORD A. WONG

Holes is a book. It was writen by a writer. It has 233 pages and no pictures. It is about many things. Many things happen in the book. There is a hole in the book and the book is about a hole. There are many chapteers about this hole and it is very impeortant hole to have a book writen about it.

(F)

Stanford, did you even attempt to read the book????

As I grab a bottle of water I hear Mom ask, "Yin-Yin, have you seen the Hamburger Helper?"

Yin-Yin answers sweetly, "Kristen, I have no idea where your groceries ran off to. Perhaps you ought to keep a better eye on them."

"What are you saying? That I cannot even manage to keep track of the groceries?"

"I didn't say that," my grandmother replies. "You did."

My mom is slamming all the cabinet doors as Yin-Yin rearranges the utensils. They used to be really close, but that was before Yin-Yin moved in with us last fall. She was supposed to move into Vacation Village. That's the lame name of the old-people's home. But there was some mix-up and she couldn't get in right away. So she's here until they have an opening, which I think means she has to wait for someone to croak.

Dad insists that everything worked out great, because my sister had just started college and suddenly we had a spare room. He didn't even ask Sarah or Mom or Yin-Yin if it was okay. One day he just moved my grandmother's stuff in with my sister's. I'll bet Yin-Yin is the only old person with a purple beanbag chair in her room, a poster of Mongo Bongo on the wall, and a green Lava Lamp next to her bed.

After a while Mom had to start working part-time instead of full-time to keep an eye on my grandmother. Sometimes Yin-Yin gets in trouble. She forgets things. She's been known to salute the mailman and put clean dishes in the oven. One time she set a doggie dish filled with dog biscuits on our front porch.

"But we don't have a dog!" Mom sounded more exasperated than usual.

"That's what you think," Yin-Yin told her.

Lately our kitchen has turned into a dim-sum factory, something my mother is not pleased with. I don't think she would mind so much, except that Yin-Yin is always following her around saying things like, "Another frozen entrée? Interesting."

I'm glad that Yin-Yin's living with us. I sort of miss Sarah, though I'd never tell her that. She's already so conceited, I'm surprised her head hasn't popped. My sister skipped a grade, got all A's, played the flute, volunteered at the animal shelter on Saturdays, and delivered meals to old people on Sundays. Sarah barely has time to visit us this summer. She works at the college bookstore, and after the Fourth of July she's going to sail around the world and take classes on a ship. Sarah didn't even have to ask twice. Dad just whipped out his checkbook and paid for it. Everything my sister does impresses him. I'll bet if she picked her nose and made a bunny statue out of boogers, he'd think it was terrific. Sarah's going to be a lawyer just like Dad. Maybe they can sue each other.

My father misses dinner again. We have sandwiches because Mom never did find the Hamburger Helper. Now she's rinsing the dishes before she puts them in the dishwasher. Dad says that's unnecessary, but she does it anyway.

The television's blasting. I join Yin-Yin on the couch as she watches her game show and yells out the answers to the people on TV. She has always wanted to win "A *NEW CAR!*"

Top Cop's up next. During a commercial, Yin-Yin pats my knee. "Stanford, did I ever tell you that I once considered becoming a policewoman?"

Wow, that's hard to believe. My grandmother a cop? But then, Yin-Yin's been full of surprises lately. "You'd sure give Top Cop some competition!" I tell her.

Yin-Yin and I burst out laughing. I see Mom standing in the doorway wiping her hands on a towel. She turns and goes back into the kitchen.

Top Cop's a rerun. As he interrogates a murder suspect, I let out a huge sigh that's been building all day.

"School?" Yin-Yin asks. She's seen the refrigerator.

I nod.

"Feeling bad?"

I nod again.

"I have just what you need."

Yin-Yin leaves the room. As I wait for her to come back, I watch a commercial where a cat is dancing. How do they get those cats to do that? I tried to get the neighbor's cat to dance, but it wouldn't cooperate. Now it runs away whenever it sees me.

My grandmother returns carrying a big blue box. It's not dim sum, which surprises me. Her answer to everything is dim sum: turnip cakes, dumplings, spring rolls, *shu mai* . . . Whenever my parents fight, she pushes dim sum at them and won't leave until they're both eating. "They can't fight if their mouths are full," is her theory.

As if she's reading my mind, Yin-Yin says, "*Dim sum* means 'to touch the heart.' But for stress like yours, you need this." She places the box on my lap.

I look down. She is right, of course. I lift the lid and reach inside for my needles and yarn. Other than basketball, knitting is the only thing that calms me down. If the Roadrunners ever found out, I'd be dead meat.

So here we are, just Yin-Yin and me. We don't talk. Instead, she yells at the television and I knit.

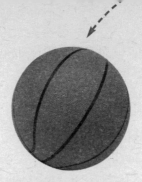

JUNE 12, 7:31 A.M.

What's wrong with this picture? It's summer and I'm up early. I'd rather be sleeping. Or playing basketball. Or hitting myself on the head with a brick. Anything other than starting summer school.

I get down to the kitchen in time to be with Dad. He's grumpy and Mom's all stressed-out again. "But you missed dinner four times last week," she's saying as she grips the coffeepot. "We hardly ever see you."

Dad's jaw tenses. "You know I'm up for a promotion." My father works for Calvin Benjamin Jacobs, the big law firm. "This Alderson case could make or break my career. You have no idea how much this means to me."

I have no idea what he is talking about.

My mother mutters something, then accidentally misses Dad's cup.

"Kristen!" he exclaims, shaking the coffee off his hand.

"Oops," says Mom.

"I'm out of here," Dad announces as he gets up.

Mom storms upstairs. She is still holding the coffeepot.

I remember the first time I tried coffee. It was a few years ago.

My dad was eating breakfast and reading the paper, like he always does on Sunday. I was looking at the paper too, only I wasn't really reading. I was just pretending.

"What's it like?" I asked.

"What's what like?"

"The coffee, it smells really good."

Dad whispered, "Is she around?" I knew he was talking about my mom. I shook my head. "Then come here."

I moved closer and he handed me his coffee cup. As I brought it to my lips, the smell was so strong I could practically taste the coffee. Cautiously, I took a sip.

Urgggggg!!!! It was all I could do to keep from spitting it out. It was like drinking hot gutter water!

My father laughed. "It takes some getting used to."

"No, no," I protested. "It's great. Really, it's great." And with my dad, it was. After that, whenever my father took his first sip of coffee in the morning, he'd raise his cup to me and wink.

He hasn't raised his cup to me in a long time.

Mom comes back in after Dad is gone. "Stanford, have you seen the Wheaties?" she asks, looking in the cupboards. "Yin-Yin, did you finish up the Lucky Charms?"

Yin-Yin just smiles mysteriously.

We usually have at least four kinds of cereal. Today there are none. For breakfast I make a cookie sandwich using Nutter Butters on the outside and an Oreo on the inside. After my fourth one, Mom musses up my hair. "Stanford, no sense in prolonging the inevitable. Off to summer school!"

I hate it when people touch my hair. I head to the bathroom to repair the damage. Sarah left a bunch of hair stuff the last time she was home. I try the mousse, but it's too pouffy. Mousse may look like whipped cream, but it tastes nothing like it. Don't be fooled. What's this gel gunk? It feels creepy/good. After slicking my hair, I practice my "cool dude" smile in the mirror.

"Stanford," my mother calls out. "What's taking you so long? You're going to be late."

The smile slips off my face.

8:50 A.M.

Uh-oh. What if one of the Roadrunners catches me walking to school with my backpack? Oh man, there'd sure be a lot of explaining to do.

I wish I were invisible right now. Then there would be zero chance of getting caught. I know. I'll be like James Bond, no one ever catches him. I'll just pretend I'm a SPY. I will sneak to and from summer school and *no one* will ever suspect a thing. Call me Stanford Spy. Or Stealth Spy. No, wait, better idea: I will be known as SSSSpy for Super Stealth Stanford Spy.

As I hop from bush to tree and duck for cover behind parked cars, I congratulate myself. I am too clever for words. I am invincible. I am SSSSpy. Hey, I should have my own theme song. I wonder where you get one of those?

SSSSpy sneaks into Mr. Glick's classroom right before the bell rings and cases the joint. Gotta be careful; there may be enemy spies here. SSSSpy counts fifteen students: six girls and nine boys. Kids from different schools go to Rancho Rosetta for summer school, so SSSSpy has a good chance of maintaining his cover.

Suddenly SSSSpy recognizes one of the boys from his English class last semester. The kid quickly turns away when he sees SSSSpy looking at him. It is clear he does not want his identity revealed either.

SSSSpy surveys the room. A normal person might believe this is a classroom, but SSSSpy can see it for what it really is: a torture chamber. The Teacher Torturer, who goes by the name Mr. Glick, has cleverly disguised his instruments of doom. Instead of stretching racks and machines that poke out your eyeballs, there are desks. If you sit at one of them long enough, you will turn to dust. The bulletin boards are plastered with posters screaming insane things like READING IS FUN and BOOKS CAN TAKE YOU PLACES. SSSSpy quickly decodes the messages. What they really say is: READING ZAPS YOUR MIND and BOOKS WILL BORE YOU.

On the wall above Mr. Glick's desk is a framed newspaper article featuring Rancho Rosetta's number-one nerd, Millicent Min. She's eleven years old but in high school. In the newspaper photo, Millicent's grinning and shaking Teacher Torturer's hand as he presents her with a trophy as big as a toilet. She is probably an enemy spy. Or worse. A double agent. No, no, wait . . . a triple agent!!!

SSSSpy silently slides into a seat in the back, the better to observe the others. He slouches down so he won't be noticed.

"Good morning, Mr. Wong," Teacher Torturer booms. Oh man! The enemy has spotted SSSSpy. "Please sit up so I can see you," orders Teacher Torturer. "And that goes for the rest of you too."

"Bummer" school has officially begun.

Teacher Torturer stands in front of the room and clears his

throat. It sounds like a machine gun firing. The dweebs who are taking the class to get ahead lean forward. SSSSpy and the kids who are taking the class so they won't fall behind lean back.

Teacher Torturer looks like an army recruiter. His hair is short, but he has a big, thick brown mustache and he wears itty-bitty granny glasses that look like they are going to slide off the tip of his nose.

"My name is Mr. Glick. I will be your English teacher this summer, and we have a lot to cover. You will be required to write three book reports," he says as he marches up and down the rows of desks. "They will count for one-third of your grade. Your final exam will count for another third, and the rest of your grade will be determined by quizzes, homework . . . ," he looks straight at me, "and attendance.

"Many of you have had me before," Teacher Torturer sneers, "so you know how I grade. But for those of you who are new, I look for your insights. I look to see if you understand what you are reading and how you bring your own unique perspective to the books. And I look for . . ."

As he yammers on, I look for scars on his face. Rumor has it that Mr. Glick killed the cook at Stout's coffee shop because the man overcooked his hamburger. Digger swears he knows someone who knows someone who was there when it happened. Tico says that it's bunk and that if it were true, Mr. Glick would be in prison, not teaching English.

I believe it really happened, but that Mr. Glick was too clever to get caught. Just by looking at him you can tell he's the kind of person who would kill you if he didn't like you. I guess I ought to start planning my funeral.

JUNE 13, 2:40 P.M.

After summer school and lunch with Yin-Yin, I head over to Stretch's house. Stretch stopped talking over a year ago when his voice kept cracking. It was funny. He sounded like a frog or a girl and sometimes both. Whenever he tried to say something we'd all just start snickering. One time Gus laughed so hard that milk came out of his nose. He's been trying to do it again but hasn't succeeded yet.

Stretch's real name is Steven. He used to be really short, so we started calling him Stretch because he had to stand on tiptoes to reach things. Before he started growing, he was so little, people always forgot he was around. Now Stretch is the tallest one of us. He's even taller than Coach Martin. My dad says that one day I will be bigger than he is. Maybe, but I'll never be smarter than my father. It's awful being the only stupid person in a family of smart people.

A couple years ago we were all watching *Make Me a Millionaire*. Dad and Sarah always made it a point to tune in because they got to show off how big their brains are. So the host says, "Soon, we'll be searching for contestants to compete in a special *Make Me a Millionaire* Family Week. Maybe it will be *your* family!"

My sister sat up and exclaimed, "Oh! Should we try out?"

Then Sarah and Dad both turned their heads toward me just as I started eating a strawberry ice-cream cone from the bottom up. Their silence told me all I needed to know.

I got them back, though. A few days later the show was on again. The final question that night was: "The Lakers beat the Knicks with a sixty-foot buzzer-beater in these finals. What was the year and who scored the winning points?"

"The year was 1970 and the player was Jerry West," I said without looking up from the dragon I was drawing. When the host repeated my answer, there was silence in the room again, but this time I enjoyed it.

Stretch opens the door. We don't even say hello, that's how tight we are. His parents own You-Pak-It-We-Stor-It and are always at work, so Stretch is home alone a lot. Automatically I head to the kitchen to get some food. I am relieved to see there's nothing on the refrigerator announcing that I've flunked English. We grab some Cheese Puffs and I follow Stretch into the living room, where the large-screen TV takes up the entire wall.

I've heard Digger tell people that we're best friends even though sometimes he acts more like my worst enemy. But really, Stretch and I are best friends. Neither one of us has ever said this out loud, but I know we are. We don't talk. I mean, I talk to Stretch all the time, but he never talks to me. He never talks to anyone anymore. It's too girly to talk about things like friends anyway.

Stretch turns on the set and we eat Cheese Puffs and watch *Sesame Street*. Elmo's acting all weird because he can't find his hat. I know this is a baby show, but neither of us mentions it. It's like this unwritten rule that once we leave Stretch's house *Sesame Street* never existed.

Usually it's easy to veg around Stretch. Today I can't sit still. I look at Stretch laughing at Elmo. He has no clue that he's sitting next to a liar.

"Hey," I begin. I have to tell him. Stretch gets really good grades, but he'll understand. He's never criticized me and I don't criticize him, even though we both do incredibly dumb things pretty much all the time.

I open my mouth, but nothing comes out. I sound like Stretch. He's waiting. "Never mind," I say. "Elmo's really funny, isn't he?"

Stretch nods and we both return to the TV just in time to see Elmo find his hat.

JUNE 14, 8:48 A.M.

SSSSpy sneaks around the garbage truck. He races past the kids on their bikes, dashes through the school door, and slips into the classroom. Another day without getting caught! SSSSpy is amazing.

SSSSpy has started wearing a clever disguise — a green-and-white baseball cap. Everyone knows Stanford Wong is *the* Lakers' number-one fan. No one would ever suspect him of wearing Celtics colors.

Once everyone is seated, Teacher Torturer makes an announcement: "Please pass your word-definition homework up to the front. I assume you've all done your homework, right? Good. Because that will really help you on the pop quiz you are about to take!"

The class moans. "Also, just to liven things up," he continues, "I want you to sit in a different seat every day. After you've sat in every seat in the room, you can start over. That way I can see some of the students who always try to hide in the back. And the kids who always sit in the front can get another point of view."

There is much grumbling as we all get up. I move one seat over, but everything still looks the same from here.

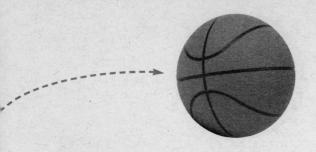

JUNE 15, 10:15 A.M.

The time in Teacher Torturer's class has been one of the most difficult assignments SSSSpy has ever had. Five days a week, three hours a day in that place. Do you know how hard it is to stay awake for three full hours while Teacher Torturer is talking? I'm surprised he doesn't put himself to sleep. And when he's not talking, he's expecting you to read or write.

After class SSSSpy had to dart around to avoid being spotted by any Roadrunners or enemy agents on his way back to home base. He changed his route every day. It was tough, but SSSSpy was up to the challenge. He had to be. If he got caught, he'd be sent to the firing squad.

I've just finished three packets of cinnamon Pop-Tarts. I was hoping Dad would eat breakfast with me, but Mom said he was already at the office. I grab my basketball and head toward the door.

"Stanford, what about your homework?"

"Mommmm, it's Saturday, gimme a break! I slaved all week in Tortur — Mr. Glick's class."

"It was a short week," she points out. "You started summer school on a Wednesday."

"Whatever."

Mom relaxes. "Look, Stanford, I know that summer school is the last place in this world you want to be, but if you fall behind now, it will only make it that much harder to catch up later."

I continue looking at my shoes. I wish they were Alan Scott BK620s.

"Tell you what," Mom sighs. "You can play basketball today, but tomorrow, *all day*, you study."

"Deal!"

I meet up with Stretch and Digger near the park. Joey and some of the other C-Team players are on the court. At my school, most sixth graders start out on the C-Team. The C-Team takes anyone who shows up, no matter what grade you're in or how bad you are. The B-Team is for really good players in any grade, and the A-Team is only for the best. This past season I made the B-Team and so did the rest of the Roadrunners, although only Digger and I got much court time.

Joey and his friends clear out when they see us coming.

"Thanks, guys."

"No problem, Stanford!" Joey says. He turns to Digger. "Here's the two dollars I owe you."

"Keep it." Digger waves him away.

"You sure?"

"Yeah, why not?"

"Wow, thanks, Digger. You're okay!"

As Joey takes off we start practicing crossover dribbles.

"How's your dad treating you?" Digger asks me. "Bet he's working you really hard."

"Yeah," I tell him. "I have to do so much stuff."

Digger misses a shot. I rebound and make it.

"Like what?" Tico asks as he and Gus join us.

We all sit on the grass and begin throwing the ball at each other. The goal is to knock someone over. It's a game the Roadrunners invented, and we think it's good enough to be in the Olympics. We call it Silent Slam Ball.

"What kind of stuff do you have to do?" Tico persists. "Do you get to work a paper shredder?"

"Well . . . ," I begin. *Thud!* The ball hits me in the chest. I slam it hard at Stretch, who doesn't even flinch. He hurls it at Digger. It would be easier to tell the Roadrunners what my job was if I knew what my dad actually did all day. "I do lots of things," I try to explain. "It's really tough work. My father says he'd be lost without me."

I can remember when I used to go with Dad to his office on the weekends. I'd sit in his big leather chair and twirl around. Once I made a paper-clip chain that was four feet long.

I'm not allowed to visit him at work anymore. Not since the last time, when my father sent me out to get sandwiches. On my way back, I told the man in the elevator that my dad had to work all the time because his new boss was a real pighead. How was I to know *he* was Dad's new boss?

Digger aims the ball at Tico, who's watching a squirrel. I want to warn him, but that's against the rules.

"I'll bet you're a gofer," Digger says.

"A gopher?"

"No, a go-*fer*." *Wham!* Tico falls over. I shake my head. He should have never looked away. "Like go-fer coffee, go-fer this, go-fer that, go-fer —"

"How's your job, Gus?" I ask, turning my back to Digger.

Gus hurls the ball at Stretch. "I've been working really hard. Mowing lawns is a tough business."

"He's making a ton of money," Tico says. He's still lying face-down on the ground.

"Millions," Gus confirms. "C'mon, let's play!"

We get up. Stretch passes the ball to Tico, who runs down-court, shoots, and makes it. High fives all around. Tico's small, but he's fast. He's great at stealing the ball, but a lousy shooter. Guess that's why he's a point guard and I'm a small forward. Stretch is a center, what else? Digger's a power forward and Gus is a shooting guard.

"Tico, sit out," says Digger. "I want in."

Tico retreats to the sideline so Digger can play. Gus growls, "How come you always make Tico sit out first?"

Stretch and I glance at each other. Gus has been mad at Digger for more than a year. We were cutting through someone's yard when Tico spotted a tall hedge with a bowling ball–sized open-ing in it. Digger dared Gus to put his head in the hole. When Gus did, he got stuck. Then, just as a bunch of high-school girls walked by, Digger pulled Gus's pants down.

"It's not like they'll ever recognize you," Digger said later.

He had a good point. Still, Gus has yet to forgive him.

"It's okay," Tico says. "I'll play next game." He's used to warming the bench.

"You want to sit out instead?" Digger asks Gus.

"Let's just play to twenty, then Tico can rotate in," he answers.

The game begins. It gets rough when Gus and Digger fight

over the ball. I swoop in and steal it from both of them and make a jump shot.

As Gus cheers and Digger steams, Stretch just looks at me and shrugs. I glance over to Tico. He's busy scratching the dirt with a stick.

Stretch and Digger are down four points. I make the winning basket and Gus whoops.

"Good game," I call out.

"I had an off day," Digger mutters.

"Can I play now?" Tico asks. "My foot fell asleep for so long it's having dreams."

Digger throws the ball at him. "It's all yours," he huffs. "I got better stuff to do."

We start a new game, me and Stretch versus Tico and Gus. This time I have fun.

JUNE 18, 2:37 P.M.

"Yin-Yin, I have to go to the office," Mom is reminding my grandmother for the one hundredth time. "Remember?"

"I'll go by myself then," my grandmother announces. "I can take the bus." Yin-Yin can't drive anymore because she failed her driving test. She claims they asked her trick questions. She showed me the test and I think she's right.

Even though I am in the next room, I can hear my mother sigh. "No, no, please don't take the bus. I'll drive you." She comes out of the kitchen and yells, "Stanford!"

I turn up the volume on *Top Cop*. He's about to close in on a murderer who's just stolen a blue 1967 Mustang.

My mom turns off the TV. "I have to take Yin-Yin to Maddie's. I'm going to drop her off, and then pick her up later. I want you to stay with her so she doesn't wander off again." I open my mouth to protest, but Mom is too quick. "There will be no discussion about this. You stay with Yin-Yin, no ifs, ands, or buts." Whatever that's supposed to mean.

So much for basketball this afternoon. I was really looking forward to it because Digger just got a pair of Alan Scott BK620s. Gus is going to have him play with a BK620 on his left foot and his old shoe on his right and see if he can tell the difference.

"Why don't you take your homework with you?" Mom suggests as she picks up a sock off the floor. "You can do it at Maddie's. Maybe Millicent will be there and she can help you."

Maddie is Millicent Min's grandmother. You'd never know they are related. Maddie is fun and Millicent is a freaky geek-a-zoid genius, totally useless, like a basketball without air.

"I've already done all my homework," I lie.

Mom smiles. "Well then, what are we waiting for?"

3:20 P.M.

Before I know what's happening, Maddie gives me a big hug. Normally I am against hugs, but I don't protest. Maddie's soft and squishy and smells like gingerbread. She reminds me of Christmas.

I start to sit down, then ask, "Millicent isn't here, is she?"

Maddie and Yin-Yin glance at each other and smile. "No, but I can ask Millie to come over," Maddie says, walking toward the phone.

"Noooooooo!" I shout, flying across the room and grabbing the phone from her hands. "I mean, no thank you. That's okay. Never mind. No need to do that."

Yin-Yin and Maddie laugh and head to the kitchen. They have known each other since they were girls. That means that they've known each other for a million years. When they get together, they don't sound like grandmas, they sound like normal people. They're always trying to outdo each other with outrageous tales. Maddie usually wins, though lately Yin-Yin's stories have been getting more and more amazing.

My grandmother used to be really active. She took salsa dancing lessons, and in art class she once won a ribbon for a painting of an airplane. Recently Maddie's been trying to get her to try yoga. But ever since Yin-Yin moved in with us, she mostly sits around and watches TV. Maddie used to compare Yin-Yin to a hummingbird. She's hardly humming anymore.

I put the phone down. After thumbing through Maddie's stack of travel magazines, I examine her collection of snow globes. One starts leaking when I shake it too hard, so I dry it on my shirt and put it back where I found it.

I head toward the kitchen, then stop when I hear Yin-Yin say, "They still want to send me to that retirement home."

"Did you tell them you don't want to go?" asks Maddie.

"Noooo . . . not really. Just thinking about it makes my head spin. It's like I don't know anything anymore. Sometimes when I wake up I forget where I am. Other days all I can do is sit in my room and stare at Sarah's Lava Lamp. The only thing I know for sure is that Kristen's a terrible cook. You should see what she makes. Maddie, I'm right there and she still insists on cooking for the family. We'd be better off with no food in the house!"

"Well, cooking aside, what does your heart tell you to do?"

"I'm not sure." Yin-Yin sighs. "Rick insists that I can't live on my own. So I'm a little forgetful, so what? But I know I can't stay with the kids forever. I feel so useless, like I'm always getting in the way. . . ."

When I was little I'd sneak under the table as Yin-Yin and Maddie drank tea and ate sweets. It felt safe there. Every so often a cookie, carefully wrapped in a napkin, would fall to the ground and I'd reach out and snap it up. Now I'm too big to fit under the table, so I flatten my back against the wall and listen to them from the next room. I think they suspect I'm there, though, because every so often a cookie, carefully wrapped in a napkin, gets thrown my way.

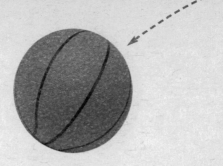

JUNE 21, 11:58 A.M.

SSSSpy is doodling skulls in his notebook. They all have thick mustaches and granny glasses. Teacher Torturer sneaks up from behind him and hands him yesterday's pop quiz. "Well, you're consistent," he says.

SSSSpy sees the D on the page and quickly crams the paper into his backpack.

The bell rings. As everyone gets ready to leave, Teacher Torturer tells the class, "Just a reminder: Most of you have turned in your list of the three books you will be reading and writing reports on this summer." He looks directly at SSSSpy. "But for those of you who haven't turned in your list yet, you'd better do so soon, or you will be in grave danger of not passing this class."

Slowly SSSSpy rips the page of skulls out of his notebook. He crumples it up and then throws it past Teacher Torturer's nose and into the trash can.

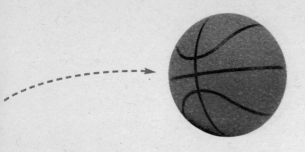

JUNE 23, 7:42 A.M.

"Stanford, you're in big trouble!!!"

I get yelled at so much these days you'd think I'd be used to it. But this time I'm getting blamed for something that's not my fault. My father just found a carton of mint chocolate chip ice cream in his sock drawer, and it was all melted. (The ice cream, not the socks.) I stand still and don't say anything because it is too totally weird: When I was putting on my shoes this morning, I found potato chips in them.

Dad's still shouting, but right when I am about to defend myself, my mom barges in and says, "Stanford! Is this your idea of a joke? Fish sticks in my purse? I'll never get the stink out!"

"I swear I didn't do it!"

By the look on my parents' faces I can tell they don't believe me.

"Look," I say, taking a piece of bologna out of my pants pocket. "*I* didn't put this here."

"Give me that!" Dad grabs the bologna and waves it accusingly at me. "You are in big trouble, mister."

"You've gone too far this time," Mom adds.

The only time they are in agreement is when they think I've done something wrong.

"I didn't do it!" I pull a piece of bologna from another pocket and then a slice of bread. I could make a sandwich, but this probably isn't a good time for a snack.

"If you didn't do it, then who did?" Dad demands.

I have no answer for him. Okay, so maybe I've done dumb stunts like gluing his briefcase shut. Or, when Sarah was living at home, sneaking onto the computer and inserting the words *butt cheese* throughout her term paper. But I don't do stuff like that anymore, not since my father made me sit out two basketball games last season because instead of doing the dishes, I threw them away.

Dad is still staring at me, waiting for an answer. Mom is still holding up her purse. It is like they are frozen. Suddenly there's a small noise in the hallway. We all look up in time to see Yin-Yin trying to sneak away.

2:15 P.M.

Digger and I arrive at the court from opposite ends of the park just as Joey is leaving.

"Hi, guys!" Joey says. He's always in a good mood.

We both nod and start practicing free throws. Digger's awfully quiet.

"You okay?" I ask.

"Yeah," he answers, looking away. He makes a couple of

baskets, then says, "Hey, Stanford, when your dad gets mad at you —"

Just then we hear a big commotion. "Put me down! Put me down!"

Stretch and Gus arrive carrying Tico. "Put me down!" Tico cries.

"Well, if that's what you want . . . ," Gus says. They dump him beneath the basket.

"*Ouch!*" Tico yells as Gus and Stretch start laughing. "You guys are total dipsticks." He starts chasing them as they run circles around us.

I turn to Digger. "What was it you wanted to ask?"

"It's nothing," he says. "Forget it."

JUNE 24, 8:53 P.M.

Mom and Dad are having another huge fight. It's what they do. Yin-Yin and I are sitting on the couch in the family room. One of her game shows is on, but the volume is way down low. We're both listening for how many times our names come up. Tonight Yin-Yin's winning. I am knitting furiously and my whatever-it-is looks like a mess. It's all lumpy and full of big holes, like a rat was chewing on it.

"...she went for a walk and then forgot where she lives again," my mother shouts.

"It happens," my father shouts back. "It's no big deal. Remember when Stanford did that?"

"He was seven then. Your mother is in her seventies." After a long pause, my mother adds more softly, "Rick, I love her too. But you're not the one home with her all day. Her behavior is getting more and more erratic. Besides, I told them at work I was only going part-time for three months. It's almost been a year. Yin-Yin was supposed to go to Vacation Village a long time ago, you know that."

"The doctor said it's just mild senility," my father counters. "Besides, Vacation Village is all booked up."

"Rick," my mother says gently, "they called today. There's an opening."

Silence. The only noise is the frantic clicking of my knitting needles and the murmur from the TV. Yin-Yin stares blankly at the screen. Someone is spinning a wheel that's as big as a house. Everyone holds their breath as the wheel slows.

Suddenly Yin-Yin points the remote control at the television and presses the volume button so that it is blasting. The wheel stops. A lady sobs and shouts, "I have always wanted a convertible!"

I have to get out of here. I stash my knitting under the couch and head out. Yin-Yin does not even notice I am missing. I look back through the window. Mom and Dad sit on either side of my grandmother. Dad takes the remote control from her and turns the TV off. Mom puts her arm around Yin-Yin. Like a little kid getting in trouble, my grandmother bows her head and stares at her hands folded together on her lap.

I start to run. I run so fast that everything is a blur. I run so fast that I'm practically flying.

Honk, honk, honnnnnk!!! SCREECH . . .

I look up. I am standing in the middle of the street. There is a car right in front of me. The driver sticks his head out the window and yells. I yell back at him, even though I know it was my fault. I almost got smushed, smashed, flattened, killed.

I take off running again. I'm not sure where I am going, but I can't wait to get there.

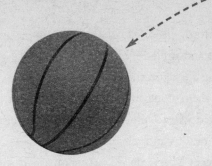

JUNE 25, 8:19 P.M.

Teacher Torturer made SSSSpy stay after class again. He told SSSSpy, "You're not off to a very good start this summer. You'd better get serious soon, 'or else.'" Mr. Glick and my father must use the same dictionary.

After dinner, Mom and Dad called me into the living room. They both had silly grins on their faces, so for a moment I thought that maybe they had changed their minds about making Yin-Yin leave. But noooooooo. Instead, total humiliation. Get this: Millicent Min, brainiac, nerd, and poster girl for Chinese geekdom, is going to tutor me in English. Maybe I should just slit my wrists now and get it over with.

Thanks to Yin-Yin and Maddie, Millicent and I have been forced together since we were little. Only she's never really been a little kid. Millicent's more like the dorkiest, most obnoxious grown-up you can imagine, only shorter.

For example, there's the time our families were at a picnic. Millicent kept hogging my dad, talking to him about global warming. I kept trying to get into the conversation by saying things like, "If the Earth is too hot, maybe they should make a giant air conditioner."

"Stanford, please!" Dad said, waving me away. He turned to Millicent and smiled. "How often is it that I get to hear a certified genius's take on the environment?"

I left them alone and went to shoot hoops. Of course, later I got blamed when Millicent discovered her briefcase was full of chopped onions and relish.

Millicent Min is always ratting on me. If she ever made a CD, her greatest hits would include "Stanford Sprinkled Sand in My Sandwich," "Stanford Squashed a Bug in My Book," and the ever-popular "Stanford Sneezed All Over My Homework."

Nobody likes a tattletale, which is probably why no one likes Millicent Min. She thinks that just because she's this genius person, everyone knows who she is. When really, no one cares about Millicent, except for teachers, parents, and fellow brains like my sister.

Now this. I am to be tutored by my mortal enemy. Our mothers agreed that starting next week I would be forced to spend three days a week, an hour at a time, with Miss Know-It-All. And get this: Millicent's getting *paid*. Money, moola, cashola. No one's paying me to have to be in the same room as her.

When Millicent called to confirm the bad news I could tell she was pretty bummed too. She said, "Listen, Stan-turd, this is not my idea of an ideal summer. In fact, it is worse than getting gout, failing the GRE, and being passed over for graduate school during a meteor shower without a telescope."

I wasn't sure what she was blabbering about (no one's ever sure what she's saying), but I did manage to tell her, "This sucks."

My whole reputation's at stake here. What if the guys or

any of the kids from school found out I'm being tutored by Millicent Min, girl geek? Just being seen with a kid who carries a briefcase is enough to catapult me right back into the nobody category.

After I get off the phone with Millicent, I head for the living room. Yin-Yin is watching one of her game shows. She's exhausted from making enough dim sum to feed a whole basketball league. Every day during the school year Yin-Yin would make dim sum for my lunch. Every day I'd throw it away. It's not that I don't like Yin-Yin's dim sum — I love it. But it would be suicide to be seen at school with weird-looking food.

I flop down on the couch next to my grandmother with a plate piled high with *cha siu bao* and *ha gow*. She reaches for one of the fluffy white pork buns without even taking her eyes off the television. I pick up a *ha gow* and bite into a shrimp. Someone on television is about to win a *"fabulous* prize!" Too bad it's not me.

JUNE 27, 3:21 P.M.

Millicent called, this time to figure out where to meet for tutoring. She didn't laugh when I suggested the moon. We finally agreed on the library. It is the one place I know the Roadrunners would never go. Roadrunners aren't famous for their brains. Tico gets decent grades and Stretch always makes Honors, but they don't want anyone to know that.

I'll bet Millicent thinks I'm some sort of freak because I'm not nearly as smart as her. It's bad enough that teachers expect more of Chinese kids. But to have someone like Millicent living in the same town, and to have Sarah as a sister, makes my life impossible.

"Stanford Wong? Are you Sarah Wong's little brother?" my teachers always ask. Eventually, when they find out that I am nothing like my sister, I can sense their disappointment. Sarah skipped a grade. So it only seems right that I flunk a grade to balance things out. Hey, maybe I'll be in *Ripley's Believe It or Not!* The headline will read: STANFORD WONG, THE ONLY STUPID CHINESE KID IN AMERICA!

Maybe if I could run Millicent and all the other "high achievers" out of town there wouldn't be so much pressure on me. What a total dweeb she is. I wonder, if Digger didn't ask me to join the Roadrunners way back then, if I didn't have basketball, would I have ended up like Millicent Min, only without good grades? Would I have been like Marley, who has not only embraced his inner geekiness but flaunts it?

I'm late getting to the library. Still, I can't bring myself to go inside, so instead I practice spinning the basketball on my finger. Finally I realize that if I don't go in, Millicent will probably come looking for me, or worse, someone might see me.

The library lady peers over the top of her glasses and smiles. I try to smile back, and then look for Millicent. She said to meet in the periods section. I wander around until I spot her. Why didn't she just say, "Meet by the magazines"? She is beyond weird.

Millicent's sitting with her back straight and her hands folded, staring at a clock on the table. Pens, a notebook open to a blank page, and some other papers are all neatly lined up in front of her. Her briefcase is on the floor, and her T-shirt reads SO MANY BOOKS, SO LITTLE TIME. How can my dad be impressed with someone like Millicent Min?

I walk toward her and she grabs a book and covers her face. I wish she'd keep it covered.

"Nerd," she says.

"Geek," I reply.

"Imbecile."

"Freak."

After about five minutes, the name-calling stops and Millicent begins to lecture me. Who does she think she is, Mr. Glick? I stop her midsentence. "You have to promise me you won't tell anyone about this."

"About this what?"

Isn't it obvious? "This tutoring business."

"Yeah, okay. Now tell me, what is it about reading that you find so difficult?"

"*No!*" I shout. The library lady almost drops a big pile of books. "No," I say more softly. "You have to swear you won't tell."

"All right, I won't tell."

I don't believe her. "Cross your heart and hope to die, stick a needle in your eye!"

"This is ridiculous," Millicent says, turning up her nose. "Why don't we just spit into our palms and rub them together?"

Finally she's said something that makes sense. I spit into my hands and hold them out to her. She acts horrified and shouts, "I'd rather eat worms!"

Worms! That reminds me. "I've eaten a worm before. I ate it on a dare and it didn't taste half-bad. It wasn't as chewy as I thought it would be. . . ." Before I can even get to the part about how I had to drain two cans of Coke to wash down the wormy taste, Millicent bolts from the table. What is her problem?

Unfortunately, after a couple minutes she returns. By then I have a plan. I know she'll go for it because Millicent's all into rules and regulations like my dad.

"A contract?" she says.

"A contract," I confirm. Maybe we can even keep it in a safe and seal it with wax. Or blood!

At first Millicent refuses. Then I tell her that if she doesn't agree, I'll plug my ears and hum whenever she talks. To prove this, I plug my ears and hum.

"Huuuummmmm . . . hummmm . . . huuummmm . . ."

"*Enough!*" she yells.

Millicent glares at me, hunches over, and begins writing something in tiny perfect letters like she's some sort of human computer. It's the contract. I make her swear on her mother's life that she won't tell anyone about our secret. She makes me swear to bring pens next time. We both sign the contract, and then Millicent has Mrs. Martinez, the library lady, add her name to "make it official."

"Can I go now?" I'm exhausted.

"No," Millicent snaps. "We haven't even begun."

I wonder if her underpants are too tight. She's sure acting like it. Man, Millicent talks a lot. I can't even understand half of what she is saying. Will she ever shut up? She's been going on for such a long time I'm getting hungry. I reach for my backpack.

"What are you doing now?" Millicent hisses.

"Eating a deviled ham sandwich." Is she so blind that she can't even tell what a sandwich is? "I have to keep my energy up for basketball. I'm the league free-throw champion."

"Put that away," she squawks, "or Mrs. Martinez will kick us out of here."

"Chill, Mill." I take another bite in slow motion. It's fun watching Millicent's face get all scrunched up. "You want a taste?"

Millicent grabs her notebook and hurls it at me. It goes flying way over my head, but I jump up and catch it. Ha!

"You pig," she shouts. "You have no regard for anyone but yourself!"

Mrs. Martinez sprints over just as Millicent is about to hit me over the head with a huge book.

"Ms. Min," she says, all out of breath. "Please lower your voice. This is a library, not a playground." Mrs. Martinez pries the book from Millicent's hands and places it on the table. "I expect better of you."

Millicent Min getting chewed out by a librarian???!!! I laugh so hard I almost choke on a piece of ham. Then Mrs. Martinez starts in on me about the evils of eating in the library. I stop chewing and stash what's left of my sandwich in Millicent's briefcase.

Millicent is glaring at me, and the library lady is lecturing me. Man, this is going to be one long summer.

JUNE 28, 2 P.M.

It's all too weird. Mom's packing. Dad's pacing. He even took off work today to be here. Yin-Yin is staring at the television and it's not even on.

My sister is home from college. Her duffel bag sits by the front door next to Yin-Yin's boxes and old-lady suitcases. Last fall when Sarah was packing for the dorms, she was so happy to be moving away. Dad was happy too, because his daughter was going to his alma mater, Stanford University. He was so proud of her. He still is.

No one's happy today.

"Hey, Squiggy," Sarah says. I hate it when she calls me Squiggy. "What's the scoop?"

"Yin-Yin's moving out."

"I know *that*. But why?"

"Because she hid the eggs," I try to explain. "Because she tells funny stories, because she salutes the mailman, and because she keeps getting lost."

I want to cry, but I can't. When I was little I cried all the time and Sarah made fun of me. Boys aren't supposed to cry. I bite down hard on the inside of my cheek.

"How long are you here for?" I ask, trying to change the subject.

"Just until the fifth," says Sarah as she takes the rubber band off her ponytail and shakes out her hair. She's really pretty like Mom, only she doesn't need to know that. She's got a big enough head already. "Did you hear I've been accepted to the Summer at Sea program?"

"Yeah, Dad told me." I wish she was staying home this summer. Why can't she just stay home?

"I heard you're going to summer school."

"I flunked English," I mumble.

"You just have to study more," she says, sounding like Millicent.

"Yeah, well, easy for you to say!" Sarah looks startled. "Not all of us can get straight A's, you know. Dad's always comparing me to you. 'When Sarah was your age, she won this award. When Sarah was in English class, she did extra credit just for fun. Sarah is such a great student, why can't you be more like her?' Sometimes I wish I never had you for a sister!"

Uh-oh. I take it back, I take it back.

"Hey, Squiggy," Sarah says softly. "I know you don't mean that. Why are you doing this to yourself?"

"Doing what?"

"Letting him get to you like that. You shouldn't compare yourself to other people, Stanford. You're a great kid. You'll get through summer school. I heard that Mom and Dad hired Millicent Min to help you."

"Yeah," I mutter. "I'll bet Dad wishes she was in this family instead of me."

Sarah musses up my hair. "Don't be such a goof. If I were home this summer, I'd tutor you myself. But I can't pass up an opportunity to study aboard a ship and sail around the world. Besides, how else can I buy my little brother souvenirs from every port? Maybe I'll even find a sword for you."

I've always wanted a sword.

"I know these next couple of months are going to be difficult with Mr. Glick's class and Yin-Yin moving out," Sarah tells me. "But Mr. Glick is not so bad once you get to know him. And you can visit Yin-Yin anytime." She looks sad. "Promise me you'll visit her, so she won't be lonely."

"I promise," I tell my big sister.

JUNE 29, 9:30 A.M.

Vacation Village does not look like anyplace I'd want to vacation at. It's a regular old building with ancient-looking furniture in the lobby and ancient-looking people shuffling in every direction. You can't even turn around without bumping into one of them. And it smells like old people's feet. Who would want to vacation in a place that smells like old people's feet?

I hold my breath and try to make it all the way to the elevator before I have to exhale. No wonder some of the old people wear oxygen masks. In the elevator my parents raise their voices, talking louder and faster to Yin-Yin like they have a lot to say before the doors open.

"You will love it here!"

"You are so lucky they have a spot for you!"

"Our house is so close by!"

We step out of the elevator and everybody stares at me. A lot of the old fogies try to touch me and pat my head like I'm some sort of dog or something. It's so creepy, but I let them because . . . well, I don't know why I let them. Old people make me nervous. Maybe next time I will tell them to stop.

Mom and Dad do not seem to notice how ugly the place is,

but Sarah and I look at each other and grimace. Yin-Yin keeps her head bowed as we make our way down the hall. The tissue in her hand is all shredded. She's shuffling like the rest of the old people. Yin-Yin didn't do that before.

"Oh look! Fresh flowers!" my mother exclaims.

Dad announces, "It says here on the bulletin board that they are serving pot roast tonight. Yin-Yin, you love pot roast."

"No, I don't," my grandmother mumbles. "You do."

"Hello! Hello! Hello!" an old man shouts at us. He is way down the hall but comes racing toward us in a weird slow-motion sort of run that makes him look like he is going to tip over. His hair is tilted to one side. "You must be the new girl," he says to Yin-Yin.

She gives him a glare. "I'm neither new nor a girl." His mouth hangs open as he watches her walk away.

"This way, Yin-Yin," my mother says as she pushes the door open into a small apartment. It is actually just a bedroom with a couch and table and a bed. Hey, the bathroom has a telephone in it! The walls are plain, but there is a tree outside the window. I can see the branches. We are on the third floor.

"Isn't this nice," Mom comments. What? Is she blind? "We'll bring some of your furniture and decorate the walls and it will be so cozy."

"A room with a view," Dad says, trying to sound cheerful.

Yin-Yin doesn't answer. She just stands by the window and stares out at the parking lot.

"Come on, Stanford," my father says. "Let's get Yin-Yin's things."

"Yes!" my mother chirps. "And while you do that, Sarah,

Yin-Yin, and I will go exploring. I hear they have aerobics and arts 'n' crafts and all sorts of fun activities here!"

Mom and Dad have been chattering away nonstop ever since we left the house. Why are they talking to Yin-Yin like she's a little kid? And why isn't she protesting? I know if they tried to imprison me here, I'd make a run for it.

Dad doesn't say anything as he hands me Yin-Yin's boxes from the trunk. The more silent he is, the madder I get. Finally I blurt out, "Why can't she still live with us?"

"It's complicated," is all Dad will say.

He thinks I won't understand. Why doesn't he ever want to talk to me? He and Sarah used to talk for hours.

As we lug the boxes into the building, the bottom breaks on the one I am carrying. I expect Dad to yell at me, but instead he puts down his box and together we pick up Yin-Yin's things.

I hand him a photo of Sarah and me on Christmas Day the year we got the new television. Dad stares at an old picture of himself standing next to his father. They both look grim. The plaster imprint of my hand that I made when I was in kindergarten has broken in two. "That's easy to fix," my dad assures me.

I like it that it's the two of us doing something together. I just wish we were doing something else.

We drop off the boxes in Yin-Yin's room. She's still standing in the same spot by the window.

"Where's Kristen?" Dad asks.

"She and Sarah went exploring," Yin-Yin tells him without turning around.

"Did you want to go with them?"

"No."

The three of us are silent for a long time. My father keeps looking like he's about to say something, but then doesn't. Finally he speaks. "Mom," he says softly in a tone I've never heard before.

My grandmother turns around. She's been crying.

Dad looks shaken. "I'm going to go get some sodas for us," he says. Then he rushes out of the room.

I go up to Yin-Yin and put my arm around her. Am I getting bigger, or is she getting smaller?

Yin-Yin keeps staring out the window. I can't tell what she's looking at. Without facing me she whispers, "Stanford, you have to get me out of here. C'mon, Stanford, help me run away."

"Sure, Yin-Yin. Whatever you say."

"*No!*" she suddenly shouts. She turns to me. Her eyes look wild. "Promise me," she pleads. Her grip on my wrist is strong. "Promise to help me!"

"I, I promise, Yin-Yin," I sputter. "I promise."

She lets go of me and calmly looks back out the window. My dad returns with three sodas. "Root beer, anyone?" he asks brightly.

Yin-Yin ignores him.

For a moment he looks lost. "Stanford?" he says, holding one out to me.

I take it and he seems grateful.

"Give it a little time," he tells Yin-Yin. "You're going to love it here."

"Please go away," she tells him.

"Mom . . . ," my father pleads.

"Go," she says firmly.

63

"Bye, Yin-Yin," I say as we leave.

She does not say good-bye to me.

We find my mom and Sarah watching some old people watching a movie about some old people who swim in magic water and turn young again. "Time to leave," says Dad.

We step into the elevator. When I was smaller, there was always a race between Sarah and me to see who would get to press the buttons. Neither of us moves, so it's up to Mom to hit the down button. We all face forward in silence and watch the numbers above the doors count down as the elevator hums its way to the ground floor.

JULY 1, 3 P.M.

I hate Millicent Min.

"Did you read the Robert Frost poem?"

Millicent doesn't even bother to say hello. Instead she just launches right into schoolwork. Not that I'd want to say hello — I'd rather be saying good-bye.

When I don't answer, Millicent makes a face. "I thought not." She pushes a book toward me. "Read this," she orders.

I grab the book and give her a good glare before staring down at the words.

"Out loud," Millicent demands. "Read it out loud."

Before I even finish the title, she barks, "Louder and with feeling! Robert Frost did not pen 'Stopping by Woods on a Snowy Evening' so Stanford Wong could mangle his poetry."

I hate Millicent Min.

I read her stupid poem. When I am done, Millicent says, "Read it again."

"Awwww," I start to protest, but her eyes are shooting lasers at me. It's amazing how frightening she can be, especially since she's such a puny little weakling.

I read the poem out loud *five* more times. When I finally finish, Millicent looks smug. "Whose woods is he in?" she asks.

"How am I supposed to know that?" I snap. "He's probably trespassing and will get arrested."

"Do you think the narrator of the poem is trespassing?"

"That's what I just said."

"Why do you think the horse stopped?"

"Maybe he had to pee. That's why you should never eat yellow snow."

She doesn't even smile. I hate Millicent Min.

"How would you describe the setting of the poem?"

"Freezing," I tell her. This is boring. "And dark. They are probably lost. They may even die in the woods and never be found until the snow thaws. Then there will be two skeletons, a man and a horse."

I imagine Millicent lost in the woods. This cheers me up a bit.

Before she can ask me something else, I ask, "Hey, aren't you supposed to be helping me? Shouldn't you be giving me the answers?"

"True," Millicent says, all prissy, "my job is to help you. But I merely lead you to the questions. The answers you have to discover on your own."

"Then what good are you?"

"I have promises to keep," Millicent growls, "like agreeing to tutor you. How is it even possible that you are Sarah Wong's brother?"

I hate Millicent Min.

"Well, how's it possible that your parents are normal and

you're not?" I ask her. "Did they adopt you from the Human Society?"

Millicent bursts out laughing, "You mean the *Humane* Society?"

"I meant to say that," I sputter. "I said it wrong on purpose."

It takes Millicent a while to stop snickering. I am still stewing as she continues to grill me about the horsey poem. The more questions she asks, the more confused I get.

"Stanford, what does the darkness symbolize?"

"Stanford, why is the imagery so important?"

"Stanford, do you agree that the second stanza has an unbroken curve of rhythm?"

How can we talk about a dumb poem for so long when the poem is so short? I can't wait to get out of here and onto the basketball court. I wish Millicent would just shut up. I feel like the guy in the poem who has miles to go.

I hate Millicent Min.

JULY 3, 2:45 P.M.

Teacher Torturer tried to trip up SSSSpy today. However, much to his tormentor's surprise, I responded, "The horse is confused because he can't find the farm and they still have to go a long way before it's time to chill out."

"Stanford," Mr. Glick said, looking at me over his glasses. "You are right on target."

"I am?"

"Yes, yes," he said excitedly. He turned to the class. "Who can elaborate on Stanford's observations? Stanford just told us that the narrator and the horse have been together a long time. Yet there are miles left on their journey. That's why the narrator says his horse must be confused that they are stopping."

I said all that? Several hands in the room shot up. Mr. Glick pointed to a girl in the front. "Kate, could you build on Stanford's premise?"

"Stanford!!!" the Roadrunners shout as I near the court. They always greet me like I'm some sort of hero. I pull my shoulders back. Stretch tosses the ball to me and we immediately start playing.

"You look happy," Gus says. "You must have had a good day at work."

"Yeah," I tell him. "Today wasn't bad."

JULY 4, 6:31 P.M.

Last Fourth of July, Maddie gave Yin-Yin some illegal Chinese firecrackers. My mother kept yelping at every pop, and my father laughed a lot. It was pretty great.

This year Yin-Yin is locked away at Vacation Village. We begged her to come home to visit, but she won't leave her room, not even to eat. Someone has to bring her all her meals. I thought all the activities at Vacation Village were supposed to cheer her up.

We all stopped by this afternoon. Sarah gave Yin-Yin a glittery Uncle Sam hat and forced her to wear it. Mom brought an apple pie from Butterfield's Bakery. The pie was untouched when we left. From the parking lot I spotted Yin-Yin staring out the window still wearing her hat. I waved to her, but she did not wave back. She probably didn't see me.

Now Mom, Dad, Sarah, and I are sitting in the backyard not talking, this time because Dad made his famous barbecue beef teriyaki sticks.

"Is that what I sent you to Stanford University for? To come home with crazy ideas?" Dad rarely uses that tone on Sarah; usually it's reserved for me.

"It's not crazy," Sarah shoots back as she crunches on a carrot. "Being a vegetarian is very healthy."

"No, it's not. Everyone needs to eat meat," Dad informs her, holding out a teriyaki stick. Sarah sets it down on her paper plate and picks up another carrot.

I'm happy he is mad at my sister for a change. To earn extra points, I eat all my teriyaki sticks and then eat Sarah's too. She lines up her baked beans with her fork and frowns. Just when the silence is going to kill us, Digger shows up with Gus.

"Hello, Mrs. Wong!" Digger says. "You look nice today."

Gus pretends to pluck bugs from my dad's hair, which is pretty funny since Dad is really proud of his good grooming.

"Can Stanford come with us to the park to watch the fireworks display?" Digger asks, adding, "Please, ma'am."

My mother glances at my father. He doesn't say anything. Dad doesn't like Digger. She looks at me. I raise my eyebrows in an attempt to signal her that I want to go, but not if it's going to be a problem.

"Sure, why not?" Mom replies. "Nothing much is happening here."

"Man, what was going on at your house, a funeral?" Digger asks when we walk down the middle of the street. When cars appear, we yell at them and act crazy.

"His grandma had to go to an old people's place," Gus explains as he finishes hooting and flapping his arms at a station wagon.

"I don't even have any grandparents," Digger says.

"I have six grandparents," Gus brags. "You should see all the stuff I get for my birthday."

We round the corner. Stretch is sitting on the curb, and Tico is stuck in a tree. The Roadrunners are now complete. After we get Tico down, we all head to the park. There's a crowd already there. Still, we manage to get a good spot on the grass.

Gus produces three boxes of sparklers from nowhere. He quickly sells the sparklers for fifty cents apiece. "One box of a dozen only costs two dollars," he informs us. "I should have gotten more, then I'd be rich."

"My mom thinks it's great that you guys have summer jobs," Tico muses. He starts to snicker. "She says that you both must be very mature."

Gus and I look at each other and make pig noses. Then he takes out one last box of sparklers. We light them and use them as swords, making sure everyone gets a chance to die.

Digger springs for sodas and popcorn and those glow sticks that light up when you crack them. I spot Marley standing alone in the crowd staring up at the stars. He is wearing his "Beam Me Up, Scotty" T-shirt. I take my glow stick from Digger, and when I look again, Marley has disappeared.

It's getting dark. A voice on the loudspeaker announces that the fireworks will begin in five minutes. A murmur crosses the crowd. As the national anthem plays, little kids run around and squeal. The adults sing "The Star-Spangled Banner," but not the Roadrunners. We're too cool for that.

At last, the first firework explodes against the night sky with a burst so loud I flinch. Glowing white ribbons tumble downward. A blast of green meets them halfway up and lights up the darkness once again. Blue, red, and gold, a rainbow of shapes and colors takes over. It is beautiful. For a moment, I forget my troubles. For a moment, it's just me watching the fireworks try to touch the moon before slowly showering back down to earth.

JULY 5, 12:48 P.M.

After English I visit Yin-Yin. I can tell that Sarah must have stopped by before she left for Summer at Sea. She's placed pictures of herself all over the place. I try not to gag.

"How are you doing?" I hand Yin-Yin a box of Sugar Babies. She loves Sugar Babies, even though they are bad for her teeth.

Yin-Yin puts on a big smile. It's so fake it hurts to look at it. "Oh, it is just lovely here. They have bingo and you can eat all you want. They even have a beauty shop." She doesn't look like she's been to the beauty shop. Her hair is all messy and her sweater is buttoned wrong. "How's summer school?"

"Miserable," I tell her.

"How's Millicent?"

"Miserable."

"Tell me something I don't know," she says, popping a Sugar Baby into her mouth. She closes her eyes when she chews, and for a moment Yin-Yin looks like she's in heaven.

"I'm getting a pimple. A big one," I say, pointing to my chin. Really, it's going to be *huge*. I've had zits before, but this one's going to be in the record books. It's like a mountain growing on my face. Stanford Mountain.

After I show Yin-Yin my pimple, I tell her how horrible Mr. Glick is and how Millicent Min is even worse. Then I give her a report about home.

"Sarah forgot to take the compass I got for her trip. And Mom and Dad had a big fight about Dad's job. So now they're not talking and when they do, they're superpolite to each other. I think I liked it better when they were yelling. At least then they were speaking."

"Your parents are acting like little kids who don't know how good they've got it," Yin-Yin says. "What they need is some of my dim sum." She looks lost for a moment. There's no stove or refrigerator in her room, only a coffeepot.

Stupid, stupid, stupid. As I head to the park, all I can think of is how stupid I am. I planned to cheer Yin-Yin up. Instead, all I did was complain. Maybe she's right. Maybe Mom and Dad need some dim sum. Maybe we all could use some dim sum.

JULY 7, 10:33 A.M.

Ugh. Tomorrow is Monday. That means summer school and Millicent Min, two of the most disgusting things in the world. At least today I can have some fun. I've already finished all my homework. I had to or else risk Millicent getting on my case with her whining, "Stan-turd, can't you do anything right????"

The Roadrunners are at the park. Gus has jumped on Tico's back, and Tico's spinning around trying to throw him off. Gus's dark curly hair flops all over the place. You can't even see his face.

"Stanford!" Digger yells when he sees me. "Duck!" He hurls the ball at me. I catch it with one hand and toss it back.

"Let's play!" says Gus as he stumbles around.

Digger is looking at me funny. What is it about him that always makes me feel like I have a booger hanging out of my nose? He stares right at you like he's daring you to look away. Never look away from Digger. He might take that as an invitation to sucker punch you, then he'd say he was joking.

I don't like Digger's jokes even though everyone at school always laughs at them. Half the kids are impressed with Digger because his dad's on television and his family has a lot of money. The other half are scared of him because of his temper.

Digger's not scared of anyone or anything. Well, maybe just one thing.

A while ago, we were walking in the middle of the street, spraying passing cars with cans of soda. A car turned the corner and Digger yelled, "Get it!"

We all shook up our cans and sprayed the car really good, then ran. Only Digger didn't run. Instead, he stood still, totally frozen. We stopped and turned around just as Digger's dad got out of the car. He opened the back door and glared at Digger. "*Get in!*" he yelled.

I had never seen Digger look scared before. We didn't see him for three days, and when Digger finally showed up he wouldn't look at any of us. He didn't offer an explanation for his absence, or the bruise on his cheek, and we didn't ask.

"You okay?" It's Digger. "You're zoning out."

"C'mon!" Gus cries. "I wanna play ball, I wanna play ball!"

I touch my good-luck charm to make sure it's still there. I wish it worked for things other than basketball.

JULY 8, 7:54 P.M.

Today when SSSSpy turned in his homework, Teacher Torturer murmured, "Handing it in on time is half the battle."

I spent the rest of the class trying to decode what he was saying.

Somehow Mr. Glick has found out that Millicent Min is tutoring me. "Millicent Min! What a delight," he gushed. I was not sure we were talking about the same person. "Please give her my regards."

"I sure will," I answered, knowing full well that I wouldn't.

This afternoon Millicent was her usual pain in the neck. She and the library lady picked three books for my summer book reports. Right now Millicent's making me read *The Mixed-Up Files of Ms. Franks and Beans*, or something like that. The other two books are *Number the Stars* and *Holes*. Forcing me to write another report about *Holes* must be Millicent's warped idea of a joke.

For this *Mixed-Up* book Millicent has me read parts of it out loud, then she quizzes me. The story is not as bad as I thought it would be. There are these two kids who run away and camp out in a museum. Some days I've felt like running away too.

It's dinnertime now. Dad's late, so it's just Mom and me. She finishes rearranging the utensils. "There!" Mom says. "Maybe they will stay that way now."

I sit down as she puts the spaghetti on the table. It looks like a plate of worms. Dead worms with blood all over them. When I add Parmesan cheese, it looks like maggots.

As I poke at my food, Mom asks, "How are you doing in English?" and "How are you and Millicent Min getting along?" and "How are you feeling these days?" Why is she always drilling me? Doesn't she trust me? It's obvious she doesn't think I'm very smart. If she did she wouldn't be paying Millicent Min to harass me.

Mom picks at a piece of garlic bread and says, "What book are you reading now?"

"Stop asking me so many questions!" I yell. "What if I asked you questions all the time? Like why did you send Yin-Yin away? Don't you love her? Are you too lazy to look after her? How hard can it be? She's really old and can't run very fast."

My mother looks stunned. I push my plate away, race to my room, and lock the door. I'm panting as I reach under the bed and pull out the blue box. I crank up my radio so that it's blasting. Still, I can hear my mother knocking on my door, calling out my name.

I open the box. My hands are trembling. I can't believe I just yelled at my mom. It's one thing for my dad and me to yell at each other, but I've never yelled at my mom like that before.

I pick up the needles and begin knitting frantically. I have no idea what I am making.

"Stanford?" Mom calls out. "Stanford? Stanford! Open this door immediately."

She knocks again and I ignore it. Finally the knocking stops. Exhausted, I abandon my knitting needles, grab my basketball, and sprawl out on the bed. I spot a small black spider dangling from the ceiling. I'll bet I can hit it with my basketball. I begin to take aim, then stop. Slowly, I put the ball down.

What has that spider ever done to me?

JULY 9, 6:37 P.M.

It's eighty-nine degrees outside and I am freezing. Yin-Yin is pacing her room. "Did you bring it?"

I nod and take the package out from under my shirt. Yin-Yin slips the box of Kwan's frozen Oh My! Shu Mai! into a pillowcase.

"Follow me," she whispers. As we slip into the staff break room, she explains, "We're not supposed to be here, so we have to hurry."

Yin-Yin is looking a little better than the last time I saw her. She is wearing matching shoes, and her dress is buttoned the way it's supposed to be. Her hair still looks kinda funky, like she slept on it funny, but I don't mention it. We are too determined to complete our mission.

After microwaving the *shu mai*, we scurry down the hallway laughing and duck back into Yin-Yin's room.

"Not so good," she says, biting into an Oh My! Shu Mai! "Not nearly as good as mine." I nod in agreement. "Well, it will do for now," Yin-Yin sighs. "But don't worry. Next time they'll be better."

JULY 11, 3:59 P.M.

If I hold the book up and stare at the pages, Millicent actually thinks I am reading. *Ha!* She doesn't have a clue. Hey, this isn't bad. When Millicent thinks I am reading, she's not lecturing me. I just have to remember to turn the page every now and then.

"Wake up!"

Someone is hissing at me. Oops, I must have fallen asleep. I hope I wasn't drooling. That happened one time in class and my notes got all smeared.

"We have to go over the parts of speech again." Millicent is shoving some papers at me. "Here, I've made a list for you with examples. Plus, you should be up to at least chapter six in —"

"No fair!" How can she expect me to read six chapters when I have important things to do like watching *Top Cop* and working on my crossover fake-out two-pointer (otherwise known as the Stanford Shake 'n' Bake)?

"Sit up," Millicent orders as she points to one of the papers.

NOUN: A person, place, thing, or idea.
The brilliant <u>tutor</u> tried to teach the ignorant boy.

ADJECTIVE: A word that describes a noun.

> *The* <u>*pea-brained*</u> *basketball player did not even attempt to study.*

VERB: A word that expresses an action.

> *The police* <u>*arrested*</u> *him and threw him in jail.*

ADVERB: A word used to describe a verb or adjective.

> *The boy apologized* <u>*profusely*</u>, *but it was too late and he was fed to the wolves.*

Is Millicent making fun of me? She's making fun of me! I wad up her list. "It's missing something," I inform Miss Priss. I execute a classic Stanford Shake 'n' Bake and hit Millicent right on the nose with her own paper. Two points! "It needs to say: 'Millicent Min: Ugly jerk.'"

Oh god . . . now she's lecturing me. . . . What have I done to deserve this?

Finally, finally, *finally* she shuts up. One more millisecond and I would have morphed into a blob of jelly or I would have disintegrated. Or, I know, I would have burst into flames. Digger says that in some countries people are just walking around and then, *boom!* They explode. He's even seen it happen once when his family was in Spain to watch the bullfights.

As Millicent and I leave the library, I hope she catches on fire, but she doesn't. Instead she turns right, so I turn left.

4:59 P.M.

I really needed to go to the right, but I didn't want to walk in the same direction as Millicent Min. So now I have to take a shortcut through the park to get to the drugstore. Some guys from school are playing soccer. One yells, "Hey, it's Stanford Wong. Hi, Stanford!"

Another boy calls out, "Stanford, if you ever give up basketball, why not give soccer a try?"

Weakly, I give them a thumbs-up and then continue trudging through the park. I have two zits now and they are really beginning to bother me. One's as big as a house. Ooooh, wouldn't that be gross? To live in a zit. You'd have to wear a scuba suit or an astronaut outfit to do that. Disgusting.

The drugstore isn't too crowded. Good. Look at all the pimple medicines. Man, there are a lot of them. There must be millions of zits out there to have so many medicines. How am I supposed to figure out which one to get? Finally I shut my eyes and just grab one.

This line is sooooo slow. The lady in front of me has bought tons of dog food. She must have a really big dog. Hey, there's a girl over there who's kinda cute. She's taller than me, but she has a really nice smile, plus she has sparkly eyes. I like sparkly eyes. I try to make my eyes sparkle back at her.

Ohmygod. She's standing next to ... it can't be ... she's standing next to Millicent Min. *No!* She's *with* Millicent Min.

This can't be happening. I try to cover my zits. The girl is looking at me and smiling and sparkling. Wow, she's cute. Oh god, now Millicent's turning around and staring at me. She looks horrified. I toss the zit medicine and run out the side door.

Beeeeeep!!!! Oh no. I went out the fire exit! I can't believe I did that. I bet that girl thinks I'm the biggest idiot. When Millicent gets through telling her about me, I might as well be on a Big Stupid Idiot poster.

I'm running, running down the street. Gotta get away, gotta get away. Hey, wait a minute. . . . I slow down. Millicent signed a contract. She's sworn not to tell anyone she's tutoring me! I guess we'll find out if she's good for her word. I can't believe that Millicent Min has the power to screw up my life even more than she already has.

JULY 12, 9:14 A.M.

Mr. Glick played a totally mean trick on us yesterday. He started reading this story called "The Lottery." At first SSSSpy didn't care. He was busy drawing the most incredible maze on his arm. Then the story started to get interesting. I thought it would be about winning money, but instead it was about this weird town that seems normal but is totally Twilight Zoned out so you just know that something bad's going to happen. Right when we were about to find out what it was, Mr. Glick closed the book.

"Awwww," several kids cried. I was surprised to hear myself join them.

"If you want to know what happens, then read it yourself," Mr. Glick chuckled. "It's your homework assignment."

Even though I didn't want to, I opened "The Lottery" before bed. The story really bothered me. Why did that have to happen to the lady? She didn't do anything wrong, and what about her little boy? Did he have to be a part of it? Just because things are always done one way, does it mean they can't change?

I couldn't sleep at all last night just thinking about it. All this homework is not healthy.

"Who read 'The Lottery'?" Mr. Glick asks now.

I raise my hand. Not too high so that I look like a kiss-up, but not too low so I don't get credit.

"Good," he says as he scans the room. "Who wants to start off the discussion?"

A couple of the kids in the front of the room shoot their hands straight up in the air, but Mr. Glick locks in on me. "Stanford? What did you think of the story?"

I check to see if I accidentally raised my hand. Nope. I hate it when teachers call on me in class. He's waiting. I mutter something.

"What's that?" Teacher Torturer asks.

"I said it was stupid," I say louder.

The kids in the front still have their hands raised and are now frantically trying to get Teacher Torturer's attention. It looks like they are going to fall out of their chairs.

"Stupid?" Mr. Glick echoes. Ooooh boy, here it comes. I'm in trouble now. "Can you explain why you feel this way?"

I mumble, "It was stupid to have a lottery in the first place. It wasn't even for money; it was to see who was going to get stoned to death. Who'd want to be a part of a lottery like that?"

Mr. Glick looks at me and raises one eyebrow. SSSSpy starts to sink lower in his seat. Teacher Torturer turns to the class. "Stanford has an excellent point. Who would like to elaborate on that?"

I look around the room. A lot of kids are talking at the same time. Everyone has an opinion about "The Lottery." I don't say anything more in class, but I don't zone out either.

4:31 P.M.

Yin-Yin always asks how I'm doing with Millicent. She really wants us to get along. One time I said, "We're making a lot of progress."

Yin-Yin nodded and smiled. "So I've heard from Maddie," she said, which means that Millicent must be lying about tutoring too.

As I head to Vacation Village, I rehearse what I'm going to tell my grandmother this time. When I get to the lobby, old ladies try to pinch my cheeks and pat my head. I grip my Celtics cap to keep it safe and run down the hall to get to Yin-Yin unharmed. She smiles when she sees me. "I'm doing really well in English," I tell her before she can ask. "Mr. Glick says that I am one of his best students. Millicent's been a big help, and she's really nice too."

Yin-Yin beams. It's easy to make her happy. All I have to do is lie.

There's a knock on the door and a perky Vacation Village lady comes in.

"Come on, Mrs. Wong. It will be fun."

"No, really, I'd rather not," Yin-Yin tells her.

The lady is practically pushing my grandmother down the hall. "Now, you know the doctor said you need to move around more. Come on. Give it fifteen minutes. If you still don't want to dance after that, you can quit."

"Fifteen minutes?" asks Yin-Yin.

"Fifteen minues," the perky lady promises.

Now they're herding lots of old people into the dining room. The tables are pushed against the walls. It's really scary. All the geezers are swinging their arms in the air and trying to wiggle their bottoms as music plays. Some of them look like they have no bottoms; others look like they have several. I can't watch.

The Roadrunners go to most of the school dances. Usually we just sit in the bleachers and look cool. Sometimes girls ask us to dance, and we do. I make sure that wherever I am dancing is really crowded so I don't have to move around a lot. Gus goes wild on the dance floor. Tico's more like me, though he's famous for this one move, the Tico Tornado. Digger's actually a really good dancer, even though he doesn't look like he'd be. Stretch refuses all offers. Girls ask him the most.

"Young man, please join us!"

Oh no, oh no, oh no! Yin-Yin's instructor is asking me to dance and all the old people are smiling at me. I think I've seen something like this in a horror movie.

"Uh, no thank you."

The dance teacher twirls around and asks, "How can you say no to the cha-cha?"

I have no clue how to cha-cha and I don't want to find out. Without warning the music starts up and the old people are shuffling toward me with their arms out like zombies!

"Gotta go," I shriek.

I run to Yin-Yin's room and lock the door. That was close! I hope they don't send one of those perky Vacation Village ladies to find me. I hate perky. Recently one of them tricked Yin-Yin into making a birdhouse. It's on her coffee table. I pick it up and examine it. It looks like her old house, white with columns in the front and a green door. If I were a bird I'd be proud to live in a house like this.

I'd like to be a bird. To be able to just fly away whenever I wanted. I know Yin-Yin hates being cooped up. She hasn't said so — in fact, she's getting better at pretending she likes it here. But I can't forget the day she made me promise to help her run away. I'll bet, if she could, Yin-Yin would fly right out of here.

JULY 13, 11:23 A.M.

I'm guarding Tico and we're heading downcourt when Gus tries to get the ball from Stretch using my famous Stanford Shake 'n' Bake move. Only Gus adds a pirouette like some sort of doofus ballerina and then trips over his own feet. We're pushing each other around and laughing hysterically when Digger shows up.

"What's so funny?" he asks as he sets a bag down on the ground.

"I'm Gus the ballerina basketball player," Tico says, running in circles on tiptoes.

Soon Stretch, Digger, and I are leaping and twirling all over the court. At first Gus tries to pretend we don't exist, but soon he's laughing and joins us. Some kids from school are watching, but we don't care.

When we finally get tired of prancing around, Digger retrieves his bag. "Guess what I got?"

"Triple-decker tuna salad sandwiches on wheat?" asks Tico.

"Does this look like a sandwich?" Digger pulls out a Road-runners baseball cap and puts it on. His red hair sticks out from the sides.

"Totally cool!" Gus says.

"It's yours," Digger says, tossing him a cap.

"Me too," shouts Tico.

"I'm in!" I add.

Stretch nods and Digger gives one to each of us.

"These are great," says Tico.

"They're from my dad." Digger doesn't sound too happy, but no one else seems to notice.

As we try the caps on, we grin at each other. We look good and we know it. No one would mistake us for ballerinas now. We're the Roadrunners.

JULY 15, 10:35 P.M.

On *Top Cop* tonight, Top Cop's long-lost girlfriend showed up and turned to him for help. Bad guys were after her because she had double-crossed them. Top Cop got the bad guys, but first they kidnapped his girlfriend and tossed her off a bridge. Bummer.

I've never had a girlfriend. Digger has had lots of them, or so he claims. We've never seen any of them, though plenty of girls act like they'd rather shove pencils in their ears than talk to him. Tico has lots of girls after him. It's because he's nice. Girls seem to like that sort of thing. Ever since Stretch started growing and stopped talking, girls have been doing strange things when he's around. Like they gather in small groups and walk back and forth in front of him a hundred times a day. I don't think Stretch notices. If he does, he hasn't mentioned it. (Ha-ha!)

Gus and I talk about girls a lot, but we can't figure them out. They are so confusing. Like, if you look at them, they get mad. And if you don't look at them, they get mad. And if you're nice to them, they think you like them. And if you're mean to them, they think you like them. And if you do like them, they think you hate them.

When I was in grade school, it was a lot easier to figure out if a girl *like* liked you. All you had to do was hit her. I don't mean slug her, but just sort of hit lightly and laugh lightheartedly while you were doing it. If the girl hit you back and smiled, she *like* liked you. But if she screamed and then slugged you really hard or worse, kicked you, it meant that not only did she not *like* like you, she hated you, which automatically meant that all her friends did too.

Girls stop by the park all the time and watch us play basketball. We pretend not to notice them, but Digger gets louder, Gus goofs off more, Tico smiles wider, and I stand taller. Only Stretch acts the same. I'm convinced they come to watch him the most.

There are lots of kids at Rancho Rosetta Middle School who are boyfriend/girlfriend. It's just sort of known who's a couple. Only if you didn't know who was together, then it would be impossible to tell. Being together doesn't necessarily mean that the couple talk to each other or even sit together at lunch.

From what Gus and Tico and I can figure, you can be boyfriend/girlfriend with someone and not even have to say anything to her. We've heard that sometimes all you have to do is nod at a girl and if she smiles back at you in a certain way, then that's it. It's official. In fact, we think that Gus once had a girlfriend, broke up with her, and then went out with her best friend, all without him even knowing it.

Then there are the couples who want everyone to know they're together. The girls write the boys' names all over their notebooks and make a big deal about wearing their jackets, even when it's hot. Some of the eighth graders hold hands and a few even kiss on campus. There's this one couple that we nicknamed

Rescue 911, because it looks like they are giving each other mouth-to-mouth resuscitation. All day long, all they do is kiss in the quad, near the big tree. They don't seem to care who looks at them, and believe me, everybody does. They have hickeys all over their necks, which, Gus swears, can kill you if it's done wrong.

None of us are really sure how to give (or get) a hickey. I've practiced on my arm, but it hasn't worked. Digger says, "You just bite the girl's neck, like a vampire." Right, like he'd really know.

There's talk that all the Roadrunners have gone to second base with girls. We don't deny the rumors. I'm not too clear on what second base is, but I'm too embarrassed to ask anyone. They'd probably laugh at me if they found out I've never even held hands with a girl before.

I keep thinking about that girl who was with Millicent Min at the store. There was something about her. Maybe it was her sparkly eyes or that she looked right at me and smiled. I wouldn't mind if she *like* liked me. That girl can slug me anytime.

JULY 16, 4:05 P.M.

Millicent is staring at me like I'm sort of alien. Who knows? Maybe I am an alien. After all, aliens live on planets, and Earth is a planet, and I live on Earth. So that makes me an alien, right?

Sometimes I feel like an alien. Maybe I'm the leader of Planet Stanford, where we just float around all day and watch *The Three Stooges*.

"Just try," Millicent whines. "Just give the books a chance. Would that be so hard?"

"I can't," I tell her. "Reading zaps my energy for important things like basketball."

"Well, what about your homework?" She sounds upset. Good. "What did Mr. Glick say about it? According to my chart, you've only completed sixty-seven percent of your homework so far this summer. Did you turn in your homework today?"

"I did it, I swear," I say. "But then, when I was going to school, there was this little brown dog and he was running away. Then Tico showed up on his skateboard, the red one, not the blue one, and he had to swerve to miss the dog. But instead of slowing down, the dog sped up, which was probably hard for him because he only had two legs. Instead of back legs, the dog had these two little wheels strapped to him, and they were spinning so fast . . ."

I am beginning to actually get interested in my own story. Maybe I'll tell stories for a living. "So then, the FedEx man is thanking me, but the dog is still running straight toward a bus when one of the dog's wheels falls off —"

"Enough!" Millicent commands, holding both hands out like she's stopping traffic. "What does any of this have to do with your homework?"

"What homework?"

"Precisely what I'd like to know," she snaps. "Here, read this. If you don't start completing *all* your homework, I'm going to tell your parents. Honestly, Stanford, if you would just listen to me, you'd pass your class. Why can't you just do what I tell you?"

I snatch the book from her and pretend to read. Millie-the-Dog-Hater gets up to sharpen her pencils. She does that a lot. The words begin to blur on the page. I am so tired. This place just puts me to sleep. It's so quiet in here. Maybe I ought to suggest to Mrs. Martinez that she play some music to liven things up.

"*Ouch!*"

"Wake up!" Millicent hisses. She kicks me again. I grab my leg. It really hurts. Millicent gives me a smug smile. Maybe since we aren't discussing my "deplorable lack of academic ambition," this would be a good time to ask her about that sparkly girl.

"Who was that person you were with?" I try to sound casual.

"What person? Stanford, as usual, I have no idea what you are blabbering about."

"The person with you at the drugstore the other day," I remind her.

Millicent tenses up, which surprises me. I didn't think it was possible for her to get any more tense than she already was. "No one you know."

"She seemed nice. What's her name?"

"Emily," Millicent mumbles.

Emily's a good name. I like that name. Stanford and Emily. Emily and Stanford. Yeah, that works.

"Did she ask about me?"

"No," Millicent scoffs. "Though we did laugh when you set off the emergency alarm."

My jaw locks. I wonder what the penalty would be for dunking Millicent in the book-return bin. Hey, wait! "Emily seemed pretty cool," I point out. "What's she doing hanging around with a nerdling like you?"

"Better me than you," she shoots back.

I know it's a long shot, but here it goes. "Maybe you could introduce us?"

"Maybe not."

I lean in and lower my voice. "Hey, Millicent. Remember, you promised not to tell anyone you're tutoring me, right? I mean, if that girl or the guys ever found out, it could ruin my reputation."

I can tell she's thinking about it. She did swear on her mother's life, and if she broke the contract it could kill her mom. Should I remind her of that? That she'd be responsible for the death of her very own mother? I'll bet there's a law against that.

"Well," Millicent finally says, "I guess if it's so important to you then I won't mention it to her."

Wow! She's going to do it. "Thanks," I tell her. I never

expected Millicent Min to help me out. Sometimes she's okay, I guess. I remember this one time when we were little kids. I was in second grade and Millicent was in fourth or fifth on account of her being a genius. Even with all the noise on the playground, I could hear Digger yelling, "I see London, I see France, I see Bettina's underpants!"

"Excuse me!" Millicent called. I came out from behind my tree to watch her drag her briefcase to the climbing bars. "London is a city, whereas France is a country," she corrected Digger. "So if you knew anything, you'd know that your song is inconsistent."

The playground went silent. Even back then, Digger had a reputation.

That day at lunchtime Digger threw a Tater Tot at Millicent Min. He missed, but since she was sitting alone nobody got hit.

"Hey, Mill the Pill, duck!" he shouted.

The second one landed on her tray and made this popular girl Bettina and her friends giggle. Soon Millicent was being showered with Tater Tots. It took about forever, but when the lunch monitor finally figured out what was happening, she ordered both Digger and Millicent to Principal Powell's office.

Digger marched away, waving as the boys cheered. Millicent slumped over like a question mark, hugging her books and looking like she was going to cry. I remember feeling bad for her, but I didn't do anything to make her feel better. The last thing I wanted was for Digger Ronster to beat me up. I didn't even want him to look at me. We weren't friends then. That would come later.

The next day, Digger started throwing hamburger buns at

Millicent. Every day, when the lunch monitor's back was turned, he threw something else, like French fries or green beans. Digger never threw dessert, though. I guess he thought it wasn't worth wasting his dessert on Millicent Min.

After a while the kids got used to Digger throwing things at Millicent. But apparently she never did. One day the cafeteria was fairly calm when all of a sudden, *boom!* Digger's covered with foam and the whole room's laughing at him. That was the last time Millicent got sent to the principal's office. Later I overheard my parents talking. Millicent got kicked out of school for rigging a salt shaker to explode. Lots of kids thought this was unfair, because Digger started it. Still, no one came to her defense.

I have never told Millicent this, but I sort of admire her for what she did to him when we were little. It takes an awful lot of courage to stand up to Digger.

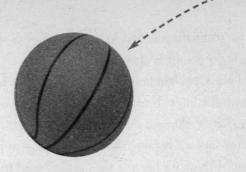

JULY 19, 7:35 P.M.

Exactly how many birdhouses can one person make? There must be at least eight of them here. Some are small, others are two-story numbers, and all are painted in bright colors. My favorite is on top of the television. There's a small satellite dish on the roof of that one.

Yin-Yin's named her latest birdhouse "Family Reunion." It has little photos of our family all over it and bits of jewelry and stuff.

"These are cool," I say, picking up a birdhouse that looks like a log cabin.

"They have a really nice arts and crafts teacher here, and the beauty shop is actually quite good."

Today my grandmother's hair looks better than it did when she first arrived. She says she paid a visit to Mr. Arturo and he gave her a bob. I pretend to know what that means. "You look really pretty," I tell her.

Yin-Yin holds out her hand. I slip her the Sugar Babies. Mom's down the hall trying to get someone to fix the TV.

"Do you still shout at the television?" I ask.

"Of course I do," my grandmother states matter-of-factly.

"That's half the fun. Besides, everyone here is so old and hard of hearing it doesn't bother them."

I guess Yin-Yin knows she's in an old people's home. I wasn't sure if she knew, because she was so spacey when she first got here. Lately, though, she's been more like the old Yin-Yin. The doctor says it's because she's "acclimating to her new environment." I think it's because she's getting used to it here. With all of the old fogies hanging around, I wonder if Yin-Yin feels like one of them. Some walk; some are in wheelchairs. A lot of them have those metal rolling things they lean on. I want one of those. I'll bet it would be fun to run up to one, grab the handles, lift up your feet, and sail away.

"Do you still watch *Top Cop*?" Yin-Yin asks.

I nod and examine one of the birdhouses. It's shaped like a stove.

"Caught any bad guys yet?" Yin-Yin gives me a wink. Only it looks more like a big squint. She's never been good at winking. I keep telling her she needs to practice.

My grandmother and I have this bet. Either she's going to win a big prize or I'm going to catch a bad guy. Whoever reaches their goal first gets to make the other person do anything they want. I'm going to make her wear her underpants on her head. Yin-Yin says she's going to make me kiss a girl. I wonder what it would be like to kiss Emily? Would she slug me really hard? Would she kiss me back?

"Nope," I tell Yin-Yin. "Haven't caught any bad guys yet, but I will." Stanford Wong, *Top Cop*'s Top Cop.

Mom returns with a screwdriver. "No one can fix the TV,

so I'm going to do it myself," she says as she fiddles with the back of it.

I try not to laugh. Mom fixing a TV, that's pretty funny.

"*A brand-new washer and dryer!!!!*" a voice on the television shouts. The audience goes nuts.

"There," my mother says, looking proud of herself. "The television's fixed." The three of us settle down on Yin-Yin's bed and watch the game show.

"Where's Rick?" Yin-Yin asks. I look at my mom. She's acting like she didn't hear Yin-Yin. "Where's Rick?" Yin-Yin asks again, this time louder.

"He had to work," Mom says without expression. "You know how much he works."

Yin-Yin and I both nod. We know how much he works.

JULY 21, 9:49 P.M.

Mom and Dad are arguing about my grades again. You'd think they would get tired of it. I know I am.

"He's showing lots of improvement."

"He failed a class. Sarah never failed anything in her entire life."

"We're not talking about Sarah; we're talking about Stanford."

"What is it with that boy? Is he just lazy? I swear he's just doing this to upset me. You'd think that with someone like Millicent Min tutoring him, he'd do better."

"Stanford's not trying to upset you. If anything, he wants to impress you."

"Well, he sure has a funny way of showing it. When Sarah was his age she skipped a grade."

"You're expecting too much from him."

"I'm expecting him to try. If we have low expectations of Stanford, then he'll never amount to anything."

So far I've done a lot of knitting. My whatever-I-am-making is about six inches wide and eight feet long. It looks like an ogre's scarf or a blanket for a snake. I've chosen some really nice yarn colors — red and yellow. I also found this one yarn that's lots of colors mixed together. How'd they figure out how to do that? Maybe I'll be in charge of yarn colors when I grow up. Do you have to go to college to do that?

Dad says, "If you don't get good grades, you'll never get into a good college." Okay, so, and then what? My life will be ruined? He's never come right out and said that, but I know that's what he means. He really wants me to go to Stanford University, where he went. He had it all figured out, even before I was born. That's why he gave me this dumb name.

"It could be worse," Mom used to joke. You could have been called Dartmouth or Hofstra."

She doesn't joke about college anymore. "There's more to life than school," I've heard her tell my father. "He's still a kid; there's plenty of time to stress over colleges later."

There are tons of things I can do besides go to college. Gus thinks that I have it in me to play pro ball. Yesterday Stretch and I slaughtered Digger and Tico. Yin-Yin says that I can do anything I want to do. Maybe I don't want to go to college. Maybe I want to sail around the world, like Sarah. Only I'd skip the study part.

When I handed in my book report on *Mrs. Franks and Beans*, Mr. Glick actually smiled at me. He says I am improving, "thanks to Millicent Min." She's getting the credit for my improvement. I'll bet he believes I am so stupid that I can't do anything on my own.

I know that's what my dad thinks. He's always saying, "That boy's like a loose cannon." I was pleased until Millicent explained, "A loose cannon rolls around the ship in an unpredictable manner and never hits its mark."

"Rick," I hear my mother say now, "if you're so concerned about his grades, maybe you could go over some of his homework with him sometime."

"The boy doesn't need me to go over his homework. What he needs is discipline. He needs good study habits and someone to make sure he does what he is supposed to."

"Oh, and I suppose I'm the one who's supposed to carry out your orders?" Mom's voice sounds icy.

"Well, I can't do everything around here. You know how swamped I am at the office."

"Excuse me." My mother takes aim. "I guess my job's not important. We can't forget that the law firm of Calvin Benjamin Jacobs would fold if Rick Wong took even two minutes off to be with his son."

"I am up for a promotion," my father shoots back. "Do you know how many people would kill to get this job?"

"I know one person," my mother says.

I shut my door and push a chair up against it, then duck for cover under my blanket. Still, it feels like every shot they take at each other passes through me first.

JULY 22, 10:26 A.M.

Strange, but English is not as totally awful as it was when it first started. Maybe Teacher Torturer is getting better at his job. Today Mr. Glick brought in a friend who used to be in the CIA. Now he writes spy novels. I've never met an author before. The guy looks so normal, boring even. The least he could do is wear a hat or carry a cane.

"Is everything you write true?" asks one of the kids.

"No, but many parts are," A. C. Griffiths tells us. He scans the room. "The boy with the basketball."

"Have you ever killed anyone?" I ask.

"If I told you, I'd have to kill you," Mr. Griffiths says with a wink. Everyone laughs.

A. C. Griffiths talks to us about writing a book and how hard it is. "The words don't just magically appear on the page," he explains. "Someone has to put them there. It might take me years to write something that someone can read in hours. But that's my reward, that someone is actually enjoying my work."

He begins telling us what he's writing next, "a spy novel set in outer space in the not-too-distant future." How cool is that?

Suddenly the bell rings and class is over. Mr. Glick thanks Mr. Griffiths and says, "Sorry, but that's it for today."

I wish class had lasted longer.

I take my time stuffing everything in my backpack. I want to tell Mr. Griffiths that sometimes I pretend I'm a spy, only he might laugh at me. So instead I slip into SSSSpy mode and listen to him and Mr. Glick. They discuss Mr. Griffiths's bad back and the quality of Mr. Glick's front lawn. I'll bet they are talking in code.

Finally they shake hands and promise to meet for dinner. After Mr. Griffiths leaves, Mr. Glick notices me standing in the back of the room.

"Need any help?" he asks.

"Uh, no, I got it," I tell him.

He glances at my *Number the Stars* book. "Excellent reading choice. Have you started it yet?"

"I'm going to start it tonight." I'm not lying either. I really am, right after *Top Cop*. "How do you know A. C. Griffiths?"

"A. C. and I go a long way back. We met while waiting in front of the principal's office. He was such a cutup." A slow grin crosses Mr. Glick's face. "Who knew he could write? And as for me, I got in so much trouble all the time, who knew I'd end up a teacher?"

Mr. Glick used to get in a lot of trouble? Before I can say anything, he tells me, "Now, Stanford, it wouldn't do my reputation any good if the other kids found out about my shady past. Let's keep this between you and me, okay?"

I zip up my backpack and fling it over my shoulder. I still can't believe that Mr. Glick was sent to the principal's office.

"Okay," I assure him. "It'll be our secret."

4:49 P.M.

I'm at the park. It's two-on-two, Tico's ref-ing, and Digger and I are ahead. Stretch passes the ball to Gus. I intercept and swerve around. I'm clear to shoot when suddenly — oh no, no, no, this can't be happening! It's Millicent Min and she's waving to me.

I miss the shot. Air ball. Everyone laughs, even the girls who are pretending not to watch us play.

Millicent comes closer. *Why?*

"Stanford," Millicent calls out. Her voice sounds funny. "I need to see you for a minute."

What a total dork she is with her briefcase. Everyone is staring at her. No one, and I mean *no one*, ever interrupts when the Roadrunners are playing. Millicent looks like she doesn't even notice she's stopped the game. She's one of those people who are so into themselves they don't care what other people think.

"Can't it wait?" I ask, lowering my voice.

"No," she insists, lowering her voice.

Everyone is still staring. "Gotta go. See you guys later," I mumble.

Digger's face turns as red as his hair. "Hey, Stanford, come back, we're not finished yet."

"No, I gotta go," I call back to the guys.

"Forget her; let's play," Digger shouts. He's staring at Millicent. I have to do something before he figures out who she is. "Stanford, come back. We need you!"

"Don't talk to me," I hiss as Millicent tries to catch up to me. "I don't want to be seen with you. What are you doing here?"

She looks hurt. "Your books," Millicent says, handing them to me. "You left them at the library. You've got a quiz tomorrow."

I stop and face her. "Oh. Yeah, well . . . ," I say, taking my books. "Thanks. Um, I'd better get back to the game."

Millicent is staring off somewhere like she's on another planet. I've noticed that she zones out a lot.

"Are you okay?"

She comes to and looks surprised to see me. "Yes, yes, I'm fine," she assures me. "Hey, good luck on your quiz."

"Right," I reply. Is she making a joke? "Like I'm really going to pass."

"You might." She sounds like she means it. "You're not as stupid as I first thought you were."

"Gee, thanks, Mill, and you're not as big a blockhead as I thought you were."

We both almost grin but catch ourselves just in time. I wait for her to leave, and when she finally does I stash my books in the bushes.

"It's about time," Digger says when I step back onto the court. "Who was that? She looks familiar. Does she go to our school?"

"Yeah, who was that?" Gus chimes in. "Your babysitter? Your parole officer? Your *girlfriend*?"

"Who, her?" I scoff. "Naw, I'd never go out with her! She's just some weirdo my parents say I have to be nice to."

Digger passes me the ball and I run down the court toward Tico. After I make the basket I look around in time to see Millicent marching past with her nose stuck up in the air.

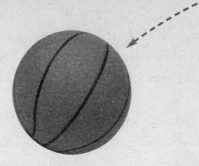

JULY 23, 12:30 P.M.

"Yin-Yin! Yin-Yin, wake up!"

I shake my grandmother and her eyes fly open. She blinks wildly. "Where am I?" she asks. "Have I died?" I take her glasses from her hand and put them on her face. "Oh." She sounds disappointed. "Still here, am I?"

I wave my English quiz in front of her. "Yin-Yin, look! I got a C-plus."

Yin-Yin sits up and examines my quiz. Mr. Glick has written "Good effort" across the top.

"Stanford, that's terrific. Can I keep this?"

"Not yet," I tell her. "I want to show Dad first."

8:05 P.M.

I am flying high. I made most of my shots at basketball, and then I won at H-O-R-S-E and everyone had to cough up a dollar. Stretch didn't have the money, so Digger tossed in two dollars to cover him. It is a great day.

Dad's home on time tonight. He's sitting in his den working. His den is off-limits, but this is important. I knock on the door and he waves me in. I try not to grin. I want my grade to be a surprise.

"Here," I say, handing Dad my quiz.

He looks up from his stack of paperwork and takes the paper from me. He stares at it for a long time. Then Dad scowls and my heart stops beating.

"A C-plus?" my father says. "Stanford, next time try to do better, will you?"

JULY 25, 3:30 P.M.

At least Mom was pleased with my C-plus. It is so far up from my F, she thinks anything is progress. My mother's going to meet with Millicent today. I'm not sure what they are going to talk about, but you can bet it's not basketball.

I wait for Millicent outside the library and hand her my quiz.

"C-plus," she reads. I grin and nod. "Okay, that's a good start."

We go inside. I hold up my quiz so Mrs. Martinez can see my grade. She smiles. I'm feeling pretty good.

"Let's get right to work," Millicent says as she unpacks her briefcase. "You passed your quiz; that's a positive sign. I think we're at a turning point in your studies and I predict that it is an affirmative one. It's a pity that you have to be nice to that weirdo who's tutoring you, though."

"What?"

"Yes, Stanford, that's right. When you opened your mouth at the park, I could hear what you were saying. Imagine that! Silly me," Millicent says, slamming her dictionary on the table. "I was beginning to think you were human, or should I say 'humane'? Oh well, there's no need for you and me to dwell on this." She delivers a wicked smile and adds, "When I meet with your mother this afternoon I'll be sure to tell her what a delight you are to work with."

7:17 P.M.

Great. The big brainstorm that came out of my mother and Millicent's meeting was that I have to read at least half an hour *before* I play basketball. This *does not* include my regular homework assignments. If this is a plot to make me miserable, it's working.

"That Millicent Min sure is a nice girl." Mom passes me a plate of lasagna. It's my father's favorite. I make sure not to eat too much, so there will be plenty left for Dad. Besides, I'm not very hungry. Right before dinner, Stretch and I had a Doritos-eating contest. He won, but only because he smashed his up so he could get more in his mouth at once. I'm going to try his strategy next time.

"I think she really likes you. It was her suggestion for you to read more. She is so concerned with you passing your class. Stanford, did you hear me?"

"Whatever."

"She's kind of cute too, don't you think?"

What is this? Is she trying to ruin my appetite for life? Millicent cute? Next Mom will say, "Don't you think greasy grimy gopher guts are cute?"

"Sure, Millicent's cute," I tell Mom as I take a big bite. Mom makes the best lasagna, even if it comes frozen in a box. "She's sooooo cute."

My sarcasm goes right over my mother's head. She perks up and says, "I agree! I'm so glad you and Millicent Min are good friends."

Who said anything about us being good friends? Wait. If Mom thinks that, Millicent must not have told her I told the guys she was a weirdo. How come she didn't fink on me?

"I know summer school is hard for you, sweetheart. Just try to hang in there." Mom looks at the clock. Dad used to call when he was going to be late. "Millicent says that you are showing some improvement, but she fears you have some anger issues."

"I don't know what she's talking about," I grunt.

"Millicent also said she thinks you could be trying harder."

I glance at my F paper on the refrigerator. How can I explain that some sort of supersonic magnetic force prevents me from getting anywhere near my English books? Mom has no clue how hard it is for me to study.

She is waiting for a reply.

"I am trying, honest," I say. "But what's the point when I know I'm going to fail?"

My mother puts down her fork. "If you were on the basketball court and a bunch of guys blocked you, would you give up?"

I laugh. "Of course not." She knows so little about basketball. "I'd fake them out or go around them. Or I'd just pass the ball to a teammate and then get it back and make a basket."

"Hmmm," she says, thinking. "Do you need to practice for a

basketball game, or do the players just step on the court and start playing?"

"Of course you need to practice." Why is she suddenly interested in my sport? "You need to warm up before every game too. Coach says you'd be nuts not to."

"Well then," Mom says, picking her fork up. "Maybe it's time for you to read some, study some, warm up before the tests, and give English your best try."

She winks at me and takes a bite of lasagna.

I hate it when parents use logic. It's totally unfair.

JULY 26, 1:57 P.M.

I was going to get one of those spy books A. C. Griffiths writes. Mr. Glick says that if we bring in the book, he'll get his friend to autograph it. I thought I'd give it to my dad to cheer him up since he's in a permanent bad mood. Then I remembered that Mom got Dad a book for his birthday, but he never read it.

"Who has time to read?" he said.

My thoughts exactly!

Before I visit Yin-Yin I have to go to the grocery store. Yin-Yin gave me a list of things to buy for the Vacation Village cook for his birthday. His name is Ramon, and Yin-Yin really likes him. "Don't tell your parents about the presents for Ramon," she told me over the phone. "They won't approve."

"What's a scallion?" I ask the store lady.

"Does oyster sauce come from an oyster?"

"Is a wonton skin something that would be on a shelf or in the freezer, and do they have to actually skin a wonton?"

"Would cornstarch be in the ironing aisle?"

The store lady snatches my list, grabs a basket, and gets everything I need. That was nice of her.

My grandmother is waiting for me in the Vacation Village

lobby. The bulletin board has changed. There are really old-looking photos of babies on one side and some really new-looking photos of prehistoric people on the other side. The sign says: THEN AND NOW. OH BABY, GUESS WHO'S WHO! Who would have thought these Vacation Villagers were ever babies?

Yin-Yin grabs my hand. "We don't have much time," she whispers.

I try to ask her what's going on, but she keeps shushing me. She's starting to remind me of Millicent Min. As we rush down the hallway, Yin-Yin suddenly shoves me through a side door. My grandmother is stronger than she looks.

I glance around. We are in the kitchen. "Ramon's running errands," Yin-Yin tells me. "I figure we have about an hour and a half to get everything done and get out of here."

Get what done? I wonder if this is another one of Yin-Yin's wacky projects, like wanting to turn our yard into a miniature-golf course. I dug fifteen holes before Mom made me stop.

"Do you have everything?" Yin-Yin asks.

I nod and surrender my backpack. It is bulging with groceries. My grandmother breaks into a wide smile as she empties it. Fish sauce, ground pork . . . she cradles the cilantro and then smells it as if it were a bouquet of flowers.

"Thank you, Stanford," she says, giving me a squeeze. "I will put all this to excellent use!"

"I thought it was for Ramon's birthday? What's going on?"

"What's going on is they never have dim sum around here," Yin-Yin says. She maneuvers around the big kitchen as if she has always cooked here. I perch on one of the long steel counters and watch her, like I used to at her house and then later at ours. This is the happiest I've seen her since she arrived at Vacation Village.

"My mother taught me how to make dim sum," she tells me as she minces scallions. "You know, Stanford, your great-grandparents used to live in China in a hut with a dirt floor."

I didn't know that. Until this moment I never actually thought about my great-grandparents.

"They cooked over an open fire and slaughtered their own chickens."

Okay, now I'm hearing more than I want to.

"When my parents first came to America they were shocked. They had never even imagined stores stocked from floor to ceiling with groceries, iceboxes in your house to keep food from spoiling, and a man in a white suit who would deliver milk and eggs to your front door. Coming from a land where food was scarce, America was like heaven to them."

Yin-Yin searches for a big bowl and finds one. "I always wanted a daughter to pass on my recipes to. But your auntie Mary in San Francisco has shown no interest in dim sum. No interest in cooking at all," says Yin-Yin as she rips open the wonton-skin packages. "Can you believe that her family goes out to eat *every* night? I've offered to show your mother how to make dim sum several times, but each time she has said, 'Thank you, Yin-Yin, but not today.' I know what that means. It means 'Not today and not ever.'"

There's a sudden twinge in my chest. I don't like it when Yin-Yin talks about my mom like that, any more than I like it when my mom complains about Yin-Yin. But my grandmother doesn't say anything more. Instead she is cheerfully cooking in Ramon's big kitchen.

I watch as Yin-Yin folds the scallions into the pork, adding a dash of soy sauce and some spices. Expertly she grabs a blob of the meat and drops it dead center onto the first wonton skin lined up on the counter. Then she uses a beaten egg to seal the edges. Together we curve the wontons into half-moon shapes. Mine don't look as good as hers.

Yin-Yin hunts around and comes up with a metal basket. She turns up the heat on the deep-fry vat. It is already filled with oil. "Thank you, Ramon," she says.

Soon the sizzling sound of wontons frying fills the kitchen. The smell is delicious. I can hardly wait to eat one. Yin-Yin hands me a plate and puts paper towels down on it. I hold it out and she dumps the golden-brown wontons on it and fills the deep fryer with more. Together we blot off the oil as we wait for the next batch.

"Careful, they're hot," my grandmother warns as we each reach for a wonton. I don't care if I burn my tongue. I've missed Yin-Yin's fried wontons almost as much as I've missed having her live with us.

It is hot, so hot that I fan my mouth as I bite into one. Ooooh, but it is soooooo good. Yin-Yin and I grin at each other and help ourselves to more.

The second batch is ready and there are no more left to cook. "With Ramon's deep fryer, I can cook even quicker," Yin-Yin says admiringly.

As she starts to empty the wontons onto another plate, the kitchen door swings open and someone booms, "*What* is going on in here?"

We both freeze.

Yin-Yin plants a sweet smile on her face. "Well, hello, Ramon. I thought you were out for the afternoon."

"I was," Ramon barks. He does not look like a cook; he looks like a boxer. Ramon's younger than my dad and more muscular, with his hair slicked back and tattoos on both arms. His eyes scan the messy countertops. "Mrs. Wong, what are you doing in my kitchen? You know this is off-limits to residents. I could get fired for this!"

Yin-Yin is now batting her eyes at Ramon. She approaches him cautiously, holding a plate of fried wontons out in front of her like a shield. "I made these for you, Ramon," she says innocently. "I thought you might like to try the famous dim sum I once made for Elvis."

"Mrs. Wong, I'm already in enough trouble with management for that rum-cake fiasco last week. I really don't have time —"

"Just one," my grandmother coos. She waves the plate under his nose. "Just one, Ramon."

"Oh, all right." He looks angry as he snatches a wonton. There is no expression on his face as he chews. "Elvis was a lucky man," Ramon remarks when he is done. "But Mrs. Wong, we both know that I'm not Elvis and you didn't make them for me today. Now please get out of here before we both get in trouble."

I grab Yin-Yin by the elbow. "You heard him," I hiss, dragging her away. As we make our way down the hall, I ask, "Did you really make dim sum for Elvis Presley?"

"Who said anything about Elvis Presley?" she replies. "I made them for Elvis Price, my old neighbor."

As we approach her room, she stops abruptly. "Wait! The other plate."

"I'll get it," I tell her.

Slowly I open the kitchen door. I see Ramon sitting on a kitchen stool. Most of the dim sum is gone. His eyes are closed as he eats another wonton. He doesn't look mad anymore.

JULY 27, 1:20 P.M.

It's Saturday. No one's at the park but Digger. I start to turn around, but it's too late. "Hi, Stanford," he shouts, waving.

I wave back. "Where are the rest of the Roadrunners?" I ask. Even when Digger's nice to me, I can't relax until at least one other guy shows up.

Digger bends down to tighten the laces on his BK620s. "How should I know, I'm not their baby-sitter. Hey, where's your fan club?"

"What are you talking about?"

"That girl you were with the other day. She didn't seem like your type. She seemed like a nerd."

I ignore him.

We play a little one-on-one. As usual, Digger's fouling all over the place. I don't call him on them because I am in no mood to argue. Hearing my parents argue this morning was enough for me.

As I attempt to forget about Digger and play against him at the same time, I see Marley watching me from behind a tree. He's writing something in his stupid Star Trek captain's logbook. I try to pretend he's being transported to another galaxy. It's hard to play basketball when you are ignoring two people, but I do what I can.

Finally I see Gus coming up the walkway. He's got an ice-cream cone in each hand and is eating both, which is a very Gus thing to do. Tico's with him. He's carrying a soda the size of a bucket.

"Heads up," Digger shouts. He tosses the ball to Gus and knocks an ice-cream cone out of his hand. "Oh hey, I'm sooooo sorry," Digger says.

Gus just glares at him. His pistachio cone is slowly melting on the ground.

"Pick it up," I urge. "Hurry, you've only got five seconds before it goes bad!"

"It looks like the Wicked Witch of the West," Tico observes. "Or is it the East? 'I'm melting! I'm melting!'" he cries.

We all watch the ice cream slowly turn into a puddle. I know if I dropped a perfectly good ice-cream cone, I'd still eat it. I'm not fussy about stuff like that, although I do have my standards. I would never eat food off the ground that didn't belong to me.

Now Gus and Digger are having a stare-down, or should I say, "glare-down"? Chocolate ice cream from the surviving cone is running down Gus's arm, but he ignores it. Finally I shout, "Hey, I thought we were here to play basketball!"

Digger and I are on the same team. To make up for Gus's ice-cream cone, I let Tico sink a couple of easy shots and I'm purposely sloppy so Gus can get in a few baskets too. Digger growls at me, but I ignore him. Even though I'm not playing my best, we still beat them.

Gus looks glum and Tico looks like he's relieved the game is over.

"We make some team, right, Stanford?" Digger says, grinning. "Digger and Stanford, the dynamic duo! Remember how good we did on the B-Team? We should be on the same team all the time."

When Digger and I are on the same side, we do get along pretty well. Mostly, when the Roadrunners play each other, whatever team I am on wins. Digger's the second-best player; that's why we're usually against each other.

I glance at Gus and Tico. Neither looks happy.

"Whatever," I say.

For a moment Digger looks hurt. Then he says in a mocking voice, "Oh, excuse me, I forgot that it's a blessing to play on the side of the almighty Stanford Wong. All bow to Stanford!"

He gets on his knees and bows to me. I just shake my head.

"Just because you made the A-Team you think you're better than us," Digger says, brushing the dirt off his knees.

"That is such a lie," I tell him.

"So now I'm a liar?"

"Forget it," I mutter as I walk away. "I'm out of here."

I head to Stretch's house. I hope he's home.

"Why weren't you at the park?" I ask Stretch as he lets me in. We head up to his room. I look around. "Oh, I see."

There are piles of clothes everywhere. Stretch starts tossing the ones that are too small into boxes marked "Salvation Army." He holds up an Alan Scott T-shirt. I nod and he throws it to me. I slip it on over my tank top. It may not be BK620s, but I'll take what I can get.

"Gus and Digger were at it again," I inform Stretch as I start going through his CDs. I put on Mongo Bongo's greatest hits. "Today was lame. Tico and Gus were off their game and Digger was out to get them."

Stretch nods. He's seen it all before.

"Sometimes I think there's not enough room in the Roadrunners for both Gus and Digger. But then, if someone has to go, it might have to be Gus, since Digger is like in charge of the Roadrunners. Hey, did you hear? Mr. Ronster said he was going to buy us all Lakers jerseys this year."

Stretch raises his eyebrows.

"I know," I tell him. "If you add that up with the game tickets and everything, it's going to cost him a fortune!"

It must be nice to be superrich. Digger's dad also donates big-time to the school's Booster Club. He's paying to get the gym floor refinished in time for the Hee-Haw Game.

Stretch finishes filling up the boxes and we carry them into the kitchen. There's a bunch of bananas on the counter. I break one off and toss it to Stretch, then peel one for myself.

"Wanna go get some ice cream?" I ask through a mouthful of banana.

Stretch grabs his wallet and we start walking like monkeys. He's really great at swinging his arms and I'm an expert at making monkey sounds. This is what I like about hanging out with Stretch. With him, I can just be myself.

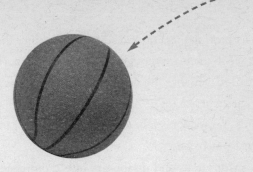

JULY 28, 3:39 P.M.

It's Sunday. Used to be that Sundays were the days my father and I would do stuff together. Of course, that was a million years ago. Today, instead of hanging out with Dad, I'm going to the mall with my mom. When did the world get turned upside down?

"Honey, how does this look?" Mom comes out of the dressing room and models a navy blue suit. It looks exactly like the other five navy blue suits she's tried on.

"Great," I mumble as I tug at a piece of rubber on my shoe. I'll bet BK620s never fall apart. "Can we go now?"

"Does it make me look fat?" she asks.

Why are females always so worried about looking fat? Skinny girls scare me. "Mommmm, you look fine," I groan. I am getting hungry. "Why can't you just wear your old clothes?"

Mom is still inspecting herself in the mirror. Now she's holding in her stomach. "I haven't bought a new suit in ages. Now that I'm back to working full-time, I think I deserve one, don't you?"

I nod. Hey! There are tons of straight pins on the floor. I

start picking them up and sticking them into the wall. I am going to see if there are enough pins to make a fancy letter *S*.

"Do you like work?" I ask. Mom works at a think tank. That's where a lot of smart people get together and solve problems. Yet we've been here for hours and she can't even figure out what suit to buy.

Mom nods and disappears into the dressing room. "I do. I feel really important there, like I'm making a contribution."

After a few minutes she reappears in yet another blue suit. "I get noticed at the office," she says as she admires herself in the mirror. "I feel like a somebody."

I wish my dad would pay more attention to my mother. Mom's really pretty, even if she doesn't think so. She has shiny black hair that she puts in a ponytail when she's at home, and she wears warm-up suits even though she's not into sports. Although from what she tells me, she used to be really good at dancing.

Mom and Dad used to go dancing all the time when they first got married. She keeps a photo of Dad twirling her on the dance floor tucked into the corner of her bathroom mirror. My father is really handsome. Lots of people say that I look like him, but I don't see it.

Nowadays the only dancing my mom does is when she takes her aerobics class.

After an eternity, Mom appears with one of the navy suits slung over her arm. "I think this was the best one, don't you?"

I agree even though I couldn't tell any of them apart. "It looked really good on you. That color flatters your complexion," I say, quoting a commercial for hair dye.

There, I've made Mom smile. I force myself to smile back even though I don't feel like it. Now that Yin-Yin's gone and Mom's working all the time, our house feels empty. Just because I ignore my mother most of the time doesn't mean I don't want her around.

JULY 30, 3:45 P.M.

We're in the middle of tutoring and I am exhausted. This reading-before-basketball routine is really wearing me down. I can't believe I'm supposed to do this *every day.*

I picked up *Holes* yesterday and before I could stop myself I was reading the book. It threw me off because I'm not finished with *Number the Stars.* Reading more than one book at a time is really tricky. Sometimes I get the stories so mixed up they don't make sense. Plus, reading is dangerous. It zaps all my energy, like right now. I'm so tired I can't even sit up. I'm slipping down my chair. Slipping, slipping, slipping . . . hey, if I keep going I'll be on the floor! That'll be neat. I haven't sat under a table in ages.

Wow! Who would have guessed that Mrs. Martinez has gum under her tables? It's amazing. Really beautiful. There are so many different colors. They look like those sagmites or whatchamacallits in caves. I could stay down here forever, even though it's pretty cramped. I almost forgot how great sitting under a table can feel.

Millicent's tapping her foot. I wish she'd keep her foot still so I can tie her shoelaces together. What's the matter with her?

"Okay!" Millicent says. "Stanford, get off the floor. There's enough dirt down there already. Let's go over plot again."

Oh no. Not that. I hate plot, whatever it is. Just as I am about to complain, I hear someone blurt out, "Ohmygosh, Millie, what are you doing here?"

A pair of purple sandals approaches.

"I just came to get my library card," the girl says, "and . . ." Oh no, oh no, oh no, she's looking under the table. I try to stand and bump my head. It's *her*.

"Uh, oh, hello there! I'm Emily Ebers, Millie's best friend. I don't think we've met."

I can feel my face burning. Even the tips of my ears feel hot. I crawl out and shake Emily's hand. "Stanford Wong," I tell her. "I'm just, uh, uh . . ." Panic. Panic. She can't know that Millicent is tutoring me — she'll think I'm stupid. What should I say?

"I'm just helping Millicent here with her studies," I blurt out.

Millicent yelps, but I ignore her because Emily is looking me over. Oh man, she's cute. Her eyes are doing that sparkly thing again. They're sort of greenish-brown, which looks really great with her blond hair. I'm having a little trouble with my balance and start to sway back and forth. "This is a superfine library," I hear myself say as I grab the table for support. "Really excellent." Ooooh, how stupid! I sound so stupid.

"It really is excellent," Emily says. How does she make her eyes sparkle like that?

"Yes, so true. Even the bottoms of the tables are clean. Uh, that's why I was under the table. I check the tables' tops and bottoms for cleanliness."

"Oh, so you're some sort of table monitor?" Emily asks, smiling at me. She has the nicest smile.

I smile back. "Uh, unofficially, yes."

"Excuse me!" interrupts Millicent. "We really should be getting back to the books."

I don't want Emily to leave. I've got to say something. Anything.

"Um, Emily, I'm sure Millicent would prefer it if you weren't here during our tutoring sessions." I lower my voice and tilt my head toward Millicent, who looks like she's just chewed on a lemon. "She gets embarrassed."

Emily looks sad. I don't want her to be sad. "Of course," I quickly add, "if Millicent ever figures out the difference between plot and theme, then maybe we could get together afterward. You know, get a burger or something."

"Oh! That sounds like a terrific idea. We'd love to go," Emily says brightly. I just love the way she talks. Her voice sounds like it's smiling.

Millicent looks like she is having trouble breathing. Emily sees this too and takes her aside. I start ripping a sheet of notebook paper into little pieces. Millicent will probably tell Emily that I'm stupid and she's the one tutoring me. It makes sense, because if Millicent's a genius, then only a super-genius would be able to tutor her, and no one has ever mistaken me for a super-genius.

I strain to hear what they are saying but can only make out snippets. "It's okay, Millie. . . . This explains a lot of things. . . . You are home-schooled. . . . Don't feel bad . . . no shame in needing a tutor. . . . It must be a hard class. . . . Not everyone can be a genius. . . ."

Wait! Something's fishy here. Millicent is not home-schooled — she's in high school. If Millicent is not correcting

Emily and announcing how smart she is, that must mean that Emily doesn't know Millicent Min *is* a genius. But why doesn't Millicent want Emily to know about her IQ? It's usually the first thing she tells people. Could she be covering for me?

Hey, wait a minute. . . . Not only does Emily think Millicent is dumb, but she thinks I am smart! I'd better do something fast so Millicent doesn't change that.

I dig through Millicent's briefcase until I find a copy of our contract. Why is it laminated? I stand behind Emily and hold up the contract for Millicent to see. She grits her teeth and gives me a small nod while Emily looks away. Relieved, I do the special wavy Roadrunners hand signal for making a good basket. Millie just scowls.

Finally Millicent returns. She stares at the huge pile of torn paper on the table. We try to continue our tutoring session, but it's hard for me to focus with Emily in the library. Emily is far more interesting than English. On the other hand, whenever she walks by, I get to raise my voice and say things like, "Millicent, you should know this by now. Why is foreshadowing important?" Millicent looks like she's constipated, but I sure am having a great time. I take one of her red pens and draw a sad face on her notebook.

"Millie, Millie, Millie, haven't I taught you anything?" I ask, shaking my head and trying to look concerned, which is totally hard to do because I'm going to crack up at any moment.

When Emily isn't looking at us, Millicent glares at me. Finally she slams her notebook shut. "Fine! It's clear nothing's getting done today. Let's just quit early, okay? Are you happy now?"

"Well, yeah! Hey, Emily." I run over to her. She's looking at the magazines. "We can go now. We got done early today."

"Wow, you must be a really great tutor!"

"That's what I've heard," I say, trying to look modest.

This is going to be so fun, pretending to be smarter than Millicent Min. But I can't figure out why Millicent is playing along. What's in this for her?

4:31 P.M.

At Burger King, Emily and I talk and talk and talk. It is so easy to talk to her. I've never met anyone like Emily before.

"So, you're from New Jersey? That's the home of the Nets. Julius Erving played for the Nets between 1973 and 1976. Drazen Petrovic also played for the Nets. Both of them are Hall of Famers." Millicent is gaping at me, but I ignore her. "Do you miss New Jersey?"

"Yes, well, some things," Emily says as she opens up a napkin and places it on her lap before biting into one of her cheeseburgers.

Wow, she's got a lot of class. I set my basketball aside and do the same.

"My father loves the Nets too. We used to live in this great old house and our backyard was on the edge of the woods. I loved that house." Emily lowers her head and adds, "But then my dad left and Mom decided we needed a 'change of scenery.'"

Oh, she looks so sad. I can't stand it. "Well, I'm glad you moved here," I tell her.

"You are? Stanford, what a nice thing to say. Are you always this nice?"

I glance at Millicent. She looks like she's dying of boredom.

"I dunno." I hope I am not blushing too much. "Uh, how did you and Millicent meet?"

"Volleyball," Emily states. "We're on the same volleyball team."

Millicent Min on a volleyball team? I start to snicker, then remember Millicent can blow my cover at any time. "Volleyball," I repeat. "That's a good sport. I play basketball."

"Are you any good at it?"

I sit up a little straighter. "I'm on the A-Team," I boast. "It's the first time a seventh grader is on the A-Team."

"Oh! No wonder you always carry a basketball." Emily blushes and explains, "I saw you once at the drugstore."

"Drugstore?" I try to sound vague.

"Yes, I was there with Millie, but it was a while ago."

"The drugstore. Hmm, well, maybe that's why you look a little familiar."

Emily lights up and then says, "Wow, Stanford, so you're on the A-Team and you're really smart too? That's a double whammy."

Millicent clears her throat. "Stanford smart?"

"Well, yes," Emily says. "After all, he's tutoring you, isn't he? He wouldn't be a tutor if he weren't smart, right, Stanford?"

Millicent and Emily both look at me, only one looks happy and the other looks horrified. Emily smiles as she sips her Diet Coke. I notice that she doesn't have a straw, so instead of answering, I jump up to get her one.

I take my time. I have to remember to breathe. Emily thinks I'm smart. She thinks I'm a smart basketball player, and I'm fairly certain it's possible she might like me.

"Hey, Emmie, lookit!" I'm back and holding up two fistfuls of straws. I hand half of them to her.

Even though I'm talking to Emily, Millicent speaks up.

"One: *Lookit* is not a real word," she announces. "And two: It's stealing when you take things and don't use them for their intended purpose. Plus, consider the unnecessary waste and its impact on the environment."

Emily bites her lip. She has nice lips. I've never really noticed a girl's lips before, but hers look really soft. Millicent's look hard since she's always frowning.

"I guess we really shouldn't waste them," Emily says as she sets down her straws. She sounds disappointed.

"Fine. Great. Terrific. I'll just put them back then," I tell Millicent. I hope she is happy making Emily sad.

I put the straws back and spot something on the counter. "Are those free?" I ask the Burger King man.

I come back wearing a gold cardboard crown and hand one each to Emily and Millicent. Emily puts hers on immediately. She looks like a princess. Millicent tosses her crown aside and grinds her French fries into her mouth like she's a pencil sharpener. She's superskinny, so I suppose it's good that she's eating so much. Emily looks really healthy and sturdy.

"Emily, watch this," I say.

I open up a napkin and press it against my face. Then I stick my tongue through it. Emily bursts into a fit of laughter. Then she tries it and I start laughing. It's like we've known each other forever. Sometimes I even forget she's a girl. Then I look at her sparkly eyes, her perfect skin, her crooked smile, and I know this is no boy I'm talking to.

"Here, Millie," Emily says, handing her friend a napkin. "Your turn."

I look at Millicent. Is she still here? She holds the napkin to her face and then wipes her mouth. "If you two will excuse me," she says, standing up, "I think I hear my mother calling."

She grabs her briefcase and storms out. This makes me happy until I realize that Emily is going with her. "Excuse me, Stanford!" she says before rushing after Millicent.

I am alone. A little boy at the next table puts a napkin to his face and sticks his tongue out at me. Is Emily ever coming back? I'll wait for her. I'll wait forever for Emily Ebers.

5:12 P.M.

I've been stood up. I just know it. She's never coming back. I'm never seeing Emily again. I might as well be dead. Millicent's told her the ugly truth and Emily has dumped me. I hate Millicent Min.

I can hardly eat my second hamburger. It tastes as bland as paper. Oh wait. I'm eating the wrapper. Hey! Look, it's her! I start breathing again.

"I'm back," Emily says, sliding into the booth.

"Where's Millicent?" I try to sound like I care as I polish off my burger.

"She went home." Emily wrinkles her forehead. "I just don't know about her sometimes."

Emily leans forward and gazes deep into my eyes. My heart is racing so fast. Can she hear it? Who used up all the oxygen in the room?

"Stanford," she says. "Please make me a promise."

Yes, yes, anything. . . . I gulp and nod. I wonder if she's going to ask me to be her boyfriend. Digger says that a lot of times girls are the ones who ask. This relationship is going a lot faster than I ever imagined.

Emily looks nervous. To help her out, I try to put on a very sincere face, a very caring face, a boyfriendish sort of face.

"Are you okay?" she asks. "All of a sudden you look weird."

I immediately return to my regular face. "I'm fine," I tell her. "I was, uh, just trying not to burp."

"Oh! Listen to this," Emily says. She takes a huge gulp of air and then burps out the words, "Hello, Stanford!"

I don't believe it. Can I be hearing correctly? She's burping *and* talking at the same time? None of the Roadrunners can do that! Emily Ebers is the girl of my dreams.

"You are too cool," I tell her. We grin like idiots. I point to Emily's second cheeseburger and ask, "Are you going to eat that?"

Her face clouds. "You think I eat too much, don't you? You think I'm fat."

"No, no, no," I protest. "Not at all, I just thought that if you weren't going to eat it, I'd help you."

Emily's face lights up again. "Well, I am kinda hungry. But I'd be happy to share it with you."

As we both eat, I remind her, "Uh, was there something you wanted to talk about?"

"Oh, right." She turns serious. "Please promise you won't make fun of Millie for being so bad in English." *What?* "She's very sensitive about needing a tutor and won't even discuss it with me. You know, not everyone's as smart as you are."

Okay, so it wasn't what I thought. But the good news is that Emily really does think I am smart.

"It's not nice to make fun of a person just because they don't get good grades," I explain to Emily. She nods. "Grades aren't everything. You shouldn't shut someone out just because they don't do great in school. Sometimes a person's feelings are more important than a stupid grade!" I suddenly realize that I am shouting.

Are those tears in Emily's eyes? "Stanford, you are so amazing," she whispers.

The people sitting near us are staring. The little boy sticks his tongue out at me again, only this time without the napkin. I try to ignore him. I'm not sure if I am trembling because of what Emily has said or because of what I have said.

Emily is still looking at me all sparkly-eyed. Suddenly it hits me — the nicer I am to Millicent, the more Emily will like me. I sit taller and thrust out my chest. "Yes, well," I say, lowering my voice. "Let's be good friends to Millie and respect her privacy."

Using a suave move I once saw in a movie, I keep my eyes on Emily as I pick up my Coke to take a sip. Ouch! Uh-oh, I forgot about the straw. Now it's lodged in my nostril and hanging out of my nose. Emily breaks out laughing. "Stanford Wong, you have the best sense of humor!"

Even though I know I should feel embarrassed, I don't. I feel terrific.

JULY 31, 10:39 P.M.

I can't stop thinking about her. Emily is actually interested in me for what I have to say and not just because I am a Roadrunner or a basketball player. I mean, she's never even seen me on the court.

I wonder if Emily likes the way I look or if I seem dorky to her. Yin-Yin and my mom are always telling me how handsome I am. But even if I looked like a smushed toad, I'm sure they would say the same thing.

I look in the mirror and practice different smiles. Closed mouth, wide grin, lots of teeth. They all look stupid, so instead I flex my muscles. My body could use some definition. I think I need to start lifting weights. I cringe every time we have to use the locker room at school. Showers are the ultimate humiliation. I try not to look at the other guys, but I can't help it. There's only so much one of those scratchy white towels can hide, so you have to make a decision: front or back.

Like everyone else, I always cover my front side and then as much of my backside as the towel can reach. That leaves my chest exposed, but Tico says that's no different from wearing swim trunks.

A few of the guys have a lot of armpit hair, and some of

them have a lot of hair *everywhere.* There's a bunch of kids like Digger who strut around showing *everything.* They're not embarrassed at all. I wonder if Digger is one of those nudist people.

Gus and Tico are like me. They hurry up and shower and then hurry up and get dressed. We don't look at each other. If you look at a guy too long, there's a chance you'll get thrown out of the locker room naked. That happened twice last year. One kid was so humiliated he had to transfer schools. The other kid got a note from his mom asking special permission for him to skip showers. Someone found out about it and now his nickname is Stinky Mama's Boy.

Whether he's naked or clothed, everyone stares at Stretch. He doesn't look like one of us. Stretch doesn't act like the rest of us either. He always has a book in his back pocket and even has been seen reading in public. Plus, there's that mute thing. Girls really go for that strong, silent type. Maybe the next time I see Emily I'll try not talking so much.

AUGUST 1, 10:45 A.M.

"Stanford, you seem to be having a good time. Care to share your daydream with us?"

Huh? Is he talking to me? Am I in trouble again? What did I do this time?

"Uh, no," I mumble.

Mr. Glick is always asking me to stay after class. He's not as bad as I used to think. I mean, he's really awful and terrible, but not really, really, really awful and terrible. English is not as totally boring now that I know what Mr. Glick is talking about. I'd never tell that to Mr. Glick or Millicent Min though.

For some weird reason, class has been going by more quickly lately. Like right now, I am surprised to hear Mr. Glick say, "That's all we have time for today. I'll see you all tomorrow!"

Even though we've been dismissed, I stay after class just to talk. Not about books, just about stuff. "BK620s are the best basketball shoes in the world," I explain to Mr. Glick.

"I'm better at watching basketball than playing it," he chuckles. "But I'm sure the right equipment can make a difference. Or at least make a player feel like a better player, and in turn he might become one."

As I try to decipher what Mr. Glick just said, he offers me another oatmeal cookie. His wife made them. I don't want to hurt Mr. Glick's feelings, so I take it. They taste like dog food. I know because when Yin-Yin put out the food for her imaginary dog, Gus dared me to eat one of the biscuits.

"You're showing a lot of improvement in class," Mr. Glick tells me. "Don't forget, your *Number the Stars* book report is due next week. Another cookie?"

I take one more, even though it will probably kill me. We both chew for a long time in awkward silence. Finally Mr. Glick says, "Stanford, can I be honest with you?" I wonder if I've screwed up again. "These cookies are horrible, aren't they?"

I grimace and nod. We both burst out laughing. "Here," I say, reaching into my backpack. I break a Twix bar in half.

Mr. Glick bites into it and relaxes. "Better, much better," he says as he deposits the rest of the cookies in the trash can.

3:29 P.M.

Millicent is waiting for me outside of the library. I greet her with, "Home-schooled! That's a good one! Hey, how come you don't want Emily to know you're in high school?"

"College," she corrects me. "I am taking a college course this summer."

"High school, college, whatever. Why would you want Emily to think you're stupid?"

"I don't want her to think I'm stupid, I want her to think that I'm normal," Millicent says quietly.

"But you're nothing near normal." She cringes when I say this. "I mean, you're a genius and you've always been, uh, different."

Millicent sighs and blows her bangs so they puff up. "Precisely why I want Emily to think I'm a regular kid. If she thinks I'm a genius, she might not act the same around me. She might shun me, like you and all the other kids our age."

I was looking forward to teasing her some more but change my mind.

Millicent is asking me all sorts of questions about *Number the Stars* and I'm trying hard to think of the answers when suddenly Emily appears. She's wearing a dress and looks really tan and beautiful, and she smells good. None of the Roadrunners smell like that, not even Gus the time his twin sister dumped perfume all over him.

I sit up straight and begin bombarding Millicent with questions about the importance of irony. "Come on, Millicent, we've gone over this a thousand times before."

Millicent gives me a hard stare, then says sweetly, "Oh, Stanford, I forgot. You'd better explain it to me again."

"Uh, uh, you remember," I say, trying not to choke. "It's, it's, irony is, um . . . think hard, Millicent; you know this. You know this," I repeat through gritted teeth.

Millicent looks triumphant. "Oh yes, now I remember. Irony can be an incongruity between what is expected and the actual event. Or it can be clever words used to convey an insult — for example, if I were to say, 'The boy was *soooo* smart,' when really he was quite the idiot."

Emily smiles at me. I can't help smiling back. The only one

who isn't smiling is Millicent. I guess she's being a pretty good sport. Maybe I owe her one.

After our tutoring session, Millie rushes Emily out of the library. Just as I am about to turn into SSSSpy and follow them, Mrs. Martinez stops me. I wonder what she's going to nail me for. I don't eat in the library anymore and I've stopped bouncing my basketball inside.

I watch the girls disappear and brace myself for a lecture. Instead, Mrs. Martinez reaches behind her desk and hands me a book. "Stanford, I want you to have this."

I can't believe she wants me to read another book. Isn't my life hard enough as it is?

"Just give it a try," she says. "You can keep it. It's not a library book, so you can read it at your leisure."

I look at the book. It's called *The Outsiders.* Is it about camping?

"Okay," I tell her. "I'll give it a try." I am just so relieved that I am not in trouble.

"I think you might be pleasantly surprised," Mrs. Martinez says.

"And I think you might be nuts," I want to say but don't.

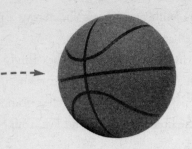

AUGUST 2, 7:46 A.M.

Every time someone shuts the refrigerator door, my F paper flutters like it's trying to get my attention. Maybe if I slam the door hard enough the paper will fall off.

I am about to bite into my peanut-butter toast when Mom strolls into the kitchen. Her hair is down and she's all dressed up in her new blue suit. She doesn't look like my mother. She looks like the "after" from one of those makeover shows.

"I've got a big presentation today," my mother tells my father. "Aren't you going to wish me good luck?"

"Good luck," he says, not even looking up from the newspaper.

I want to shake him and say, "Doesn't Mom look great? Look at her. Tell her she looks great."

"Kristen?" Dad says.

Mom turns around and perks up. "Yes . . . ?"

"Can you pick up my blue shirt from the dry cleaner's? I'll need it for tomorrow."

Mom walks out without saying good-bye.

Dad puts down his paper. "What did I say that was so bad?

I just asked her to get the dry cleaning. It's on her way. Would that be so hard for her to do?"

I start to answer until I realize he's asked a rhetorical question. Mr. Glick just taught us about those. They are questions people ask when they don't really want to hear what you have to say.

AUGUST 3, 2:04 P.M.

Oh man, it's worse than I thought. Millicent is *really* bad at volleyball. If I were her I'd be too embarrassed to even step on the court. She's trying to serve right now, only both of her arms are stiff and her face is all scrunched up. She looks like Frankenstein trying to dance.

Emily's not a terrific player either, though I'd never tell her that. At least she doesn't look like a total dweeb with a volleyball. She looks like someone who should have her own television show. I know I'd tune in.

I'm sitting in the top bleachers watching Emily's team. The girls on both sides keep looking at me and giggling. I'm not sure why. Is it my hair? I spiked it today. It took me an hour to get it just the right amount of messy.

"You look nice, Stanford," my mom said when I left the house. Then she winked at me and added, "Say hello to Millicent for me."

The game just ended. Emily's team won and she's jumping up and down looking all happy, and I can't help but grin. After my team loses a basketball game, the only person more miserable than me is Digger.

Emily comes running up the bleachers toward me. I imagine us running toward each other in slow motion through a field of flowers, except that I have allergies. So instead, I shift the dream to the beach. No, wait, even better, Emily and I are running toward each other in slow motion across a basketball court . . .

"EXCUSE ME!" It is Millicent Min. "Are you even on this planet?"

Oh. I didn't notice her with Emily.

"Millie and I were just going to get some ice cream," Emily says. Her cheeks are still flushed from playing volleyball. She always looks good.

"Ice cream? Really? I was just thinking about ice cream." I don't tell her that I had a double cone right before I came here.

We head to the ice-cream parlor with Emily walking in the middle. There's not enough room on the sidewalk for the three of us, and Millicent keeps falling into the street, which gets really annoying after a while.

"You again?" the ice-cream lady says. I signal her to be quiet, but she doesn't get it. "Another double chocolate mint cone with sprinkles?" she asks loudly. "That's two in one day."

I look at Emily, but she's busy studying all the ice-cream flavors. Millicent manages to give me a smug look, however. Does she have to know everything?

I remember my manners and pay for Emily's cone. Millicent orders chocolate in a cup and makes a big deal about getting her money out of her briefcase. She is so strange. I don't let her get to me. I'm too busy talking with Emily.

"I hated volleyball at first," she confides. "But it's not as bad as it was before. And since Millie's there with me, I know we can make faces at each other when one of us messes up. It's always great to have friends you can count on, don't you think? I'll bet you have a lot of friends, Stanford."

"Well, I do have the guys from basketball."

Emily smiles and I melt a little. "You're lucky you're so good at basketball. You must have real talent."

I don't mention my good-luck charm. Instead I say, "Actually, I do practice a lot. But I don't mind. I love playing basketball. It's not work; it's fun."

Emily looks interested, so I tell her about when the B-Team won the league championship, thanks to me. I've relived it in my mind millions of times, but this is the first time I've said it out loud.

. . . The crowd was screaming; the clock had run down. I was all alone at the free-throw line.

"Stan-ford! Stan-ford! Stan-ford!" everyone shouted.

I focused on the net. Then, I did what I always do when the pressure is on me to make a free throw: I pushed the ball into the left hand, then the right, then the left, then the right. Hold the ball up. Wait. Bounce the ball. Dribble. Dribble. Dribble. Left hand. Right hand. Both hands.

As if by magic, the crowd was suddenly silent. It was like I was all alone in the gym. A feeling of complete calm washed over me. Before I took my shot, I knew. I knew what would happen. I bounced the ball one more time, then sent it floating into the air.

All at once, the crowd went wild! I had made the basket. I had won the B-Team league championship for Rancho Rosetta!!!

As Emily cheers, Millicent frowns. Emily notices and says, "How are you doing in your English class, Millie? What are you and Stanford working on these days?" Emily is just way too nice.

When Millicent doesn't answer, I jump in. "She's reading

Holes right now. It's a pretty good book, actually. It's about belonging, isn't it, Millicent?"

Millicent grits her teeth and does a fine imitation of a grizzly-bear growl.

"Go on," says Emily as she eats her strawberry ice-cream cone. It goes nicely with her red dress. Millicent's wearing another one of her dorky T-shirts. This one says REALITY IS MERELY AN ILLUSION.

Clearly, Emily finds me fascinating, so I continue; only I'm running out of things to say about reading. "The wonderful thing about books is that they have so many pages. I mean, have you ever seen a book with only one page? Now, some books are shorter than others, but they still have a lot of meaningful words in them . . ."

Suddenly Millicent has a coughing spasm. I wish she'd stop. I can't think when she's making all that noise.

". . . and, as I keep telling Millicent," I say, raising my voice to cover her hacking, "*Holes* has a story within a story."

Emily says, "It sounds like a great book."

"It is!" I hear myself answering. "There's this kid in it who's totally misunderstood. People think he's bad, but he's really not, only no one will listen to him."

6:32 P.M.

Emily, Emily Ebers. Emily, Emily, Emily. Emily Ebers.

Emily. It's the most beautiful name I've ever heard. *Emily. Emily. Emily.* Just thinking it makes my stomach do flips.

I am at Burger Barn with the guys. I can't finish my Barnstormer, so I hand it over to Digger. Technically it's his anyway since he treated again.

"What are you so happy about?" He plucks the pickles out and tosses them up on the ceiling. The ketchup and mustard make them stick, and then eventually they'll fall down on some unsuspecting dope's head.

"That's cool," Gus says, tossing his pickles up.

"Nothing," I say, trying to look depressed. "I am not happy."

"You should be," Gus tells me. "You aced Glick's class and you're on the A-Team. Life doesn't get much better than that."

I would love to tell the guys about Emily. But if I did, they'd want to meet her. And if they did meet her, Emily's so friendly she'd want to talk to them, and if she talked to them, she'd probably mention that I am tutoring Millicent Min. And if they heard that, they'd laugh, because everyone knows that never in a million years would I be anyone's tutor. Then I'd be found out and my name would be mud. No, it would be worse than mud, it would be mud puke, stinky, slimy mud puke. Stinky, slimy mud puke on burnt toast.

Guess I'd better not mention Emily Ebers.

Emily, Emily Ebers. Emily, Emily, Emily. Emily Ebers.

I don't know what's happening to me, but I think I like it. When I look at Emily, I feel like I can jump so high that I can make free throws from the clouds. Only Emily's always with Millicent, and when I look at Millicent it makes me fall back down to earth. *Crash. Splat.* Guts everywhere.

What does Emily see in her? Sometimes Millicent just makes me want to barf. Then I look at Emily and I want to melt. Man,

I get all confused, wanting to melt and barf at the same time. Whenever I am around them, my head says to get out of there, but I don't really want to. Then my feet and my arms and legs just get wild and I end up racing around Emily and getting all hyper while Millicent glares at me.

"How's work, Stanford?"

Huh?

"I said, how's work?"

Why is Digger always so interested in my job?

"Really tough," I tell him.

"Anyone have any more pickles?" asks Gus.

Digger hands him one and says, "Maybe me and the guys will stop by some time to say hello."

"No, that's okay," I say. "My dad'll get really mad if I have any visitors."

My feelings of wonderful Emily-ness have been replaced with a pit in my stomach. Gus leans his head back as he waits for a pickle to fall from the ceiling.

"We won't stay long," Digger says, taking a huge bite of my hamburger. "We'll just pop in, say hi, and then leave. Don't worry, Stanford," he assures me. "It'll be like we were never there."

Just then a pickle falls on Gus's face.

"Bull's-eye!!!!" he shouts.

AUGUST 4, 7 P.M.

This might be impossible to believe, but I'm reading the book Mrs. Martinez gave me. It's the first book that I can't seem to put down. I'd better be careful or the next thing I know, I'll be wearing a calculator on my belt.

Mom sees me reading *The Outsiders* and kisses the top of my head. Usually I squirm when she pulls stunts like that, but this time I just brush her away and keep reading. This book is exactly like my life, except that I am not in a gang and I don't get in a lot of fights and my parents aren't dead. I asked Mr. Glick to stay after class Friday and we talked and talked about *The Outsiders.* Well, I talked and talked. He just grinned.

I thought maybe I had food on my face or something and finally asked, "What's so funny?"

"Nothing," he said. "I'm just happy that you are enjoying the book. These are the kinds of moments a teacher lives for."

I'm not sure what he meant, but then he added, "Stanford, I'll make a deal with you. You read this book and just tell me about it. No report to write, no quiz. And I'll give you extra credit."

"Deal!" I told him.

I may pass English after all.

10:07 P.M.

Something weird's going on. Millicent Min is being nice to me. She's a lot easier to be around these days, and she hasn't held it against me that I told the Roadrunners that she was a weirdo. She almost seems like a normal person.

Maybe Millicent's sick. Or maybe Maddie slipped her some secret potion or something. Maddie has always been into herbs and weird stuff like acupuncture. That's where they stick a billion tiny needles into you to cure a knee pain. If I had a billion tiny needles in me, it would sure make me forget my knee.

I wonder why Millicent turned out so strange when her family is so fun. Maddie's a blast, Mr. and Mrs. Min are always goofing off, and her grandfather was really cool. He died last year.

One time Mr. Lee was in the park hiding from Maddie. He claimed they had had an argument about free-range chickens and he was scared to go home. I'm not sure if he was really scared, because Mr. Lee was grinning when he challenged me to a game of H-O-R-S-E. I won, but he got H-O-R, which is pretty good considering I didn't know that old people could even bounce a ball. I wish my dad would play H-O-R-S-E with me sometime. I'd even let him win.

Dad and I have never done any sports together, although he did try to teach me how to play chess a long time ago. I tried really hard to learn, but I kept making the knights go sideways and finally my father gave up on me.

Maybe after summer school's over I'll ask Millicent to teach me chess and then surprise my dad for his birthday. I'll bet she's really good at it.

AUGUST 5, 3:10 P.M.

I am waiting at the side of the library. When Millicent appears, I jump out and scare her. After she finishes screaming, Millie checks her watch.

"Am I late? Stanford, you're *early*. A volleyball in addition to your ever-present basketball? What's that for?" She shifts her briefcase to the other hand.

"It's to play volleyball."

"I know that," she bristles. "But why do you have one?"

"Well, I noticed that you could use some help with your serve," I explain.

"There's nothing wrong with my serve," she declares. We both know she is lying.

"Watch," I tell Millicent as I demonstrate her serve. She laughs at my imitation. I retrieve the ball from the parking lot and toss it to her. "Here," I say. "You have to strike off your palm and the ball will go in the direction your palm faces. . . . Okay, that's good. Now hit it."

For once, Millicent Min doesn't argue. Instead she hits the ball, and it wimps out, going straight toward the ground.

I frown. This isn't going to be easy. "Hold it again, and watch your palm when you strike the ball. And this time, also bend your wrist backward. That way it'll go up higher."

I can tell Millicent is actually listening. She follows my advice and we watch in amazement as the ball forms a perfect arc in the air. We try it a few more times and Millicent keeps getting better and better. I can tell she's getting more confident. She wants to keep going, but I have to stop her.

"We'd better get to the library now," I say. "I've got a book report due soon."

5:15 P.M.

Yin-Yin always wants to know everything that is going on, but I still haven't told her about Emily. I haven't told anyone. It's like the most wonderful secret. I'm afraid to talk about it in case I jinx it. Besides, Yin-Yin might tell my mom and then my mom would get all weird and my dad would probably tell me to stop thinking about Emily and start thinking about college.

Instead I tell Yin-Yin about *Number the Stars*.

". . . and so their neighbors, who were also their friends, tried to hide the Jewish family so they wouldn't be captured by the Nazis."

Yin-Yin gets quiet. "That was not so long ago," she says. "Things were very different just a few generations back. It is important not to forget."

"Were things different for you?"

She hesitates. "I'm a first-generation Chinese-American. Your father is second generation, and you are third.

"My parents left China long ago. They never meant to stay in America. It was their plan to return to their homeland someday, but that never happened.

"They did their best to raise us as good Americans. It was very hard for them. People didn't trust them because they were immigrants and looked different. Sadly, many people are still suspicious of immigrants, even today."

My grandmother has a far-off look in her eyes. I wait for her to continue.

"My parents were hard on me and my brothers because they wanted the best for us. That included making sure I was married. Your grandfather and I had an arranged marriage."

"What's that?" I wonder, will Emily and I have an arranged marriage?

"It's when your parents pick who you will marry," Yin-Yin explains.

I shudder. My parents would probably pick Millicent Min for me.

"Your grandfather and I met one week before we were married. He didn't want an arranged marriage any more than I did."

"But it turned out okay, right?"

"Well, I had some silly plans that I was never able to follow through on. But that was a long time ago." Yin-Yin fiddles with one of her birdhouses, then looks up and puts on a smile. "Anyway, I had your father and then your auntie Mary. And my children gave me you and Sarah and your cousin Jordan. So yes, it turned out great, and you turned out great! Come here, you."

She opens her arms to hug me and doesn't let go for a long time.

AUGUST 6, 4:12 P.M.

"What now?"

"Who is that supposed to be?" Millicent points to my note-book. "Some sort of monster in a dress?"

I slam it shut. I drew pictures of Emily all over the inside cover. No one's supposed to see that.

"It's nothing, just some doodles."

Millicent is still looking at me like I smell or something. I sniff my armpit, but it doesn't reek. She looks horrified. What is with her? I'll bet her farts stink as bad as everyone else's. She probably does the SBD kind. You know, Silent But Deadly.

Last year the Roadrunners had this really great fight over whether your own farts smell as bad to you as they do to other people. Tico and I were firmly on the side of your farts smelling worse to others. Digger, Stretch, and Gus claimed that all farts smell the same no matter who deals them.

To really test this, we all went down to Taco Heaven and scarfed down three bean burritos each. Then we went to Stretch's (this was before the Jell-O fight and the "only two Roadrunners in the house at one time" rule). Tico made a bunch of scrambled eggs with Tabasco sauce and we ate those too. Then we each drank several cans of soda and waited.

It took a while for the farts to start happening, but once they did it sounded like the Fourth of July. Man, the place stunk worse than the boys' locker room on a rainy day! Digger started gagging so much that he had to leave the room. Gus had the good sense to pour Stretch's mom's perfume over the couch cushions we were sitting on. It wasn't until after Stretch emptied two cans of room freshener that Tico suggested we open the windows. We were all laughing so hard we never did figure out who was right and who was wrong.

"Are you really reading?" Millicent asks.

"Duh, what does it look like I'm doing?" I hold up the book as proof.

"Never mind," she says, going back to her chart of my progress.

Has Millicent's hair always looked like that? All straight and black and flat? Has she always had bangs? Emily's hair is so beautiful she could star in a shampoo commercial. Alan Scott just got a new haircut and it looks awesome, all spiked with blue in it.

Tico has the best hair in our group. Sometimes he spikes his hair with one main spike in the middle and lots of little spikes around it. Digger's hair is a reddish-orange color that looks fake, but it's not. It's always a mess and he looks like he has a squirrel sitting on top of his head. Stretch has a buzz cut that's so short that from far away he looks bald. Gus's hair looks exactly like his twin sister's, all black and curly. He's been mistaken for a girl from behind. This really ticks him off. Still, he refuses to cut his hair.

"Hey, Millie?" I put *Holes* down. "Do you think I should cut my hair? You know, maybe get a buzz cut or something?"

Millicent studies my hair. I know she will give me an honest answer. If anything, she's too honest, which is one of her many major flaws.

"You could use a haircut," she finally concludes. "Or something. You could definitely use something. Maybe you should try cleaning your glasses."

Stupid reading glasses. They make me look like a nerd. I clean my glasses on my shirt.

Everyone's said that they've seen an improvement in my studies since I started working with Millie. That I am doing well in English is astonishing to us both. Millicent doesn't even know I've read *The Outsiders* too. It was hard to finish. Not because I didn't want to read it, but because I didn't want it to end. Mr. Glick and I talked a lot about the book, and he gave me extra credit just like he promised.

"Thanks, Stanford," Millie says now.

"For what?"

"For yesterday. For helping me with my serve." She looks embarrassed.

"It was nothing." Am I blushing?

"No, really. You didn't have to help me."

"Whatever," I say. I pull something out of my backpack and hand it to her.

"What's this?"

"My *Number the Stars* book report. Could you look at it? It's due pretty soon."

I pretend to be absorbed in *Holes,* but really I'm watching

Millie. Her face is blank as she reads. She looks like what a zombie would look like if a zombie looked like Millicent. I worked really hard on that report. I even read the whole book and not just the first and last paragraphs of each chapter.

Finally she looks up. My back stiffens. "You need to proofread it better — there are a lot of spelling mistakes," Millicent tells me. "Your conclusion is weak, but your work is solid. Overall, nice job, Stanford."

I relax. "Thanks, Millie."

AUGUST 7, 1:02 P.M.

I was afraid Yin-Yin might be sad that I'm late. Instead, she's talking to a stranger. He looks like one of those shifty criminals that Top Cop is searching for, except older.

"Oh! Mr. Thistlewaite, this is my good-looking grandson Stanford, who I've been telling you all about," Yin-Yin brags. Her hair is combed today, and her clothes look normal.

Mr. Thistlewaite struggles to stand up. He is ancient but has a full head of dark brown hair. He smiles widely at me and I can see that several of his teeth are missing.

"The basketball player!" he shouts. "Pleasure to meet you!"

Mr. Thistlewaite edges toward the door. "Mrs. Wong, so wonderful to see you again! I was especially impressed that you climbed the Himalayas! I thought I was the only one at Vacation Village who had done that!" He bows to me. "Stanford, I hope we meet again!"

Yin-Yin and I watch Mr. Thistlewaite totter out the door. My grandmother is beaming.

"Did you really trek across the Himalayas?" I ask. I would have thought that if she had, she'd at least have a photo to show.

"I can envision it like it was yesterday," my grandmother tells me.

"Okay, Yin-Yin. Whatever you say."

3:01 P.M.

I've memorized Emily's volleyball schedule, so sometimes I sort of show up and watch her play without her knowing it. It's not like I'm stalking her or anything, like some of those weirdos on *Top Cop.* I'm just secretly watching her.

The problem is that she's always with Millicent and I want to see Emily by herself. Since it's impossible to get to her alone, sometimes the three of us do stuff together. I'll hear either Millie or Emily say something like, "Let's go to the movies this afternoon." Then I'll run as fast as I can to the movie theater and hang around the entrance. When they show up, it's not like I've been following them. Instead, they've bumped into me.

The game just ended and Emily and Millicent are still in the gym talking. What do they talk about? Do they ever talk about me? They're walking toward the door. I slip into SSSSpy mode and sneak around the bleachers to try to listen in. Emily and Millie are saying good-bye. I follow them out of the gym. Hey, I don't believe it! Millicent is walking in one direction, and Emily is walking in another.

I know, I'll race around the block and then when I run into Emily it'll look like I was coming from the total opposite direction. Brilliant! Millicent's not the only genius around here.

I take off like Alan Scott and charge down the street. Running, fast, faster, faster, faster . . . *CRASH!* Oops, oh noooo, I've knocked Millicent over. I guess I forgot Millie was also going in the opposite direction of Emily.

Do I help her up? She seems upset. Her briefcase stuff is scattered all over the sidewalk, and she looks like she's in shock. But if I help her, I might miss Emily.

Oh, all right already. My mission comes to a screeching halt as I hand Millie her books, her pens, her notebooks. Her chocolate bars, her pencil sharpener, her calculator. A comic book? She snatches it out of my hand and shoves it into her briefcase.

There! Finally we are done. Before she can say another word, I take off. I have to hurry if I am going to accidentally-on-purpose bump into Emily. I turn the corner. Then I turn another corner. I am too late. I don't see her anywhere. Stupid Millicent Min.

There's only one thing to do. Ice cream. That always makes me feel better. I take my time heading to the ice-cream parlor. There's no reason to rush, since I've lost Emily.

As I push the door open, I stop and stare. *She* is standing in line. And she's alone! She sees me at the exact same moment I see her.

"Hi, Stanford!" Emily exclaims, doing that sparkly-eyed thing. "Can I buy you an ice-cream cone?"

I try not to faint. It just wouldn't be cool.

"Uh, sure, an ice-cream cone. Yeah, okay. Why not?"

Oh man, oh man, oh man, Emily must like me. She's offered to buy me an ice-cream cone. No girl has ever offered to buy me an ice-cream cone, although Millie once said she'd buy me a one-way ticket to the moon. But this with Emily? This is major. This is big-time. It's practically like we are boyfriend/girlfriend.

"What flavor would you like?"

"Uh . . ." I stare at the flavor board. What if I order a flavor she hates? Will she think I'm weird? "What are you having?" I say, trying to sound casual.

Emily wrinkles her nose as she decides. She looks so beautiful. I just stare at her. How come her skin is so clear? Her hair smells good. It smells like flowers. I want to touch her hair. It looks so soft. Before I can stop myself, I am reaching for her hair . . . reaching . . . reaching . . .

Suddenly Emily faces me. My hand is still reaching out toward her. There's not enough time to yank it back, so instead, I do the first thing that comes to mind. I whack her on the shoulder.

Emily looks shocked. "Stanford?"

"A bug?" I stammer. "You had a bug on you."

"Oh! Euwww. Thank you, Stanford. Was it a big one?"

"What?"

"The bug."

"Oh, the bug. Yeah, it was huge."

"I'm so glad you got it," Emily gushes. "I hate bugs."

The ice-cream lady yawns.

Emily goes on, "I think I'm going to try chocolate peanut butter."

"That's exactly what I was going to order," I tell her.

Emily's eyes widen. "Really? That is just too incredible. Stanford Wong, it's like we're totally in sync."

I feel my face turning red enough to melt all the ice cream in all the countries in all the world.

As the lady scoops out the ice cream, I watch Emily. Usually I watch the person scooping the ice cream to make sure they don't skimp on my cone. But I can't help staring at Emily.

She's taking out a little wallet from her purse. It has a monkey on it. Should I show her my monkey imitation? The lady hands us the cones, and Emily hands her a credit card. Wow! I've never heard of a kid who has her own credit card. She sees me staring. "My dad gave it to me," Emily says modestly. "He's so great."

I doubt my dad will be getting me a credit card any time soon.

I watch as Emily signs her name on the credit-card receipt. She has a nice signature, all loopy. I should practice writing my name so it looks better.

We go outside and sit on a bench. We're sitting close, but not too close. I wonder what she is thinking. As we eat our cones, there is an awkward silence. I am working up my nerve to give her a present that I have been carrying around forever.

I try to sound casual, hoping my voice doesn't crack. "Um, Emily, I just read a great book and thought maybe you'd like to have it."

Emily turns toward me. "Really? Wow! You must read a lot of books, so I am sure it's a good one."

"Oh, it is," I assure her.

"*The Outsiders,*" she reads.

"It's the best book I've ever read," I hear myself saying.

She grins. "I'll be sure to get it back to you after I'm done."

"No, no, it's for you to keep. Look, I've signed it on the inside."

It took me two hours to figure out what to write. I didn't want to be mushy; I wanted to be meaningful. Finally I wrote:

To Emily,
I hope you enjoy this super terrific book.

I had considered signing "Love," but that might be taken the wrong way. "From" seemed too formal. So finally I signed:

Sincerely yours,
Your friend,
Stanford A. Wong

As Emily is reading the inscription, I tell her, "Please don't tell Millie about this. She might feel bad about her poor reading abilities if she finds out I'm giving you books." Actually, Millicent will get all smug and think that she's the one who should get the credit for me reading.

Emily looks at me for a moment and I wonder if she can tell I am lying. "Well," she says thoughtfully. "I certainly don't want Millie to feel bad. I mean, she tries so hard to use big words and everything. Like she wants me to think she's really smart. I get the feeling she won't even talk about summer school because she feels that someone who's home-schooled shouldn't have to go." Emily bites her lip. "Okay, I won't mention it to her. That's really thoughtful of you to think about her feelings, Stanford."

We continue eating our cones in silence, only it doesn't feel awkward anymore. It feels comfortable, like when I'm with Stretch, only she smells so much better.

"Stanford," Emily says suddenly. She startles me. I was so busy thinking about Emily that I forgot she was sitting right next to me.

"Yes, Emily?" I like to say her name out loud.

"Thank you for the book."

I look deep into her eyes. They are sparkling like crazy. "You're so welcome," I whisper.

My ice-cream cone is melting all over my hand, but I don't care. What I do care about is that I am sitting here on this bench with Emily Ebers. Emily Ebers who bought me an ice-cream cone. Emily Ebers who accepted the book I gave to her. Emily Ebers with the sparkling eyes.

The mere thought of being this close to Emily makes me start to sweat and I can't breathe. My stomach gets funny, like it's turning itself inside out. My heart pounds so fast I'm afraid it's going to fall out of my chest. I can't talk, and I can't focus. I'm dizzy. Oh man, I have never felt so good in my entire life.

11:37 P.M.

There! I've finally finished revising my book report. I reread it and it sounds pretty good to me. I reach across my desk and turn on one of those mushy music stations that always play love songs. Why didn't I ask Emily for her phone number? Dumb! Next time I see her, I'll get it. Or maybe I can talk Millicent into giving it to me. In the meantime, at least I can practice.

I pick up the phone and pretend to dial. In my deepest voice I say, "Hello, Emily, Stanford Wong here. What's happenin'? What's up? What's goin' on?"

That sounds stupid. Let me try again.

In a surprised voice, I say, "Oh, hi, Emily, is that you? I must have accidentally dialed the wrong number, but now that you're on the phone perhaps we ought to chat a while."

Nope, too lame. How about, "Emily! I missed *Top Cop* last night and was wondering if you saw it?"

This casual conversation is going to take a lot of work. I take a break and grab some Oreos. I can put six in my mouth at once. Some guy on the radio is spilling his guts out to a low-talking DJ named Lavender. He wants to dedicate a song to a girl named Susie who dumped him.

"Gee, Elliott," Lavender tells him, "that's rough. Two days before your wedding? Well, here's a song to soothe your broken heart."

I listen to the words and it's all about love and how true love always wins. I find myself thinking about Emily, Emily Ebers. Emily's all I can think about. Everywhere I turn, I see her face. On the television . . . on my wall . . . at dinner I swear I could see her face staring out at me and smiling through my meat loaf.

I think of Emily as I watch the black spider spinning a web for herself in the corner of the ceiling. I would do anything for Emily. Anything. I wonder if she feels the same way about me. If she wanted me to, I'd even get her name tattooed on my arm.

Last year, there was an eighth grader who had an incredible tattoo of an eagle on his left bicep. It looked so real everyone wanted to touch it. Then one day his tattoo started peeling off and he dropped from the cool list to the loser pile.

Gus says that he's getting a tattoo of a tiger cub, our school mascot. Digger wants a skull tattooed on his skull. Tico doesn't want a tattoo, and neither does Stretch. I'm still thinking about it. My dad would kill me if I got a tattoo. I asked him about it once.

"But your father had a tattoo," I reminded him.

"Just because he did something stupid doesn't mean you should too," Dad snapped back. He doesn't like to talk about his father.

Even though my dad is totally against it, I still think it would be worth it to get an Emily tattoo. I pick up my pen and slowly write her name on my right arm. I've been lifting weights for almost a week now. Well, okay, not real weights, but I have been lifting big bottles of water. I can't see any results yet, but according to Digger it takes about two months.

Digger's got a full set of real weights at his house. He says we can use them anytime. But even though the Ronsters have a swimming pool, a pool table, and even a jukebox, none of the Roadrunners are comfortable at Digger's. We're always afraid we're going to break something. Digger's house is the kind that my mom says "is more to look at than live in."

There, I'm done. *Emily* looks good on my arm. I draw a heart around it and then some arrows. Then I add my name, which takes up a lot of space, especially since I am using my fancy lettering. The word *forever* has to go down toward my elbow because I can't reach the back side of my arm.

I put in a bird, and then another one, and then one of Yin-Yin's birdhouses. My grandmother would like that. Now I add the date that I first saw Emily at the drugstore. I also include the cover of *The Outsiders* because it is the first gift we have shared, and I put a waffle cone on there too to signify the day I gave her the gift.

I look at the clock. How did it get so late? The sappy music is still on. At least my parents are no longer yelling at each other. A lady wants Lavender to dedicate a song to her first boyfriend, who she hasn't seen in years.

I admire my arm. My fake tattoo goes all the way down from my bicep to my wrist. I fall asleep dreaming of Emily as the lady on the radio murmurs, "You're listening to *Love Songs with Lavender.* This one is for all those first-time lovers out there. . . ."

AUGUST 8, 8:04 A.M.

I wake up and scream. My arm looks hideous, plus I have spelled Emily's name wrong. *Emely?* I have to wash off my tattoo before anyone sees it. Dad would kill me. Mom would want to know who Emily is. The Roadrunners would never let me live it down.

Oh man, oh man! The ink won't come off. I am a dead man. I scrub and scrub and scrub. Never in my life have I used so much soap. Finally some of the letters start to smear, but not all of them. Shoot! My arm is all black and smudgy and it looks like it says, "me tan orever."

What to do?

My mother gives me a funny look at breakfast and tucks my good-luck charm under my sweater. She knows I don't like it to show.

"You look nice. Very preppy. Going to see Millicent Min today?"

I just grunt as I shovel down my Swamp Marsh cereal. I wish there were more marshmallow bits in it. Even though it has turned the milk green, it tastes kind of plain.

"How's Mr. Glick's class going?"

"Fine," I mumble. Why is she always asking me so many questions? "I gotta go."

I grab my backpack and make sure I've got my book report. I worked really hard on it. I hope Mr. Glick appreciates all that I am doing for him.

9:10 A.M.

I am so stinking hot in this stupid sweater. Mr. Glick is collecting our book reports. When I hand him mine he smiles at me. I start to smile back, then remember I have a reputation to uphold. Maybe after Mr. Glick grades my book report, I'll stay after class to talk to him about the book. Did you know that people were killed just for being Jewish? Stretch is Jewish, and so is Emily. I wonder if they know about this.

I didn't like reading *Number the Stars*. It made me uncomfortable. It made me nervous wondering if that girl was going to be sent to the death camp. It made me think about things I didn't want to think about. By the end of the book, I was a wreck. Millicent claims that's a good thing.

Mr. Glick announces, "We are about two-thirds of the way through this class. Two book reports down and one to go. Most of you have shown a lot of improvement. I look forward to reading these." He motions to the pile on his desk.

The rest of the class goes by quickly. We break up into teams and write stories. My team comes up with a story about a swimmer who can swim across the ocean but is scared of going down the drain in his bathtub. Mr. Glick congratulates us and says that we have very active imaginations.

As I walk across campus I notice that it isn't nearly as crowded as during the school year. Oh no! There's Digger. Then I look again and he's gone. Then I see Gus, but it can't be him because he's mowing lawns. I must just be paranoid, or maybe I've forgotten to turn off my imagination from our swimmer story. To be safe, I duck back into Mr. Glick's class.

"Stanford?"

"Oh hey! I, uh, I forgot to give you something."

He watches as I fumble through my backpack. I take as long as I can. Finally I say, "Here. I want you to have this."

"Thank you." He peers in the Cheetos bag. It is empty except for a few crumbs.

"No problem!" I reply. Mr. Glick looks perplexed as I pull my Celtics cap down and my sweater up over my face. "Well, nice talking to you. See you around!"

2 P.M.

I'm at Stretch's house. Bert and Ernie are on TV arguing over how they are going to split three cookies. Stretch is staring at the television and eating cheddar cheese–flavored potato chips.

"Hey, can we talk?" I ask.

He grunts, which means "yes."

"Well," I begin, "you aren't going to believe this when I tell you, but first you have to swear you won't tell anyone."

Stretch stops chewing.

"Okay, good," I tell him. "It's just that, it's, well, I met this girl. You can't tell anyone though because, um, because her family's in the witness-protection program. So I'm not even going to tell you her name or how we met or anything, to protect her identity. Not that I'm her *boyfriend* boyfriend. I'm just a boy who's her friend, but I wouldn't mind being boyfriend/girlfriend with her, if you know what I mean."

Stretch nods.

"It's just that I wanted to tell someone about her, and you're the only one I can really talk to, and I know that you'd understand. It is so great when . . ." I try to think of a code name for Emily. "When Ms. X and I are together I can't believe how great I feel. She makes me feel like I'm some sort of hero or something. Just thinking about her makes me all spazzed out, but in the good way."

I take a breath. I didn't mean to say so much, but I just had to tell someone about Emily or else I would have burst.

Stretch tilts his head, the way he does when he is thinking. I'm fairly certain he is reviewing what I have just told him and agreeing with me that I am right to feel the way I do about Emily. That I did the right thing by telling him and that he is my best friend and would never betray my secret. He is happy for me.

Stretch is back to eating his chips and watching television. Now Oscar is angry because someone cleaned his garbage pail. Without taking his eyes off of *Sesame Street*, Stretch tips the bag of chips toward me, and I grab a handful. I feel so much better now that Stretch and I have had this talk.

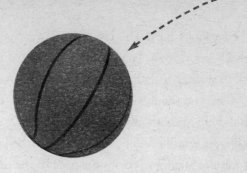

AUGUST 9, 1:45 P.M.

It's just three of us on the court today. Gus froze all of his sister's underwear and is grounded for three days. Stretch left for vacation today with his family. Every year they rent a Don Ronster Monster RV with a kitchen and bathroom and everything and hit the road like the pioneers. To figure out where they're going, Stretch's stepdad throws a dart at a map of the United States. He really wanted to see the London Bridge in Arizona and had to throw the dart five times to get there.

Digger and Tico are practicing free throws. Neither looks natural doing them.

"Hey," I call out. "Loosen up when you shoot. Flick your wrist, then push with your arm and follow through, like this." I bounce the ball twice and then execute a smooth shot, leaving my arms extended as the ball sails smoothly through the net.

Tico nods and gives it a try. He makes a basket. Digger looks at me and says, "Oh, now you're a coach too? Don't you have enough to do this summer?"

"Forget you," I say to Digger, half-joking.

He smiles, so I know something's up. "Mr. A-Team," Digger sings. "I need a moment alone with you."

Tico looks hurt. The last thing I want is a moment alone with Digger. "Sorry, but I just stopped by to say hi. I gotta get back to work. My dad's lost without me."

"Can't you shoot with us for just a while?" Tico begs. "I need you to help me with my layups."

Digger is still grinning. He looks like the Joker from *Batman*. "Oooh no, Stanford's got to get back to the office. He's quite a hard worker, aren't you, Stanford? Did you go to *school* to learn how to be such a hard worker? Did you go to hard-worker *school*?"

I take off without answering. *Digger knows! Digger knows! Digger knows!* I run all the way home and start knitting slowly, then fast, then faster. After a while I stop and gawk at what I have made. It doesn't look like anything. It just looks like a mess. A big mess. A big ugly mess. A big ugly Stress Mess.

I grab the ball of yarn and fling it hard across the room. It unravels as it flies through the air, almost hitting the black spider. I pick up the yarn and throw it again and again until my room looks like it's blanketed in a colorful web.

I try to untangle myself but finally give up and collapse onto my bed. I remember Yin-Yin used to say that when bad thoughts get you down, think of something happy. I shut my eyes.

Emily, Emily, Emily, Emily Ebers . . . Before I know what's happening, I'm digging through my backpack. When Millicent was giving Mrs. Martinez tips on alphabetizing, I found Emily's number in her organizer.

I dial quickly so I don't chicken out.

"Hello?"

"Uh . . ."

"Stanford? Is that you?"

Is it too late to hang up?

"Stanford?"

"Hi, Emily, it's me, Stanford Wong, Millicent Min's tutor. The boy who gave you the book."

"I thought it was you! I was hoping it was."

My heart is racing so fast I'm about to pass out.

"What are you doing?" Emily asks.

How can she sound so natural when I can barely talk? I hope my voice doesn't crack. What am I doing? What am I doing? I look at the yarn draped all over my room. There is no way on earth I can tell Emily I was knitting, so instead I hear myself say, "I was just lifting weights. A lot of them. Really heavy ones."

"That's cool. My dad lifts weights too."

I am glad she can't see me biting my nails. "All this weight lifting has made me hungry," I tell her. "Um, want to meet me for something to eat?"

I screw my eyes shut and wait for her answer.

"We'd love to!" Emily says.

3 P.M.

Emily is waiting for me in front of Pizza Wheels. She smiles when she sees me. I smile back; then, uh-oh, my smile slides off my face. Millicent Min is standing behind Emily, like her shadow. I forgot she was going to be here too.

"Hi, Emily! Hello, Millicent."

After getting pizza, the three of us, Emily in the middle, walk around and around the mall. Somehow Emily manages to talk to both of us at the same time. She is so amazing. At one point the three of us are debating whether it would look better to have three nostrils or three ears.

"Can you cover up the third ear?" I want to know.

"No," declares Emily. "It would be on your forehead."

"Would the nostril be on your nose?" Millie asks. She looks really intense.

"That would be on your forehead too," Emily states. "And when you sneeze or have to blow your nose, then stuff would come out of there."

Millicent and I look at each other and cringe. Emily looks pleased with herself.

"All things considered, I'd go for the extra nostril," Millicent declares. "The ear on the forehead would just look too funny."

"Yeah," I agree. "At least with the nostril, you could say it was a bullet hole."

"Well, I'd go for the extra ear," Emily says, laughing. She has a deep laugh.

"No way!" shouts Millie.

"Sure." Emily winks at me. "That way, I can wear more earrings."

"Let's go in here," Millicent says, making a sharp left into the bookstore.

When she turns, Emily and I bump into each other. It feels like I have been hit by a billion-volt electrical shock. I say, "Sorry" to Emily and then silently freak out.

Millicent heads straight toward the adult section. I clear my throat. "This way, Millie."

"Huh? Oh!" She spins around and together we make our way

to the kids' department. As we pass the sci-fi section I do a double take. Marley is eyeing me from behind a *Star Trek* comic book. He is wearing his Mr. Spock ears. I pick up speed. When I look back, the comic book is on the ground and Marley is gone, as if he's vaporized.

I shake it off and point to a display of *Holes* and a real shovel on the table. "Excellent book," I tell Emily.

Emily takes the book from me and looks at the back cover. "Aren't you reading this, Millie?"

Millicent sputters, "Well, yes, I —"

"We're reading it together," I jump in. "You won't believe what the boys at this horrible detention camp have to go through. Right, Millie?"

"Right, Stanford," Millie says, giving me a small smile.

In a strange way, our lie has bound Millicent Min and me together. Who would have ever guessed that we'd be cruising the mall and agreeing about third nostrils and books about delinquents?

"We have to talk later," Millie whispers to me while Emily is looking at magazines.

"About what?"

"About Emily."

Millicent looks worried. Whatever she has to say, I am certain I don't want to hear it.

AUGUST 10, 7:15 P.M.

Millie and I are at McDonald's. We're eating near the play area so no one will see us. A little kid and his mother look startled when I shout, "She can't find out you're tutoring me. Emily will think I'm stupid. You swore on your mother's life that you wouldn't tell, remember?"

"Well, what about me?" Millicent whispers loudly. "If she finds out I am a genius then she'll know I've lied and think I'm a total nerd."

"That's true," I confirm.

"We have to tell her," she insists. "She deserves to know."

"I know," I mutter. "It's so hard pretending to be smart. Sometimes I even bore myself when I talk about books." I take a bite out of my Big Mac and then shove a bunch of French fries in my mouth. "Emily thinks I'm smart. No one's ever thought that I was smart before."

"Please don't talk with your mouth full."

"Sorry." I swallow my food and continue. "Emily's different. Not like a weirdo or anything, she's different in a good way." I lower my voice. "When I'm around Emily, I feel important."

Millie nods and takes a sip of her milk shake. "You know,

when school starts you'll be seeing her on campus and she's bound to find out. Stanford," she says, channeling my father, "you have to think ahead, otherwise things might turn into a big mess."

Oh god! She's right. I hate it that Millicent is right all the time. It is so annoying.

Just then I spot Joey and some other seventh graders. They can't see me here with Millicent Min!

"C'mon," I grab Millie's arm. "Follow me. Hurry!"

"Stanford," Millicent whines. "Why are we sitting in the ball pit? This is so unhygienic. How often do you think they clean this area?"

"No one can see us here," I whisper. "Some kids from school just came in."

Millie sighs. She looks very uncomfortable. I'll bet it's the first time she's ever been in a PlayPlace.

"You're not going to say anything to Emily, are you?" I ask. Millicent is examining a red plastic ball like it's some sort of alien object. "Please don't say anything," I beg. "If she finds out I flunked, she won't like me anymore. No one can know about this. The Roadrunners think I'm working for my dad this summer."

Millie makes a lame attempt at tossing the ball. "Stop acting like a baby," she snaps. "You're not going to flunk. You can pass if you want to. I can understand wanting to keep it from Emily, but I thought those Road Runt boys were your friends."

"Yeah, well, they like me because I'm good at basketball."

"I had a friend who only liked me because I could help her with her homework," Millie muses. "Emily doesn't even know

I'm in high school." She picks up a green ball and throws it. It hits the wall, then bounces off my head. "What we're doing is wrong, Stanford. I don't want Emily to know. But at the same time, I feel like I'm living a lie."

"It's not like we're lying about murdering someone," I insist. "We're just not telling the exact whole truth right now. Besides, you want to keep Emily as a friend, right?"

Millicent looks sad as she nods.

"Well, if she finds out you're some sort of freak genius it might scare her off."

Now Millicent looks like she's going to cry.

"Awww, don't do that. You'll get the balls all slimy."

"Okay," she says, sniffing. "I won't say anything for now. But we have to tell her sometime soon, promise?"

"Promise." I don't ask her what "sometime soon" means. I don't want to know. "I'll even shake on it," I say, spitting into my hand.

"Uh, no thank you, you're good for your word."

A little girl jumps into the ball pit and freezes when she sees us. I toss a ball to her and she throws it back. Millicent watches. Then a little boy joins us. He starts pelting the girl with balls. I'm afraid she's going to cry, but instead she starts throwing balls back at him so fast he starts sobbing.

Just then Joey and his friends start walking in our direction. "Duck!" I hiss.

Millie and I dive under the balls just as the guys pass.

"I thought you said Stanford Wong was over here?" one guy says.

"I was sure I saw him eating with some girl," Joey remarks.

"Hey, maybe he's in the ball pit," the other boy jokes.

"Right," says Joey. "Like Stanford Wong would ever do something like that. Did you hear? He got an A out of Glick!"

"Wow," says the first guy. "It's like he's the luckiest person on the planet. I wish my life was half as good as Stanford Wong's."

AUGUST 11, 4:53 P.M.

Digger called and asked me to meet him at the soccer field. My stomach is queasy.

"What's up?" I ask, trying to sound casual.

Digger doesn't answer right away. Instead we watch the players run up and down the field. They're all starters on the school soccer team. When the striker scores a goal, Digger comments, "I wonder if he's kept up his grades. Can't play for Rancho Rosetta if you've flunked a class, you know."

Digger knows. I know he knows. And he knows that I know he knows.

"I have it on good authority that you've been seen at school."

Without taking my eyes off the soccer players, I say, "Maybe I just like to hang around there."

Digger laughs. "Right. Everyone knows you hate school and teachers like Glick."

That's not true! I don't hate Mr. Glick, not anymore.

"So what if I've been seen at school," I shoot back. "It's a free country." I lower my voice. "What do you want, Digger?"

"I'm guessing you didn't get an A in English like you told

us. You flunked," he says, sounding smug. "You have to go to summer school, and if you don't pass you don't play basketball next year. And that girl who interrupted our game, I saw her hand you some books. She's your little study buddy, isn't she?"

When I don't answer, he goes on. "Listen, I'm not stupid. I didn't buy your 'I'm working for my daddy' story like the other Roadrunners. So I asked around. One of the guys from the football team told me he sees you at school all the time, so I dropped by the other day." He plants himself in front of my face. "Guess who I saw coming out of Mr. Glick's room?"

"What do you want, Digger?"

"In exchange for not telling the Roadrunners that you are a regular bookworm, you have to let me beat you at basketball whenever we play."

It feels like I've been punched in the gut.

"Well?" Digger is waiting. "Oh, and as you think it over, just remember that it was me who invited you to be a Roadrunner in the first place. You owe me one."

"That's blackmail!" I protest.

"Noooo," he says slowly. "I like to think of it more like a handicap, like in golf. Tell you what, I'll give you a couple days to think it over. I'm in no rush." I just stare at him. I can't even speak. "You can thank me later."

Thanks a lot, Digger.

AUGUST 12, 9:13 A.M.

Stupid Digger, stupid Digger, stupid Digger. No! Stop!

Emily, Emily, Emily, Emily Ebers. Emily, Emily, Emily . . .

"Good job, Mr. Wong."

Huh? Mr. Glick is holding out my *Number the Stars* book report. I sit up. B-minus. I got a B-minus! "Thank you," I say.

"Thank *you*," he says back. "I enjoyed reading your paper."

Right on the front, in red ink, Mr. Glick wrote, "Good job, Stanford. Keep it up!"

I nudge the girl in front of me. "I got a B-minus," I say, trying to sound modest. She gives me a blank look. I'll bet she's jealous.

I can't wait to show Millicent my grade. My mom will be so happy. My dad will be happy too. What's not to like about a B-minus?

4:30 P.M.

I'm dreading seeing Digger, but the need to play ball is stronger.

The Roadrunners are on the court. When I walk up, Digger shoves the ball into my chest so hard that I can't breathe for a moment. He laughs and winks at me. "I'll guard Stanford. Tico, you're on my team."

We start to play. Without thinking, I steal the ball from Digger and make a tough jump shot. As I take a bow and the guys cheer, Digger comes up to me and whispers, "Here's a little song I learned in *school: a, b, c, d, e, F, g . . .*"

Back on the court, Tico steals the ball from Gus and passes to Digger. It would be so easy to block him, but instead, I let him muscle past me and drive to the net. He shoots and misses. I get the ball and do a blind pass to Gus. He gets it and then misses his shot. Digger has the ball. I pretend to trip and he makes an easy basket. Everyone cheers Digger this time.

After the game, the Roadrunners are shouting and jostling and laughing, but it's too painful to watch. Instead I think about *Emily, Emily, Emily Ebers.* What would the guys think if they knew about her? I wonder.

"Off day?" Gus startles me.

"Yeah, you weren't yourself out there," Tico chimes in. "Digger got lots of points off of you."

"Hey," Digger interrupts. "Maybe I'm the one who should have made the A-Team."

"But you didn't, did you?" says Gus.

"Like anyone can stop Stanford," Tico snorts.

Right. Nothing but English. And nobody but Digger.

8 P.M.

It's past dinnertime and no one is home. I'm standing in Sarah/Yin-Yin's room. My sister and grandmother left behind enough things to look like they were here but not enough to look like they are coming back. Sarah's prom dress hangs in the closet next to Yin-Yin's brown winter coat, and a collection of Winnie-the-Poohs shares shelf space with a dozen ceramic teapots. Finally I hear the garage door open and close.

My mother looks beat as she enters the living room. "I'm not sure if I can keep up with those young MBAs," she says. "They don't have a family to take care of."

I'm not sure how to respond, so I say, "What's for dinner?"

"Dinner!" Mom exclaims. "I completely forgot about dinner. You must think I am a horrible mother." She goes to the phone. "How about pizza?" Before I can answer, she's ordering a Hawaiian Delight pizza with Spam and pineapple, my second-favorite food.

Mom hangs up the phone and flops on the couch, which surprises me — that's my move. I hand her my book report. She takes it and sits up. "You got a B!" she exclaims, leaving off the "minus" part. "Stanford, this is wonderful." I try not to grin. "You should be very proud of yourself," Mom says.

Come to think of it, I *am* pretty proud of myself.

10:35 P.M.

Dad's finally home. Mom and I walk into the den together. The man on the news is talking about a war in some country whose name I can't pronounce. My father likes to watch the news to unwind.

"Stanford did really well on his book report," Mom informs him. "You should be pleased."

He takes my paper. I hold my breath. "A B-minus," he says flatly.

"Mr. Glick says he enjoyed reading my paper," I tell him. "And he wrote 'Good job,' see, right there." I point to the red ink.

"Well," Dad replies, putting the book report down. "You are making some improvement. Let's try for an A next time, okay, Stanford?"

An A? Is he out of his mind?

"Yes, sir," I answer.

My mother glares at my father. I hope they don't have another fight over me. "Isn't there anything else you'd like to say to your son?"

"Oh, right," Dad says. "Stanford, you could use a haircut."

AUGUST 13, 3:31 P.M.

I check the clock again. Yep, the unthinkable has happened. Millicent Min is late. I wonder if it will be on the news tonight.

I'm hoping Millie will get here soon. I want to tell her about Digger. She's about the only person in the universe I can talk to about this. Millicent knows how Digger can be, so she might have some good advice. She's pretty smart. Plus, I really want to show her my book report.

As I wait, Mrs. Martinez walks by, pushing the book cart with the squeaky wheel. We look at each other and shrug. Millicent has never been late to tutoring before.

After twenty minutes I figure Millie is probably not going to show up. Maybe she's been hit by a bus. Or maybe she had a nervous breakdown because all her pens ran out of ink at the same time. Or maybe she's in the hospital because her brain finally exploded. I consider calling her but don't.

As I leave the library, I squint in the sunlight. It is a beautiful day. The kind of day Emily would love because it is bright and sunny, like her. I dedicate the afternoon to Emily Ebers. *Emily, Emily, Emily Ebers.* Maybe I'll call her. No, wait! What if I call her and she wants to meet? How do I look? Do I look okay?

I know! I'll get my haircut. Then I can make Dad happy and impress Emily at the same time.

Usually I just go to SuperFast Cuts. But today I want to go to someplace different. Someplace really good. Someplace worthy of Emily Ebers.

I stop in front of Salon Ferrante and peer through the window. It's fancy inside, and empty. A lady with a confusing hairdo sits at the desk leafing through a magazine, licking her finger each time before she turns a page. She looks bored. Suddenly she glances up and waves me in. I hesitate, but she smiles, gets up, and opens the door.

I am inside. The place is small and it looks like a living room with fancy hanging lights and bright red curtains along the back wall. Did I accidentally walk into someone's house? Am I in that lady's house? Wait, there are two of those chairs that go up and down, and a big sink. Candles are flickering. It smells like oranges. I hear strange music playing. It sounds like it could use a lot more bass. The lady runs her hands through my hair. I try not to flinch.

"I assume you are here to be styled?" I nod stiffly. At least it really is a haircut place. Still, it's too weird here. I wish I were at SuperFast Cuts. They have rows of chairs and sinks and someone whose job it is to sweep hair all day. There you know what to expect.

The lady winks at me. "Mimi will be with you momentarily. You're lucky. We had a cancellation." I nod again. Maybe if I run now, I won't have to go through with this. I inch toward the door.

A very tall black woman suddenly appears from behind the red curtains. Her hair is really short and bronze, and her nails are long and painted red. She looks like one of those scary fashion models from the magazines my sister loves to read.

"Mimi, look what I brought you!" the desk lady exclaims, taking me by the shoulders and marching me over to her.

Mimi scowls as she looks at my hair. Then she purrs, "Let me get my hands on this one!" I wonder if that means she is going to kill me. What would Top Cop do?

Before I can stop her, Mimi reaches for my basketball. I grip it harder. We scuffle until it's in Mimi's hands. I try to block her, but she tosses it to the desk lady, who catches it and tucks it under her desk. Then Mimi pushes me into a hairstyling chair and flings a silver cape over me. There is no escaping now.

The desk lady asks, "Can I get you something to drink? Bottled water? A Coke? A glass of wine?" She winks again.

"Coke, please," I gulp. I wonder if I have to pay for it.

Mimi is twirling my hair. "Shorter?" she asks. I nod. "Any particular style?"

"I want to look good," I stammer. "I want to look like Alan Scott."

"Who's that? What kind of hair does he have?"

"He's the best basketball player ever," I explain. I can tell that this is not registering with her, so I add, "He has really short hair. Sort of like a buzz cut, only not like a buzz cut. The front of his hair kind of swoops up a little into like a wave thing. And the back is sort of longer, but it's short on the sides."

Mimi smiles for the first time. She is wearing braces. "I love it!" she shrieks, turning to the desk lady. "This boy really has a sense of style. Of adventure."

I feel myself turning all red again. Maybe she's not going to kill me after all. I am surprised to hear myself ask, "Uh, Mimi, what about my hair color?"

"Color?" Mimi repeats blankly. "Your hair is a nice color. Black."

"Yes, but could you, you know, put some purple in it?" I know that girls like purple, so if I have purple in my hair, Emily will just fall all over me.

"Highlights?" she asks.

"Yeah, purple highlights," I answer. I am feeling braver. I look at a poster of a guy with highlights. He is leaning on a Porsche and there are three girls staring at him.

"A free spirit!" declares Mimi. "I think you just might be a free spirit like me!"

"What's that?"

"A free spirit is someone who's a nonconformist." Mimi twirls my chair round and round. "Someone who goes places no one else dares to go and who can create their own happiness." Mimi cranks up the music and begins to dance. "Let's do this!"

I am not allowed to look at myself while Mimi is at work. "I want to unveil my masterpiece all at once," she explains. "So tell me, a good-looking boy like you must have a girlfriend, right?"

"Well . . . ," I begin cautiously, but soon I'm telling Mimi everything. I describe Emily's sparkling eyes, her credit card, her curly-ish blond hair, her volleyball serve, her clear skin, her funny laugh, her fancy sandals, her great personality. I could go on forever.

5:25 P.M.

I have never had a haircut take so long. At SuperFast Cuts, I'm in and out of there in ten minutes. I've been here for over an hour and Mimi has put foil all over my head. I try to pick up radio signals. Maybe Lavender's on right now. I can't hear her.

Uh-oh, what if there's a fire and I have to run into the street looking like this?

"Say, Mimi, do you mind blowing out the candles? I'm, um, allergic to wax."

"Sure, no problem," Mimi says.

Emily, Emily, Emily —

A buzzer goes off and I jump.

Mimi fusses with my hair for an incredibly long time. The desk lady clasps her hands together and then applauds. Slowly, Mimi turns my chair around to face the mirror.

I stare. Is that me? I mean, it looks like me, but then it doesn't. My hair's swoopy where I want it and short on the sides like I asked. And purple, it's covered with purple streaks!

"Well, Stanford . . . ?" Mimi sounds worried.

I break out grinning. "I like it!" I really do. Mimi fakes a faint as I admire myself in the mirror. My hair is exactly the way I wanted it. Watch out, Alan Scott — you have competition!

I go to the desk lady to pay. "That will be one-twenty," she says.

Dollars? I gulp. "For what?"

"For a cut and color."

At SuperFast Cuts it only costs $12. I empty my pockets. In one I have the phone list my mom makes me carry, an Alan Scott basketball card, and a mint. In the other I have lint, some cash, and a rock that I've been saving for Yin-Yin because it sort of looks like her.

What I don't have is $120. All I have is $24.

"What's going on?" Mimi asks.

The desk lady tilts her head toward me. Am I shrinking?

"Stanford," Mimi says, "it's awfully expensive here, isn't it?" I nod and do not look at her. What if I get sent to jail for not paying? What if my dad has to bail me out? Oh god, now I'm a criminal.

"Tell you what," Mimi continues. "Pay what you can, and the rest will be a gift from me." I look up. "I had a cancellation, so if you hadn't come in I wouldn't even have had a customer."

"Are you sure?" I ask. My voice cracks.

Mimi smiles and her braces glisten. "Stanford, if you don't do what I tell you, I'm going to put glitter in your hair."

I quickly push the contents of my pockets across the desk. The desk lady picks out the money and puts it in the register. "I'll keep this," she says, taking the mint and winking. I shove the rest of the stuff, including the lint, back in my pocket.

Mimi walks me to the door. "Come back in three months and I'll touch up those highlights for free."

"Thanks," I say. She is so nice. "But I'll come in sooner, and with the money I owe you. Only I may not be able to pay you back all at once."

"You take your time. And Stanford," Mimi adds, "I'm sure she will love it."

"Who will love what?"

"Emily, your girlfriend, is going to love your new hairstyle."

"Emily's not my girlfriend," I say, though I am secretly

thrilled to hear the words *Emily* and *girlfriend* in the same sentence.

Mimi pushes me out the door. "Well, girlfriend or not, Emily's sure to be impressed."

I hope she's right.

I've crossed the street when someone shouts, "Stanford!"

I turn around. Mimi is holding up my basketball. I start to head back to Salon Ferrante, but she signals for me to halt. Then Mimi hurls the ball across four lanes of traffic right into my hands.

AUGUST 14, 1 P.M.

As I near the park, I spy the guys playing Silent Slam Ball. Gus has knocked Digger over, and he's rolling around on the grass pretending to die. Tico spots me first.

"Whoa, whoa, whoa, get a load of Stanford!"

Digger is about to throw the ball at Gus but stops short and jumps up. The others follow and circle around me, checking out my hair. Finally Gus strokes an invisible beard and in a weird accent proclaims, "Vell, es note toe-toe-lee ugg-lay."

"It looks good," Tico weighs in.

"It's okay," Digger adds.

"But purple?" Gus says, laughing. "That is such a girl color."

"It's a color girls like," I inform him.

The guys are quiet as they absorb this information. Finally Tico nods knowingly. "Smart thinking," he says. "Purple."

"Hey, Digger, you should dye your hair," Gus tells him. "Or maybe you should dye your whole head. Or even better, maybe you should wear a bag over your head."

"Shut up," Digger says. He gets ready to hit Gus with the ball but does a fake and throws it at me, hitting me in the head. I pretend to die, and all the guys burst out laughing.

I'll say one thing about the Roadrunners. We know how to have a good time.

2:22 P.M.

"Stop! Stop! Who's that?" Yin-Yin yells. "Get away from me, you criminal!"

"It's me, Yin-Yin!" I dodge the knitting needles she's stabbing in my direction. "It's me, Stanford Wong, your grandson."

Yin-Yin puts down her needles. "Ah, it is you. Luckily you said something. I was going to poke your eyes out."

She squints at me, then puts on her glasses. "You look different."

"I got my hair cut," I say proudly.

The door flies open and Mr. Thistlewaite shuffles in, brandishing a half-eaten Three Musketeers bar. "Vamoose, you cad!" He sees me and straightens his bow tie. "Well, hello, young man! Good to see you again!"

"Doesn't Stanford's hair look nice?" Yin-Yin asks.

Mr. Thistlewaite takes a big bite out of his candy bar. His hair is tipping to one side. I am starting to suspect it is fake. "Yes," he says, walking around and looking me over. "It's got purple stuff in it too."

"Highlights," I tell them both.

"Highlights," Yin-Yin and Mr. Thistlewaite say together approvingly.

"What does your mother think of your highlights?" asks Yin-Yin.

"She said it's not what she would have done, but it's my hair and I'm entitled to have my own style."

"And your father? Does he approve?"

"He didn't notice."

"How could he not notice?" Mr. Thistlewaite barks.

"Mr. Thistlewaite?" my grandmother asks sweetly. "Do you think I ought to get highlights?" She poufs her hair up and blinks at him.

"Certainly not, Mrs. Wong," he bellows. "Why tamper with perfection!"

"But Mr. Thistlewaite, maybe if I dyed my hair I'd look more youthful," Yin-Yin says.

"*Au contraire*, Mrs. Wong," Mr. Thistlewaite tells her. "You radiate youth! Why, just being around you makes me feel ten years younger! And now, my beautiful lady," Mr. Thistlewaite says, "would you honor me by finishing the story you began yesterday right before Ramon gifted us with his chocolate mousse?"

"Which story would that be?"

"The one about you flying over the mountains," he reminds her. "You had just taken flight, I believe."

I haven't heard that story. Mr. Thistlewaite and I settle in as Yin-Yin begins, "There was a time when I was told it would be impossible for me to fly. But no matter what anybody said, I knew that they were wrong. I could fly if I wished hard enough. . . ."

I listen to Yin-Yin's amazing story of what the Earth looked like from the sky. If I could fly, I'd take Emily with me and we'd fly away from Digger and from summer school and from my parents. We'd fly through the clouds, across the desert, and over the ocean. And when we got tired, we'd have a picnic on the top of a mountain and then take our time deciding where to go next.

Yin-Yin looks happy when she talks about flying. I imagine her soaring with her arms spread out. I know my parents think she's getting senile, but I think she's just becoming more of who she is — a free spirit.

AUGUST 15, 3:10 P.M.

It's almost time to meet Millicent at the library. I hope she shows up today. Right now I am standing in front of Dad's dresser. I like looking at his stuff when he's not around. I pick up the cuff links he wears to client dinners. They are heavier than they look. I examine his watch and try it on. He has two. One with a black band and one with a brown band. He must be wearing his black one today.

Dad has three bottles of cologne. I take off the tops and sniff them. They all smell good. I spray myself with all three. How much are you supposed to use? This much? I give myself a few extra sprays to be safe.

3:30 P.M.

Millicent is waiting for me at our table. She looks really upset. Is it my hair? I bet she hates my hair. Oh man, if she hates it, then Emily might hate it too. I can't believe I let Mimi talk me into getting this dumb haircut.

I sit down, and before Millie can open her mouth I cut her off. "I know what you are going to say."

She looks surprised. "You know?"

"Yes, and it's not my fault."

"I never said it was your fault," she replies. "What are we going to do now?"

"We?" I ask.

"Yes, 'we.' If it weren't for you we wouldn't be in this mess." She scrunches up her forehead. "What is that smell?"

I shift in my seat. I can smell something sort of woodsy, bakery, gas station-ish.

"How did you find out?" Millie continues, waving her hand in front of her nose. "Did Emily call you?"

Whoa, wait . . . what does Emily have to do with my hair? "What are you talking about?"

"I'm talking about Emily," she spits. "About the fact that Emily *knows* that I am the one tutoring you." Millicent gasps for air, then adds, "Stanford, you stink!"

Emily knows? Emily knows that Millicent Min is tutoring me?

"How could you tell her?" I yelp. "Why did you do it? You swore on your mother's life! What happened? Did you have a massive brain fart or something???!!!"

Mrs. Martinez signals for us to keep our voices down, even though there is no one else in the library.

"I didn't tell her." Millicent pinches her nose. "She found my certificates and diplomas. I just thought you'd want to know. I'm doing you a favor, okay?!!!"

I slump back like I've been shot. "Now I bet she hates us both. It's all your fault."

"No, it's your fault," Millicent shouts. "Hey, is your hair purple, or is it just bad lighting in here? What's going on with you?" Before I can answer, she cuts me off. "I wanted to tell Emily the truth, but noooo, you wouldn't let me!"

Almost an hour drags by. Millicent and I are still arguing when Emily walks in and heads straight toward us. Millie and I glance at each other. She starts to stand but sits back down really fast, like her legs have buckled.

"Stanford. Millicent," Emily says, giving us each a formal nod. Her eyes are not sparkling at me. Instead they throw off poisonous darts that attack every inch of my body. "I don't have much to say to either of you," she continues, "other than I hope you had fun with your little charade."

I open my mouth, but Emily raises her hand to stop me. She reaches into her purse and pulls out *The Outsiders*. "Here, you can have your book back," she says, tossing it in front of me. She takes one whiff in my direction, then backs away. "Even though you raved about it, I don't think I want to read it anymore."

Millicent looks at the book in amazement, then at me. Emily turns to her. She takes off her necklace. "I think this belongs to you," she says, slapping it down on the table. "I hope the two of you have fun together making up lies. Good-bye."

Then she is gone. *Poof!* Just like that. I wonder if Millicent feels as bad as I do. For once she isn't saying anything. This is all her fault and she isn't even apologizing for ruining my entire life.

"You're such an idiot," I shout. I push everything off the table and storm out of the library.

"You're such a cretin!" Millicent Min calls after me. "And your hair looks stupid and you *stink!*"

I don't care that she's yelling at me. I don't care that I have no clue what a cretin is. I don't care about anything anymore.

10:07 P.M.

My life is lousy. On the Lousy Meter with ten being worst, I rate a fifteen. Digger's blackmailing me. Then Millie just had to go spill her guts to Emily. And now my father's finally decided to notice my haircut.

"You look like a delinquent."

"I do not, I look cool."

"Purple hair! What will people think?"

"They will think I look cool," I mutter.

"Can you wash it out? What can we do about this?"

My mother speaks up. "It's not so bad, Rick, a lot of kids are doing interesting things with their hair these days. At least his hair isn't pink. I think Stanford looks very independent."

Mom winks at me and I give her a weak smile.

"Didn't you ever do something crazy when you were a kid?" she chides him.

"No," my father replies, shaking his head. "I was a good kid. I always did what my father told me to do."

I guess I'm not a good kid.

Instead of sleeping, I stay up and listen to the stupid sappy songs on the radio as I knit. I can hear Mom and Dad fighting about my hair. Maybe if I didn't live here anymore, they'd stop fighting. They don't fight as much about Yin-Yin now that she's gone to Vacation Village.

I heard Mom tell Dad that his mother is really improving. The doctor said, "Now that she has a place of her own, she probably feels less anxious. Plus, all the stimulation is really helping her get out of the rut that she was in."

I'm in a rut. Does that mean I belong at Vacation Village? Do they let kids live there?

I wonder what Emily is doing right now. The songs Lavender is playing are about breakups and lost loves. A man who didn't pay enough attention to his wife suddenly found the time to call Lavender and tell the entire world what a rotten husband he was. He cries as he asks Lavender to play a song.

"Gee, Dennis," Lavender says softly, "breaking up is hard to do, isn't it?" Then, get this, she plays a song called "Breaking Up Is Hard to Do"!

It's unreal. How bad I feel is unreal. I'm still not sure what I am knitting, but I don't want to mess it up. I want to make sure there's at least one part of my life that hasn't unraveled yet.

AUGUST 16, 9:03 A.M.

"Good morning, Stanford," Mr. Glick says, smiling. SSSSpy shoots him the death glare. If it weren't for him none of this would be happening with Emily or the A-Team or my dad. This isn't a good morning. It is a bad morning. A bad day. A bad life.

"Stanford!" Teacher Torturer is still standing next to my desk. What does he want now? "Your homework, please." His hand is out, waiting.

I stare straight ahead and do not answer him.

"I see," notes Mr. Glick before moving on to the next student.

4:30 P.M.

Stretch and I are losing by a million points. And not just because of my pact with Digger. I'm off my game. I've never been off my game like this before.

AUGUST 17, 10:12 A.M.

My father is reading a postcard from Sarah. There is a picture of a sunset over the shore on it. He frowns and hands it to my mother, who reads it, bites her lip, and hands it to me.

The postcard says:

NUKU'ALOFA, KINGDOM OF TONGA

Hi Mom, Dad, and Squiggy!
Summer at Sea is wonderful.
We sail around and man our own ship. I've
met a really neat guy named Matt. He's
going to be a lawyer too. We're having
so much fun I'm almost forgetting to
study!!!
   Tell Yin-Yin I said hello!
   Love,
   Sarah

The Wongs
124 Monterey Drive
Rancho Rosetta, CA
92219

"Matt?" my mother asks no one.

"'I'm almost forgetting to study'?" remarks my father. "She thinks that's funny?"

"It *is* funny," I tell him. "Why is it always so important to you that we study all the time?"

"You've got to think about the future, Stanford," Dad lectures. "Just to float through life not knowing where you'll end up will lead you nowhere."

Why do grown-ups worry so much about the future? Why don't they worry about what's happening right now instead, like how everyone's always mad at each other?

Sometimes I worry that my parents are going to get a divorce. Stretch's parents divorced when he was little, and his mom remarried. His dad remarried too, and now Stretch has stepbrothers and stepsisters he barely knows. He only sees his real dad a couple times a year and says that it's weird. Even though his stepdad is really nice, Stretch once told me that he feels guilty about liking him so much.

Lately my father's been like a ghost. You never see him but can hear him bumping around the house at night. He tries to be quiet so as not to wake us. I don't care if he wakes me up. I want him to wake me up. He can come talk to me anytime. I have locks on my door to keep my parents out. But if they ever tried them, they'd find out that the locks don't really work.

At Vacation Village they have a security guard. I'm not sure if he's there to keep the bad people out or the old people in. I wish he'd do something about all those ladies who always try to pat me on the head. Next time they try that, I think I'll bark at them.

Arf! Arf! If they're going to treat me like a dog, I might as well act like one.

When Yin-Yin first got sent to Vacation Village I promised to get her out of there. She hasn't brought it up lately, but that doesn't mean she doesn't want me to. Just because a person doesn't talk about something doesn't mean it's not important.

AUGUST 19, 9:17 P.M.

I called Emily three times today. When the machine answered, I
hung up. When her mom answered, I hung up. And when Emily
answered, I panicked, then hung up.

"Don't despair," Lavender says. "True love always wins in the
end." I hope that what Emily and I have is true love. I hope that's
what my parents have too.

This morning, when Dad asked me how summer school was
going, I answered, *"Arf, arf, arf, arf!!!"* Then, before he could lecture me, I ran off to school.

Later Teacher Torturer asked me what a proper noun was. I
just looked at him and barked. The other kids snickered and
I stood up and took a bow. Teacher Torturer did not look amused
when he said, "Rover, see me after class."

I expected a lecture. Instead, Mr. Glick told me, "We're coming
down to the end of summer. How you do in the next couple of
weeks will determine your grade. You know that, don't you?"

I nodded.

"Stanford? Is everything all right?"

"Arf."

"I noticed that you didn't turn in your homework." Mr. Glick didn't sound mad. He sounded disappointed. "You were doing so well. Stanford, you've really come a long way this summer. I was so proud when you read *The Outsiders.*"

I started to get choked up. *"Arf,"* I said.

"Woof," he replied.

"Can't talk now," I told him as I bolted out the door.

"Stanford, may I talk to you for a moment?" It's my mom. She's still dressed in her business suit even though it's nighttime. I had to make my own dinner — three peanut-butter-and-banana sandwiches. I put potato chips in the last one to give it some crunch.

"What?" I turn off Lavender and open my door.

"Stanford, did you bark at your father this morning?"

"Arf."

"Does that mean yes?"

"Arf, arf."

"Well," she says, looking like she's trying not to smile, "that's not how we communicate in this family."

"How do we communicate then?"

Mom gets serious. "I'm not sure," she tells me. "I wish I knew."

AUGUST 20, 3:45 P.M.

I don't know why I bother to show up at tutoring. All Millicent Min and I do is glare at each other. I still can't believe she told Emily our secret. She claims that Emily figured it out. I say that if she really didn't want Emily to find out she should have hidden her stupid certificates better.

Dad's going to be so angry if he finds out I've stopped doing my homework. He still has a math test I took in second grade. I got an A-plus on it. He holds the test up whenever I fail and says, "You got an A-plus once, you can do it again."

I peaked in the second grade.

"I told you we should have told Emily the truth earlier," Millicent is carrying on. "But noooooo, you wouldn't listen to me, would you? You were too interested in playing with plastic balls at McDonald's. I told you she'd find out sooner or later. I told you —"

I get up and leave before Millicent can tell me one more thing.

AUGUST 21, 2:03 P.M.

Last night I called Emily again. I don't know what to say, but I like hearing her voice. "Hello? Hello, is anyone there?" It makes me feel good, if only for a few seconds, before I hang up.

I'm coming up on the basketball court when I see the Roadrunners huddled together. Something's weird. Stretch, Gus, and Tico are all slouching around wearing their Roadrunners caps. Digger looks annoyed.

"What's up?" The guys look at each other and start snickering. I panic. Maybe Digger told them. Oh man, this is it. This is where I turn back into a nobody.

"Guess what?" Gus says.

"What?" I ask, hoping my voice does not crack.

"One, two, *three!!!*" Tico and Gus shout. The Roadrunners rip off their baseball caps and toss them into the air.

I don't believe it. Is that for real? They have purple highlights! I begin laughing hysterically and soon the guys join me. All but Digger, of course. His hair is still the same.

"It was all my idea," Gus says, tossing me a tube of Wash 'n' Wear Hair highlighter dye. His hands are purple.

"You lie!" Tico cuts in. "It was my idea."

Stretch grins as Gus and Tico pretend to strangle each other.

"Ladies, ladies," Digger says. "Let's stop fussing over our hair and start playing basketball."

Stretch grabs the ball. He's on my team. Digger and Tico start. Gus sits out with Joey and some girls who are watching us play.

Digger has the ball. He comes charging at me and almost knocks me over. He misses the net. Stretch rebounds and passes to me. I have a clear shot, but then I let Tico take the ball from me. He tosses it to Digger; Stretch intercepts and passes me the ball. I look at Digger, shoot, and miss. It kills me to do this. It was a shot I could have made in my sleep. But now that I've lost Emily, I can't lose the Roadrunners too.

Digger rebounds and makes a basket. Tico high-fives him. Stretch throws his hands in the air in protest. I turn away.

We have the ball again. I start to make a layup but stop midway and pass the ball to Stretch, only I purposely throw it high. Digger elbows Stretch and makes another basket.

Tico hoots, "Way to go!"

Game's over. We've been slaughtered.

Stretch just stands with his hands on his hips and stares at me.

Tico asks me, "Did you eat some bad ham or something? You weren't yourself out there."

"Yeah, what was with you?" asks Gus. "Digger was all over you."

"Aw, leave me alone," I say.

"I know why Digger's been doing so well lately," Tico

announces. Digger and I both face him. "It's the shoes. It's the BK620s. They're finally kicking in, right?"

"Right," Digger and I say at the same time.

"Maybe you could work with me on my bank shots," says Tico.

"Sure," I say.

"Thanks, Stanford. You can help too, but I was really asking Digger."

"Oh yeah. Of course. I'm busy anyway. You know, work and everything."

"Hey, Digger," I hear someone call out. I glance around. It's Joey. "Great game. Not many guys can score points off the mighty Stanford Wong!"

Coming up behind Joey are Marley and a couple of his friends. One of them is wearing a rubber Borg mask, even though it's boiling outside.

I gotta get out of here. I'm about a block away from the park when someone taps me on the shoulder.

"Oh, hi, Stretch." His forehead is all wrinkled, the way it gets when he's worried. "I'm okay, just having a bad day."

Stretch nods like he knows what I mean. We walk in silence, except for the sound of Stretch bouncing the ball. When we get to his house, I turn on the television while Stretch makes popcorn. *Sesame Street* is on.

Stretch hands me my own bowl. "Thanks," I tell him, adding, "Your hair looks good purple. Hey, I wonder what color Digger's hair would have come out if he added purple to it."

This cracks up Stretch so much he spits out his popcorn.

Some lands on me. I shove a whole handful in my mouth and spit it out at him like a machine gun firing. We keep this up as the TV kids leave the farm and wave good-bye to the animals. But when Ernie comes on and starts singing "Rubber Duckie," we stop out of respect. That song's a classic.

AUGUST 22, 4:15 P.M.

I wonder if Millicent Min still gets paid when all she does is sit and snarl at me. We have been having this stare-down for most of the hour. You'd think Millicent would give up, but nooooo, she's too stupid to do that. So instead, we shoot each other evil looks that cancel each other out.

Finally an alarm beeps on Millicent's watch. It is the most complicated watch I have ever seen. It even has a compass and calculator on it. What a nerd. We both get up and walk out without even looking at each other.

"Good-bye, Millicent. Good-bye, Stanford," Mrs. Martinez's voice trails after us.

I am going to see Yin-Yin. When I near her room I hear voices. I can tell it's not Mr. Thistlewaite. This voice is much softer. I push the door open.

"Stanford!" Millicent's grandmother jumps up and hooks her arm through mine. "Yin-Yin, this handsome boy is going to walk me to my car. I'll send him back once I start burning rubber."

Yin-Yin laughs. "Go on . . ." She waves us away.

It takes a long time to get out of the building, since Maddie stops and passes out dim sum to every person she comes across. Everyone seems to know her.

"Where did you get that?" I ask, pointing to the *shu mai.*

Maddie grins mischievously. "Your grandmother and I made it. Ramon has such a lovely kitchen. Although I did have to move some things around to give it the proper feng shui treatment."

We near Maddie's car, an old Dodge Dart. It looks cool, like something I wouldn't mind driving when I'm old enough.

"How are you doing?" Maddie asks as she digs through her giant purse for her keys.

Why are grown-ups always so interested in how I am doing? "Fine," I say.

"Are things going all right between you and Millicent?"

"Millicent is a big double-crossing spaz," I start to tell her. Then I remember that Millicent is her granddaughter and she probably doesn't want to hear stuff like that. So instead I answer, "Everything's fine."

"You probably already know that I'm going to London for a while," Maddie says. I didn't know that. "Most likely, Millie will be lonely when I'm away. Maybe you could call her sometime. Go bowling or something."

Oh right. Millicent Min bowling. That would be good for a laugh.

"Bowling," I say, pretending to think about it. "Sure thing, Maddie. What are you going to do in London?"

Maddie clears her throat and announces, "I'm going to harness the positive energy flow of the masses by studying the ancient

Chinese philosophy of feng shui, and then bring it back to Rancho Rosetta."

I stare blankly at her.

"Okay," Maddie confesses. "The truth is, I'm going to Fenwick and Feldie's Feng Shui Academy in London. I figure I can visit Europe and at the same time learn why putting a sofa in a certain place will ward off evil spirits. Feng shui's a really big business these days.

"Yin-Yin thinks it's ridiculous," Maddie goes on. "Instead of placing her well-being and safety in the hands of the elements, she'd rather do things like put dog food out to trick burglars into thinking there's a German shepherd in the house. But then, you know your Yin-Yin, she's got lots of interesting ideas!"

I watch the cars pass for a moment, then ask, "Maddie, you know all those stories Yin-Yin's been telling lately? Are they true? Like the one about her dancing in a Broadway show?"

"Do you think they are?"

"Not totally."

Maddie eases herself onto a bench near her car. "Your Yin-Yin was a very adventurous young woman, Stanford. Would you like to hear about some of her adventures?"

I sit as Maddie sets aside the dim sum and begins her story.

"Yin-Yin and I were spirited girls. *Strong-willed* is the word they use today. We zigged when everyone else zagged. We told people what we thought, and we knew how to have fun.

"We each had a dream. I was going to change the world, make it a better place. Your grandmother was going to become a pilot and fly through the clouds. She was heaven and I was earth, we used to joke."

"A pilot? Yin-Yin wanted to be a pilot?" I always thought she wanted to fly like a bird. "A pilot?" I say again.

"A pilot," Maddie assures me. "There were not that many women pilots back in those days. There still aren't. But that didn't stop Yin-Yin.

"She read everything she could about Amelia Earhart and even found a flight school that agreed to take her. She was close to getting her pilot's license.

"Unfortunately, her parents had other ideas. While my parents were happy to let me fight my battles and support my causes, hers felt that the best thing they could do for their daughter was secure her future. That meant marrying her off to a man who would take care of her."

"An arranged marriage," I murmur.

Maddie nods. "Because your grandfather was older, he wanted kids right away. He expected her to stay home, as most women did in those days. So she set her dreams aside and took on new ones, of being the best wife she could be, of being the best mother and then grandmother.

"As for dancing on Broadway or dining with the queen of England, those are things we talked about. We just never got around to it, though I still might give it a try." Maddie winks at me and then grows serious. "Stanford, have your parents talked to you about what's happening to Yin-Yin?"

I shake my head.

"Your grandmother may seem different to you these days

because she is living in the past as well as the present. Like many people who keep secrets, Yin-Yin kept her dreams hidden close to her heart. Now that she is getting older, she can't hold on to them as tightly as she used to. Her dreams are seeping out. Her mind is taking her on the adventures she never had a chance to take in real life."

"So she's lying?"

"A lie is when you tell someone something that you know is not true. Yin-Yin really believes her stories. Sometimes her mind plays tricks on her. When people are depressed that can happen." Maddie adds softly, "I know."

She perks up and pats me on the back. "Try not to worry too much. Your grandmother is in good physical health. And Vacation Village is a great place for her. They know how to exercise her mind as well as her body. Yin-Yin is in better spirits than I have seen in a long time!

"Stanford," she continues, "these so-called stories Yin-Yin tells may seem outrageous. Yet to me, it doesn't matter if they really happened or not, if they make her feel good. So if telling tales makes her happy, then I am all for it. What harm is there?

"I know this is hard for you to understand, but I would encourage you to listen to your grandmother. She is quite a storyteller, and as with any great storyteller, she likes an appreciative audience.

"Now then," Maddie says, standing up and smoothing the front of her skirt. "I'd better get going. I have a protest to organize. They are considering turning Main Street into four lanes, and we can't have that, can we?"

Before I can answer, Maddie has disappeared. I am so mixed up. When exactly did the world get so complicated? As I watch the Dodge Dart chug away, I notice something. I pick up the plate of dim sum and call after her, but it's too late. Maddie is gone.

I look down at the plate. There is only one *shu mai* left. I pick it up and eat it. No sense in it going to waste.

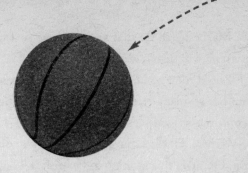

AUGUST 23, 12:01 A.M.

Mom and Dad are arguing again. I am in my room furiously working on my Stress Mess and listening to Lavender. I have called Emily's house twice today, which is once more than yesterday.

"People who need people are the luckiest people in the world," Lavender advises a distraught listener.

I need people, but I sure don't feel lucky. Mom and Dad are probably headed toward a divorce. Digger's probably going to tell the Roadrunners I'm a big fake. Now that I'm not even turning in my homework, I'm probably going to fail English and the sixth grade. Then I'm going to get kicked off the A-Team and everyone will know that I'm a nobody. Or worse than a nobody: I'm a nobody who was pretending he was somebody. Not only won't I be able to play in the Hee-Haw Game, I'll probably be the kid who has to clean up when it's over. I'd be better off running away before the game begins.

Hey . . . maybe that's not such a bad idea. In *The Mixed-Up Files* those kids run away and solve a big mystery, and in *The Out-siders* Johnny and Ponyboy run away and save some children's lives. Maybe I will do that and be some sort of hero and then everything will turn out okay.

I'll need money. Dad's always got money in his wallet, and Mom has so many credit cards she won't notice one missing. I can hide out at Ronster's Monster RV World. There are millions of RVs there, I'll bet I can sleep in a different one every night for a year. Oh man, this is going to be great. I'll buy lots of food so I don't have to cook, and I'll get tons of Oreos, and no one will tell me to "stop eating those or you'll get sick."

When my parents find out I'm gone they're going to go bonkers. Mom will cry and Dad will feel totally guilty. They will be so worried they will fall into each other's arms and swear never to argue again. Then Dad will go on television and announce to the whole world, "Stanford Wong was the best son a father could have. I was a jerk to ignore him. I only wish I had been at every single one of his basketball games to cheer him on. Stanford, son, come home and I swear I will be a better dad if you'll just forgive me!"

It's settled. I am going to run away. No one will notice anyway. Well, Yin-Yin will miss me. Wait! I know: I will take Yin-Yin with me! After all, she made me promise to help her run away. She can teach me how to drive. Oh, that's good! It'll be just like in Dad's favorite movie, *Easy Rider,* with me and Yin-Yin traveling all over the country, meeting people and having the best time being rebels.

Maddie said that Yin-Yin liked adventure, so I'm going to take her on one. I'll just need a little time to prepare.

AUGUST 26, 12:14 A.M.

Mom is asleep in Sarah/Yin-Yin's room. Dad's conked out on the couch. The television is on. A happy lady takes a bite of turkey jerky. "You made this?" she shrieks, turning to a man wearing an apron. "This tastes so good *and* costs only pennies a serving! Amazing!"

She seems like a nice lady. I'll bet she has a good life and no one in her family fights.

I've had three days to plan. I check to make sure I have all my supplies. I've got $114 from my savings, Mom's purse, and Dad's wallet. When I opened his wallet, I stared at a photo he had tucked away. It was a picture of me when I was about five. I suppose I wasn't as much trouble when I was five.

In my backpack I've got a flashlight, hair gel, and *The Outsiders*. I make sure to take plenty of food: Oreos for me, Sugar Babies for Yin-Yin, and six cans of tuna. I grab a couple of cold sodas from the fridge. When I shut the door, my F book report taunts me for the last time. I finished my *Holes* book report this afternoon. It's pretty good. I'll mail it in from the road.

12:48 A.M.

The security guard in the lobby of Vacation Village is snoring so loud I'm surprised he doesn't wake himself up. This is going to be a lot easier than I thought. I sneak up the stairs so the elevator will not disturb him. Even though it is after midnight, all the lights in the hallways are on and the glare hurts my eyes.

As I tiptoe past the rooms I hear televisions blaring. I thought old people liked to go to bed early.

Softly I knock on Yin-Yin's door. There is no answer, so I turn the knob slowly and push. She is asleep. The only light is from the full moon hanging outside the window.

"Yin-Yin, wake up," I whisper. "Wake up."

Her eyes fly open. She looks scared. "It's just me, Stanford," I quickly assure her. "It's okay."

"Who . . . ?" She squints and then reaches for her glasses. "Stanford?" She sounds confused. "Is everything all right? What are you doing here at this hour?"

I drop my backpack on the floor and sit on the side of her bed. "I'm going to get you out of here, Yin-Yin. We're going to break out of this joint and run away! Come on, get your things."

I stash some of her photos in my backpack and try to force her Family Reunion birdhouse in it, but it won't fit.

Yin-Yin has not moved. Maybe she doesn't understand how serious I am about this. "What's wrong?" I ask. "Didn't you hear what I said? We're getting out of here. C'mon, hurry before we get caught."

"Stanford," my grandmother says slowly. "I don't think we should be doing this." Slowly I turn around to face her. "I probably need to stay here," she says. "I'm not always myself these days."

"That's not true," I insist. "How can a person not be themselves?"

But then I remember Family Night at my dad's office. I had been forced to get a dork haircut and wear a starched white shirt and blue blazer. When I lumbered out of my room, my mother cried, "Oh, Stanford, you look so nice, I hardly recognize you!" Dad slapped me on the back and said, "Now this is a Stanford Wong I'd like to get to know better." They were actually happy that I didn't look like myself.

"Yin-Yin, remember when you were young and wanted to fly but couldn't? When we get out of here, we can do whatever we want, whenever we want. We won't have to follow anyone's rules. Don't you want to run away?"

My grandmother gets out of bed and leads me to the couch. "Stanford," she says calmly, "let's think this through."

"I have! I've thought of everything. Look!" I show her the contents of my backpack.

Yin-Yin spies the Sugar Babies and signals for me to give her a box. When I hand her the candy, she wraps her hands around mine. "If you're doing this for me, stop. It's not so bad here, Stanford. Not as bad as I first thought. They take good care of me and I've made some nice friends."

"Like Mr. Thistlewaite," I guess.

A small smile appears. "Yes, there's Mr. Thistlewaite and some others, like Ramon. You remember Ramon. He's quite a good cook, even if he underspices."

"No, no, no," I insist. "Yin-Yin, you've always wanted to fly and be free, remember? We can be free together!"

Yin-Yin releases my hands and takes the Sugar Babies from

me. As she opens the box, she says, "Yes, that is true. But some-times knowing you can be free is just as good as being free."

Huh? I don't understand. Maybe she *is* crazy.

"Stanford, look around the room. See these birdhouses?" I nod. "Even birds who fly free like to have a place they can call home. These days, Vacation Village is my home. I am safe here. I know who I am here."

"So you're not going with me," I say dully.

"No, Stanford, I am not." She doesn't sound like a free spirit; she sounds like a grown-up. "I really think that running away is not going to solve your problems."

"Who says I have problems?"

Yin-Yin puts down her Sugar Babies. "Come here," she says. She hugs me. It feels so good to be hugged. I start to cry on her shoulder and keep crying for so long and so loudly that it sounds like there is a donkey in the room. I can't stop. I don't want to stop. The more I cry, the better I feel. Is this why little kids cry all the time? Suddenly the door opens.

"Everything okay?" asks one of the Vacation Village ladies.

"Fine, just fine," Yin-Yin says, motioning her away.

"Mrs. Wong, you know that visiting hours ended a long time ago."

"Yes, yes, we know that," my grandmother assures her.

The lady looks at me, still hugging Yin-Yin. She nods and closes the door softly.

"Stanford, I want you to go now. I want you to go home; it's where you belong. It might not seem like it right now, but things will work out. Promise me you will not run away."

I dry my tears on my sleeve, kiss my grandmother, and take the birdhouse and her photos out of my backpack.

"I promise not to run away."

Before I go, I put all the boxes of Sugar Babies on her bed. I slip her a couple of cans of tuna too in case she gets hungry.

"Thank you, Stanford," Yin-Yin says. "You're a good boy."

1:30 A.M.

When I get home, Mom and Dad are sitting silent in the living room. My dad looks angry. My mom looks sad. The TV is muted and the turkey jerky lady is still smiling. This time she is marveling over mops that can clean the ceiling.

"Stanford Andrew Wong . . . ," my father says, rising from his chair.

"Rick . . . ," my mother warns him.

He sits back down. Dad starts to say something, but Mom cuts him off. "I'll handle this." She turns to me. "Yin-Yin called us."

I can't believe Yin-Yin would do that to me!

"Why, Stanford? Why did you run away?" I shrug my shoulders. "Is it something we said? Something we did?"

How can I tell them that it is something they did not do? They did not stay in love. How can I tell them it is because Emily hates me? They don't even know who Emily is. How can I tell them I will probably flunk English and disappoint them yet again? How can I tell them anything?

I wish there was someone I could talk to who wouldn't tell

me what to do or how to act or how to feel. I wish I knew someone who just liked me for myself and didn't expect things from me that I can't deliver.

"I'm tired," I grunt. "I want to go to bed."

"Young man!" my father begins in his low voice.

"Don't use that tone with Stanford," my mother orders him.

For once, my father does what she tells him. He softens. "Stanford," he says. "Stay. Talk to us." I turn around. My father is asking me to talk to him?

"Please," my mother pleads.

I look at them both and finally ask the question that has been hanging over my head. "Are you guys getting a divorce?"

They both look startled. Neither speaks. They keep looking at each other.

Finally Dad asks, "Whatever made you ask that?" He sounds nervous.

"Well, you and Mom are always fighting, and you stay away from home all the time. And you're always mad, so I just thought you'd be happier without us."

For once my father is at a loss for words. He looks like I have just punched him. He turns to my mom. She shakes her head and says, "Talk to him."

"Is that what you think? That I'm mad all the time?"

"That's what he said, isn't it?" Mom answers.

"I'm asking Stanford, not you," he tells her. I wonder if they are going to start fighting again. "Stanford?"

I hesitate, but he's asking and he may never ask me again. "Well, it sure does seem like you're mad a lot."

"I have a lot of pressure on me," he says. Suddenly Dad

doesn't sound like he is in charge. He sounds like me when I'm making excuses. "My job is very stressful. But I am doing it for you two and for Sarah. If I get this big promotion —"

I cut him off, "Then you will have more stress and see even less of us."

My mother covers her mouth like she's hiding a laugh.

My father looks at the clock. "Stanford, you'd better get to bed. We can continue this conversation later."

"But I want to talk now," I plead.

He's already standing up. "It's after two A.M. and I'm all talked out. Come on, let's go."

Both parents escort me to my room, as if afraid I might run away again. My mother tucks me into bed and gives me a kiss. I am too tired to protest. My father stays after Mom has left. "Stanford," he says, "running away doesn't solve anything."

"Hiding doesn't either," I tell him.

Instead of getting upset, Dad nods. "Point well taken."

After he's gone, I get up and dial Emily's number. I hang up before the phone rings. Lavender is talking. Does she ever sleep? "To all my listeners out there at this lonely hour of the night, just know that when you listen to Lavender, you've got a friend. . . ."

Through the wall I can hear the murmur of my parents' voices. They don't sound angry. Not this time. Reaching across the bed, I turn down the volume on my radio and strain to listen to what they are saying. I fight hard to stay awake but in the end finally surrender to sleep.

8:59 A.M.

SSSSpy sneaks across the school yard and slips into Mr. Glick's room. He has to sit near the front today because Mr. Glick is still insisting his students play musical chairs. SSSSpy has already sat in every seat in the room.

Mr. Glick is collecting our book reports. All of a sudden class is over. SSSSpy opens his eyes. Mr. Glick is at his desk grading papers. The room is empty of other students.

"You fell asleep, Mr. Wong," Mr. Glick says. "That hasn't happened in a long time."

"I know. I'm sorry," I mutter. "I was up really late last night."

"Studying for the final exam?"

I don't answer.

"You know, Stanford, you failed your first *Holes* book report. Did you read the book this time?" I nod. "Good." Mr. Glick smiles. "Stanford, I hope you know that I'm rooting for you."

3:30 P.M.

At the library Millicent Min looks up at me and doesn't even try to hide how much she hates me.

"Did you hand it in?" she asks.

"Yep."

"Did you do a good job?"

"Yes."

"All right then." Millicent whips out her calculator and starts stabbing the buttons. "Stanford," she says, "let's assume you get a C on your *Holes* book report. You've done a decent job on your papers, but because of some of your test grades, and the fact that you didn't turn in a lot of your homework assignments, your entire grade rests on your final exam. In order to pass English, you must get a C-minus or above tomorrow. Anything less than that and you will flunk."

The last three words ring in my ears. *You will flunk. You will flunk. You will flunk.* She just had to say that, didn't she? Millicent Min thinks she's so smart. Just once, I'd like to see her fall apart. Wouldn't that be funny.

Wait! What's happening? Millicent is packing up. I win!

She looks at me and shakes her head. What now? I pick up a pen and doodle on my arm. Before I can stop myself, I blurt out, "I tried calling her, you know."

Millicent hands me one of her Sharpie markers to draw with. "What did she say?"

I tell her how I hung up the phone before talking to Emily. Millie looks sad for a moment, and I wonder if she is human after all. "I've been meaning to ask you," she says. "Did you really read *The Outsiders* before you gave it to Emily?"

There she goes again, thinking I am stupid. "That's for me to know and for you not to find out," I say.

"Be that way then."

Before she leaves, Millicent shoves a paper in my face. "Here, these are the main points you should know for your final. Read it. It will help you. Not that you deserve any help."

Then she is gone and I am left with my test to cram for and my totally messed-up life to sort out.

11:57 P.M.

It's late, but I'm up cramming for my final exam. Mom fell asleep on the couch while watching television, so I put a blanket over her and turned the sound down. Dad comes home. He looks exhausted.

"Hi," I say to him as he sets his briefcase down in the living room.

"What are you doing up?"

"Studying."

He smiles.

"Hey, Dad, can we talk?" He promised we'd continue our conversation.

He rubs the back of his neck. "Stanford, I'm bushed. Can we do this some other time? You ought to get to bed and get some rest for your test tomorrow."

"But Dad," I plead, "this is sort of important."

"It's not about basketball, is it?" I shake my head. "What is it then?" he asks.

"It's about my test."

He sits down. "Are you prepared? I don't want you goofing off during the test and getting Mr. Glick mad at you, do you understand?" He stops, then asks, "So what was it you wanted to ask me?"

"Nothing," I mumble. "Never mind." Why can't he just wish me good luck?

He turns the volume up on the television. My mother stirs. I leave as Dad starts flipping through the channels. Mom asks, "Was Stanford just here?"

I stand in the hallway and listen. "Yes, he said he wanted to talk, but I think he was just going to try to get out of taking his test tomorrow."

"Rick, you should talk to him. He needs you. He's under a lot of pressure."

"Kristen, *I* am under a lot of pressure. The Alderson deal is coming to an end and I'll find out about the promotion soon. It's now between me and one other guy. Besides, I did talk to Stanford."

"Did you lecture him or talk to him?" asks Mom. "He stayed up late to wait for you. You know, he never goes to sleep until he knows you're home."

The television shuts off. "Oh, all right," my father grumbles. "But if he starts making excuses about his grade, I'll have to tell him a thing or two."

I run to my room and jump into bed.

"Stanford. Stanford?" My father is knocking at my door. I don't answer. "He's asleep," I hear him tell my mother. "See, whatever he wanted to talk to me about couldn't have been that important."

AUGUST 27, 12 P.M.

I was so tired that I almost fell asleep while taking the test.

Mr. Glick asks me to stay after class. I expect a lecture. Instead he says, "Stanford, I've just finished grading your *Holes* report. Would you like it back now?"

Do I want it back? I guess so, since I am making my way up to his desk. He hands me my paper. I look down at my grade and then lock eyes with Mr. Glick.

"You got what you deserved," he says, breaking into a smile. "A B-plus. Nice work."

I smile back.

I leave his room and start running. I'm surprised to find myself at the library. Millicent's not here. Why would she be?

I sit in the periodicals section and just look around. Then I get up to leave. I remember to thank Mrs. Martinez on my way out. "My pleasure, Stanford," she says. "I hope you'll visit me during the school year."

"Uh, sure," I tell her. Then I add, "Mrs. Martinez, would you like to see my book report?"

She nods as she reads it. "Very nice, Stanford. I can see why you got a B-plus!" I can't stop grinning. "I was hoping you'd stop by," she adds. "I took the liberty of getting this for you."

Mrs. Martinez hands me something. It's a library card with my name on it.

4:47 P.M.

It's like this whole summer is coming down to the last minute of the last quarter of the biggest game of my life. I have no idea how I did on the final exam. The game could go either way.

I feel nauseous, like the time Stretch and I ate all those frozen fish sticks and then drank hot chocolate to see if they'd cook in our stomachs. I have so much stuff going on in my head, Dad would be shocked.

Last night a guy named Junior called Lavender. He dumped all this stuff out about how he was a jerk and his wife left him *and* took the dog. After speaking with Lavender, he told her he felt better, and she played a song just for him.

"Sometimes," Lavender explained, "it helps to talk to someone. Thank you for choosing me, Junior. I care about you."

I thought about calling Lavender and using a fake name like Top Cop does all the time. I picked the name Scott Alan. Then I chickened out. What if someone recognized my voice?

If I don't talk to someone soon I might explode. But who? Can't talk to my parents about my parents. Can't talk to Emily about Emily or the guys about the guys. Can't talk to Mr. Glick about Mr. Glick or Yin-Yin about Yin-Yin, and Millicent hates me. Who's left?

"Sorry, Stanford, Mimi isn't working today," the desk lady tells me. "Is this about your hair? Have you been using enough product? It looks a little flat."

"Never mind," I tell her. I slap seven dollars on the counter. "This is for Mimi. I'll bring in more next week." I take three mints out of my pocket. "And these are for you."

The desk lady smiles widely. "I'll be sure to let Mimi know you were here."

As I step outside I am blinded by the sunlight. Suddenly I see a vision. No, wait! It really is Emily. I turn into SSSSpy and tail her. For two blocks she puts money in every parking meter. Then, as quickly as she appeared, she's gone.

What's that about? As if I'm not confused enough.

I don't know what to think or who to turn to. Then it hits me. I check my shoe. Sure enough, the phone number is still there.

5:20 P.M.

Coach Martin is wearing referee clothes. His whistle hangs around his neck. "Did you just ref a game?" I ask. We are outside The Locker Room, the biggest sporting-goods superstore in Rancho Rosetta. It's where I get my basketballs.

Coach laughs and looks at his shirt. "No," he says. "This is my uniform. Teachers don't get paid when they don't teach, so I always get a summer job at The Locker Room." We walk over to the curb and sit down. "Speaking of summer, how are you doing in Mr. Glick's class?"

I hesitate and then it all pours out in spurts. "Mr. Glick . . . flunk . . . Emily . . . lie . . . stupid . . . Mom and Dad . . . fight . . . Yin-Yin . . . dim sum . . . Digger . . . blackmail —"

"Whoa, whoa, slow down there," Coach Martin says. "We're both going to be on overload in a moment. Stanford, let's take these one at a time, okay?"

I wonder if I am going to cry. Man, why do I always start to cry? This is so embarrassing. I suck it up, slow down, and tell Coach about my horrible summer. He listens as I go through all the reasons why my life is a total failure.

When I am done, Coach whistles. "Well, son, you certainly do know how to keep busy. You know, no one can solve your problems for you. But maybe I can help you put some of this in perspective. That is, if you are willing to listen."

I sigh. "Bring it on."

"Life is sort of like basketball," Coach Martin begins. "There are a lot of guys on the court, each with his own agenda. So it's important to know who your teammates are. You may not know what they are going to do, but you know that they are there for you."

I am hoping that some of this will start to make sense very soon. Why do adults talk in riddles?

"Stanford, the first thing you need to get straight is that you are not stupid. Do you think athletes like Alan Scott and Michael Jordan are rocket scientists?"

I shake my head.

"Right, they're basketball players," he goes on. "They might not have been straight-A students in school, but you have to be smart to play well. And Stanford, you play extremely well. You make split-second decisions on the court. You anticipate what the other players are going to do. You know basketball strategy inside and out. A stupid person couldn't do that, could he?"

I shrug. Maybe he's got something there. But Coach is not finished. "Stanford, I'm not sure why you think the world is against you. From what you've told me, you've got a lot of people rooting for you."

"Right, and I'm going to let them down," I mumble.

"You are capable of much more than you give yourself credit for," Coach Martin says. "But until you start believing in yourself, nobody else will."

What is his point?

"Don't underestimate your family and your friends like Stretch, Tico, Gus, and even this Emily. They're your teammates. Be honest with them. They like you for who you are, not what you do."

"What about Digger?"

Coach hesitates. "That one you will have to figure out for yourself." He looks at his watch. "I have to go back now — we're having a big sale on yoga mats and it gets crazy in there. Call me again if you want to talk, okay?"

I nod.

"Stanford," Coach Martin adds before disappearing into the store, "I probably know you better than you know yourself. You have great leadership qualities. You don't hog the ball and you always give others credit. That's one of the reasons I picked you for the A-Team, because of what a great teammate you are." He hesitates, then adds, "Stanford, I would suggest you put yourself back into the game."

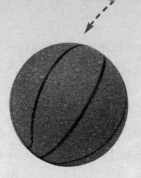

AUGUST 28, 9:11 A.M.

Mr. Glick looks solemn as he passes back our finals. He stops at my desk. From the look on his face, I know I've blown it. I've failed English, not once, but twice.

"Mr. Wong," Mr. Glick says without expression. He puts my test facedown on the desk. "I'd like you to stay after class. There's something important we need to discuss."

I slump back in my chair. My face is burning. Finally I pick up my test and slowly turn it toward me.

I choke. I do not believe what I see . . . a C-plus!!! I got a C-plus on my final exam. That means I passed! That means I don't flunk the sixth grade. That means I will play basketball on the A-Team for Rancho Rosetta Middle School!

Mr. Glick lets the class out early. "No sense in sitting in here all day," he says. "Go out and enjoy what little's left of your summer vacation."

Everyone is in a hurry to leave but me. As hard as I try, I cannot stop grinning. "You did it," he says proudly. "Stanford, you made it. Congratulations!"

He extends his hand. I extend mine, and we shake. Then he

walks to his desk and starts packing up his briefcase. He has the same one as Millicent.

I hang around for a while, not saying anything. I study the bulletin boards. The READING IS FUN poster is still up. While I would never agree that reading is fun, I would have to admit that reading won't kill you. I look at the newspaper clipping of Mr. Glick and Millicent Min. At the beginning of summer, I would have never believed that these two would be on my team.

"Mr. Glick?"

"Yes?"

"Thanks," I tell him, adding, "you know, for the cookies and everything."

Mr. Glick bursts out laughing. "You're welcome, Stanford. I'm glad you decided to give me and English a chance." Then he adds, "Once you gave yourself permission to try, you did okay. You're a smart kid when you apply yourself. Don't ever forget that."

Wow. Mr. Glick said that I am a smart kid.

I am so happy that I forget about SSSSpy and race outside doing zigzags in front of the school. I am free! I am on the A-Team! I am . . . *baammmmm!!!!!*

Stuff flies in the air. I go down hard. I must have bumped into someone. Oh man, my head hurts. I look over and there's another kid rolling around on the ground. He's holding his head too.

"Hey, sorry, man," I say, rubbing my forehead.

"No, my fault," he says. "I shouldn't have been running like that."

I stare at the kid and he stares back.

"Stanford?"

I feel around for my glasses. "Gus?"

"What are you doing here?"

"Nothing," I sputter. "What are you doing here?"

"Nothing," he says quickly.

We both scramble to our feet.

"Nice day," I comment.

Gus looks up at the sky. "Yeah. It's going to get really hot, though."

I nod like he's said something important.

For the longest time we both just stand in one spot and look at everything except each other. Neither one of us speaks. Finally I confess, "I flunked English and had to go to summer school."

It feels good to be honest with Gus. Maybe Coach was right about being up-front with my team.

Oh no, Gus is laughing so hard that no sound is coming out. This is exactly why I didn't want the guys to know. Coach was so wrong. What does he know? Now Gus is hysterical and rolling around on the ground.

"So what?" I mutter. "I passed."

Gus can barely breathe. He wheezes, "I flunked science and had to take it over again."

"No way!"

He grabs my ankles and takes me down with him. Now I'm laughing too. We punch each other hard.

"Idiot!"

"Numbnut!"

"Weasel!"

"Toe jam!"

"So is this your 'summer job'?" Gus asks when he can finally breathe normally.

"Yeah, this is it," I tell him. "What about mowing lawns? You make that up?"

"Sort of," he says. "I mow a couple of lawns every afternoon, but I spent my mornings here, trying not to let anyone see me."

"Me too!" I roar. "You know," I say, getting serious, "if I flunked English again, I would have gotten kicked off the A-Team."

Gus's eyes get wide. "Get outta here!" he shouts. "You earned your spot on the A-Team."

"Well, now I did. Now that I passed English."

"I was afraid I'd get kicked off the B-Team if I didn't bring up my science grade," Gus confesses.

We both sit silent. Finally I say, "It wasn't so bad going to summer school."

"Yeah." Gus nods. "It was no big deal. I knew I was going to pass all along. I just didn't want to mention it because, because . . ."

"Because there was no point in making a big deal about it?"

"Right!" he agrees. "Plus summer school's a good thing because if it weren't for students like us, teachers would be out of a job."

"It's not a biggie having to repeat a class," I tell him.

"Oh, I know," Gus jumps in. "A lot of kids have to repeat a class. In fact, I heard that almost every kid has to at one time or another."

"I think I heard that too." I nod. "There's no shame in it."

"Definitely!" Gus pauses. "Stanford," he says, looking around, "swear on your life you won't tell anyone I had to repeat science."

"I swear."

Without any further words, Gus and I spit into our palms and shake on it.

11:07 A.M.

It's fun to shoot hoops with Gus. No one's keeping score. Nothing's holding me back. I even spill my guts about Digger. Just as I make a hard shot clear across the court, I see him coming our way.

"What?" Gus asks. Before I can answer, he spots Digger. "You can't let him be the boss of you," Gus whispers. "Besides, you passed. You're on the A-Team. He can't blackmail you anymore!"

"Yeah, but if Stretch and Tico find out I've lied all summer . . ."

Gus moans, "I know. Tico will hate my guts."

"Give me the ball," Digger orders.

"Yes sir!" Gus replies, shoving it hard into Digger's chest.

"Let's just shoot free throws," Digger says, "and see who can get the most in a row. I'll go first."

"One, two," Gus counts. "Okay, my turn."

He misses his first shot and tosses the ball to me just as Tico and Stretch walk up.

"One, two . . . ," Gus counts.

Digger clears his throat to get my attention, but I ignore him.

"Three, four, five . . . looks like Stanford's the winner," shouts Gus.

We play a few more games of H-O-R-S-E, and each time I win, Digger turns a deeper shade of red.

"Hey, guys," I say, tossing the ball to Tico. "I gotta go see my grandma. We're having lunch at her place today."

"Don't choke on your food," Digger says.

"Thanks for your concern," I tell him. "It's nice to know you care."

12:12 P.M.

It's International Food Festival Day at Vacation Village, something the perky ladies have dreamed up. The whole place is decorated with flags from different countries. Everyone who works here is wearing funny-looking outfits, and someone hands me a sombrero. "It's a Small World" is playing over and over again. I'll never get that song out of my head.

I spot my mother. She looks really sharp in her navy blue suit. She's wearing one of those French hats that look like Frisbees.

"Stanford!" she says.

I rush up to her. "Mom, I passed. I passed!"

"Oh, honey," she says in a way that makes me choke up. "You did it!"

"I'm going to the seventh grade," I tell her. "I made the A-Team."

"Stanford." My mother brushes some dirt off my shirt. "You have always been on the A-Team, with or without basketball."

What a mom thing to say.

"I thought you had work?" I ask as we walk toward the cafeteria.

248

"I do, but this is important to Yin-Yin, so I took some time off."

"You really like your job, don't you?"

Mom smiles. "Yes, it's my version of basketball. Thank you for asking, Stanford. That means a lot to me." She gives my arm a squeeze and whispers, "Did I tell you that I am so proud of you?"

"Yes, Mother," I say, trying to sound like it's no big deal.

We head to the buffet table. Yin-Yin is nowhere in sight. There are mini-pizzas and tacos; there's sushi and curry. Then we spot the dim sum. "Uh-oh," Mom says. I grimace.

Mom takes a bite of a *shu mai*. I take a *cha siu bao*. We both look at each other and frown. It tastes good, really good. This will not make Yin-Yin happy. She fancies herself the best dim sum chef around.

Just then Yin-Yin appears. "Hi," she says. She's dressed in a nice new outfit Mom bought for her. Everything matches. "Did your father make it?"

"No," I mumble. "The Alderson whatever is coming to an end and he's got a lot of work."

"Oh well, that is to be expected," Yin-Yin chirps as she gives me a hug. "At least you're here and not someplace you shouldn't be."

I hug her back and whisper, "I passed English."

Yin-Yin lets go of me and looks into my eyes. "You made the A-Team," she says. "You're moving up. Guess that teacher of yours wasn't so bad after all?"

"Naw," I tell her. "Mr. Glick was okay in the end."

"Mr. Glick sounds like a person worth knowing."

I nod in agreement.

"How's the dim sum?" she asks, taking a plate. Mom and I glance at each other. Yin-Yin bites into a *ha gow*. "Not bad," she says.

"It's not awful," Mom agrees. "But no one makes dim sum like you."

"It's true, Yin-Yin," I say, backing her up.

Ramon approaches us. "It's going well, wouldn't you say, Mrs. Wong?"

"You've outdone yourself, Ramon."

He looks nervous. "The dim sum?"

"Wonderful," she tells him. "Next time I'll teach you how to make *chow fun*."

"I'd love it!" he exclaims, before hurrying off to check on his *carnitas*.

Yin-Yin turns to us and explains, "Ramon is the perfect person to carry on my legacy. He's a fine cook on his own, but with my coaching he's been flourishing."

"Thank goodness for Ramon," my mother whispers to me.

We all fill up our plates and are soon joined by Mr. Thistlewaite. "Hello, hello, hello!" he booms. "Mrs. Wong, you're looking magnificent today."

Yin-Yin laughs. "You need glasses," she jokes, and gives him a light punch in the arm.

"Attention everyone!" a perky Vacation Village lady wearing a kimono says. "It's time for our grand-prize raffle for a new thirteen-inch color television!"

A murmur travels through the room. Yin-Yin and Mr. Thistlewaite put down their plates and take out their raffle tickets.

"And the winner is number one-seven-two-one!!! Will number one-seven-two-one please come forward!"

Everyone claps as Yin-Yin makes her way to the front and blows kisses to the crowd. She's all smiles as we settle down to eat. "Remember our deal?" she whispers to me. "I won a big prize, so now you have to kiss a girl!"

"Congratulations," Mom tells Yin-Yin.

"Congratulations to Stanford too," she replies.

"You are so right!" Mom picks up her water glass and announces to our table, "A toast to Stanford, for passing his English class."

Mr. Thistlewaite stands up and shouts to the room, "Listen up, everyone! We are doing a toast to Stanford!"

All at once, the Vacation Villagers raise their water glasses and say, "A toast to Stanford!"

"Who's Stanford?" I hear an old man behind me ask. "Is he that new fellow with the fish tank?"

"I don't know," the lady next to him says. "But I'm sure he must have done something wonderful."

AUGUST 29, 7:30 A.M.

Even though I can sleep in today, I get up early to be with Dad. He's already eating breakfast by the time I join him.

"Did Mom tell you?" I ask as soon as I see him.

"Tell me what?" he says, taking a sip of his coffee.

"That I did it. I passed English!"

"Yes, yes, she did mention that." I wait for him to say more. When he doesn't, I ask, "How's your Alderson thing going?"

"We're almost done. I'll be glad when it's over," he tells me.

I nod. "Me too." We both eat in silence for a while. "Since I passed, it means I'm still on the A-Team," I say.

Dad looks at me. "Stanford, is that the only reason you wanted to pass English? So you could play basketball?"

I stir my cereal. Well, it was the main reason. Is there something wrong with that? He's waiting for an answer. "I really wanted to make the A-Team. Lots of kids are counting on me. And I wanted to pass so you wouldn't be mad at me anymore."

"You think I was mad at you?"

"I know you were."

He sighs. "Okay, maybe I was upset, but for good reason. Your teachers always say the same thing about you: 'Stanford could do better if he tries.' And Stanford, let's face it, you don't try very hard in school. If you put half the effort into your schoolwork that you put into basketball, you'd be at the head of your class."

"Well, grades aren't that important," I tell him.

"Really now?"

"Yeah, not for what I'm going to be when I grow up."

"And what's that, Stanford?"

"I'm going to be myself, only older."

"Ha-ha, very funny," my father snorts. "You need to get good grades. This is not some sort of a joke. In this family we don't flunk."

"Then maybe I don't belong in this family."

Dad looks at his watch. "I don't have time for this," he mutters as he grabs his briefcase. Before I can say anything else, the door slams shut.

AUGUST 31, 2:44 P.M.

It's Fiesta time! The Rancho Rosetta Labor Day Fiesta always marks the end of summer at Wild Acres Amusement Park. I've gone to the Fiesta as long as I can remember. I used to go with my parents, but now I go with the Roadrunners. Only a dork would go with his parents.

I meet Gus at the park. We'll hook up with the rest of the Roadrunners at Wild Acres, but first we've got to find some really good sticks, the kind that are smooth, with some give but not too much. Never underestimate the importance of a good stick.

After sword-fighting invisible enemies for a couple blocks, I tell Gus, "You know, my dad asked me if the only reason I wanted to pass English was to play basketball."

"Was it?"

"At first I thought it was all about making the A-Team. Then I kept thinking about it, and finally figured that I wanted to pass to prove to myself that I could."

"I know what you mean," Gus says. "I didn't want to be known as the guy who flunked science. Plus, my father offered me fifty dollars if I passed."

"You got *paid*?"

"Yeah," he admits. "Don't tell my dad this, but I would have tried to pass even if he didn't bribe me."

From far away we can see Monstroso, the big roller coaster. The music and noise of the Fiesta pull us toward it. We drop our sticks and run inside to look for the rest of the Roadrunners.

It is hard to find anyone, it is so crowded. I like being in a crowd. No one expects anything of me here. I wonder if Emily is at the Fiesta. I hope so. I have some things I need to say to her.

As Gus and I head to the stage we can hear music playing. Maybe I'll start a band. All the guys will be in it, and of course it will be called The Rockin' Roadrunners. It doesn't matter that none of us can play a musical instrument or sing. Just to be in a band automatically raises your cool factor by 5,000 percent.

Gus points to Stretch, Digger, and Tico waving. Only they're not waving to us, they're waving to someone else. We inch closer. It is wall-to-wall people. At last, I can see who all the guys are waving to. Oh no, oh no . . . I can't believe it! Emily is waving back to them, and Millicent is right behind her.

Hey, if Emily's not mad at Millie anymore, maybe she's not mad at me either!

Gus starts pushing through the crowd. "Meet you there," I tell him. I don't want Emily to see me just yet. I'm not sure I'm ready to face her. What's she doing waving at the guys? Is Digger hitting on her? He's smiling at Emily! Digger better stay away from her!

The band on the stage is full of old guys playing some loopy love song. Emily and Digger are talking. He's such a scumbag, I'll bet he's telling her a bunch of lies about how great he is. I wonder if Millie and Digger recognize each other. I hope not. It's been about five years since Millie made the salt bomb explode all over him and got herself expelled from elementary school.

Uh-oh. Now I see Digger saying something to Millicent. What if he's figured out who she is? Wait . . . I don't believe it! Digger is taking Millie's hand and leading her to the dance floor. Millicent looks like she is in severe pain.

Digger and Millie are now dancing, or at least trying to dance. Millicent is even dorkier on the dance floor than she is on the volleyball court. Emily's smiling at them. It looks like Digger is whispering into Millie's ear. Either he's forgiven her or he really has no clue who she is. I move even closer and find myself standing next to Emily.

Suddenly Millie's briefcase drops to the floor. Millicent shouts, "Get away from me!" and shoves Digger. The couples around them stop dancing and stare.

Digger's face takes on that look he has before he explodes. "You're still just a little nerd," he announces, loud enough to be heard over the music. "You lost me ten bucks!"

Millicent looks totally panicked. I wonder if she's going to pass out.

I turn to the guys. They all have their hands in their pockets and won't look up. I spot Marley on the sidelines taking notes in his captain's logbook. Millicent's mother is holding on to her father; they look horrified. Emily sees me and starts to say something, but I don't stay long enough to listen.

"Hold this," I say, handing her my basketball.

I head to the dance floor. Millicent sees me and turns pale. She squeezes her eyes shut and covers her face.

"Hey, Stan-dude!" Digger says, suddenly smiling. He holds

up his hand to give me a high five. With everything that's happened, he still acts like we're best friends. "What's up?"

"That's what I wanted to ask you," I say, keeping my arms crossed.

Millie peeks through her fingers.

"I just lost me ten big bucks because this geek-a-zoid here can't dance," Digger explains, pointing to Millie. "I bet the guys I could get through a whole dance with Miss Smarty-Pants."

Millicent looks at me. I can tell she's scared. To both our surprise, I hold out my hand to her. She hesitates and I am afraid she is going to start crying.

"It's okay, Millicent," I assure her. "It's okay."

Her body slumps. She takes my hand and I give it a small squeeze to let her know I am on her side.

I turn to Digger. "Get lost, loser. Millie knows how to dance, she just doesn't want to dance with you."

Digger looks shocked. "Hey, Stan the Man, can't you take a joke? It's just that I made a bet and this nerdball —"

"And nothing," I cut him off.

Digger's eyes narrow. "You'll be sorry," he hisses before disappearing among the dancers.

Without looking at Millie, I put my other hand on her waist and whisper, "Even if you don't know how to dance, pretend you do."

I am glad that my mother made Sarah teach me how to dance. As Millie and I march around the dance floor, we both pretend we're not stomping on each other's toes. Finally she looks right at me and says, "Thank you."

"You're welcome," I reply, adding, "and thank you. In case you haven't heard, I passed my class."

Millie gives me a genuine smile. I guess she really is on my team.

It is not totally awful dancing with Millicent Min, though I'd much rather be dancing with Emily. Just as we are getting the hang of it, Mr. Min cuts in. "May I have this dance?"

As Millicent dances with her father, I approach Emily. She keeps looking up at the sky. My guts feel like they are going to burst, but there's something I have to do.

"Emily?"

"Oh hi!" she says, like she didn't know I was there. My heart skips a beat when she looks at me.

"I need to talk to you." I hope she will forgive me. Even if she does not want to *like* like me, I still hope she will like me. Emily is a person worth knowing. "I lied about tutoring Millicent. It was the other way around."

"Millie explained everything," Emily says.

"She did?"

Emily nods.

"And you're okay with it?"

"I will be."

"I tried calling you a couple times," I confess.

Emily bursts out laughing. "I know. We have caller ID."

Oh man, I could just die, until Emily touches my arm and says, "It's okay, Stanford. I thought it was sweet that you kept calling. The only thing sweeter would have been if you actually said something."

"Uh, like what?"

"Gosh, I don't know. How about, 'Emily, I'm sorry'?"

"Emily, I'm sorry."

"Nope, too late!"

I am about to die when she slugs me in the arm and laughs. "Just kidding!"

Wow, I think she *like* likes me!

I know I should probably ask Emily to dance, but my legs are all rubbery, like when we first met. Good thing she seems content just to stand next to me as we watch the other couples glide past us. Maybe I should hold her hand. But what if she jerks her hand away? What if my hand gets all sweaty? Do people ever use antiperspirant on their hands?

I glance at the guys. They are making kissy faces and pretending to swoon. I decide not to hold Emily's hand for now. It is far too dangerous.

Emily leans in to me to tell me something. "I like your hair," she says. "Especially the purple."

Millie is now standing on her father's feet as he leaps around the dance floor. I wish my parents were here dancing together. That would make Mom happy. There's a picture on the fireplace mantel of my parents waltzing at their wedding. One time I caught Mom dancing around the room holding the photo. She's weird like that when she thinks no one's watching.

After the song ends, I go with Emily, Millie, and her parents to Monstroso, the giant roller coaster. Mrs. Min refuses to join us, claiming she's had too much bratwurst. That doesn't stop Mr. Min. I wonder if Millicent knows how lucky she is to have a dad who likes roller coasters.

On our fifth trip on Monstroso, Millie sits with her dad and

I sit with Emily. While Millie looks like she's trying to get the nerve to hold her hands up in the air, I've got my hands up, trying to get the nerve to put my arm around Emily's shoulder. Neither of us succeeds.

Millie wants to go on Monstroso one last time, but I'm afraid that if I do I'll vomit. "Pass," I say without explanation.

Mr. Min nods in agreement.

Emily speaks for us. "If I go on that thing again I'm going to barf. You go ahead, though."

Millie is the lone rider on Monstroso. Instead of screaming, she's got a wild look on her face as she grins and holds her hands high in the air. I would have never pegged her as a roller-coaster person. Then again, if someone had told me at the beginning of summer I'd be asking Millicent Min to dance with me, I would have said they were crazy.

It's starting to get dark. We are making our way from the food area to the games. Millicent's leading the way as Emily and I follow. Emily likes to talk, and I like to listen to Emily talk, so we make a pretty good pair. Suddenly the conversation shifts from basketball to books to brains, and Emily asks, "So you thought I only liked you because you were smart?"

I gag on my all-time favorite food — peanut brittle.

"Exactly how shallow do you think I am?"

I feel myself turning bright red. Then I notice that Emily's eyes are sparkling and she's grinning. Phew!

"I don't think you are shallow at all," I tell her as I pop a big piece of peanut brittle in my mouth. Millicent is trying to figure out the odds on the coin-toss game. "It's just that, well, I thought that, um, I figured that since you thought I was so smart, you'd hate me if you found out I was dumb."

"Are you dumb?"

I stop munching. My mouth is full, but still I manage to sputter, "I'm not exactly what you'd call an A student."

"Just because you're not an A student doesn't mean you're dumb," Emily muses as she takes the bag from me, digging in to find a piece that's not crushed.

"Right!" I agree. "I'm not dumb. I mean, I do dumb things sometimes, but I'm not dumb. You can ask Mr. Glick — I passed his class and he's the toughest teacher at Rancho Rosetta. Plus, Coach Martin says you have to be smart to be a good basketball player."

"Stanford." Emily moves closer and tugs on my shirt, sending life-altering shock waves through me. "I think we are being followed."

I turn around to see Tico, Gus, and Stretch tailing us as we make our way through the Fiesta. They try not to be obvious, but you can't miss Stretch, even when he slouches.

"It's cool," I assure her. "Those are my friends."

Suddenly Digger joins the other Roadrunners. This can't be good.

"Excuse me, Emily," I say. She rushes over to Millie and whispers in her ear, then the both of them disappear.

Though I have not been summoned, I join the guys.

"Pardon me," Digger says dramatically. "I have a small announcement to make."

Okay, this is it. My jaw tightens.

"Our boy Stanford Wong has lied to you all summer," he says smugly. My stomach drops to the floor. "He wasn't working for his dad and he didn't get an A in Glick's class. Instead he flunked it and had to go to summer school. He's a liar, that's what he really is. What do you think of your Boy Scout basketball player now?"

There is silence, except for the shrieks escaping from the House of Horrors. Then, out of nowhere, a deep voice says, "Zip it up, Digger."

We all look around but don't see anyone but us. "Leave him alone," the voice says again. Tico, Gus, Digger, and I stare in disbelief.

Stretch has spoken.

He sounds like a man. The last time we heard him speak he sounded like a girly frog. He looks uncomfortable. "What?" he asks. It's almost creepy to hear him talk. It's like we're in one of those Japanese monster movies where the people's mouths are moving, but the voices don't match.

"You spoke!" I say.

"Big deal."

"Why haven't you said anything before?" asks Tico. "Did you have a spell on you or something?"

"I didn't have anything to say," Stretch answers. I can tell he doesn't want to talk about this.

"Makes sense," Tico says. He turns to me. "Hey, Stanford, did you pass your class?"

I nod. "I didn't go to basketball camp, but I'm going to seventh grade."

Gus stands next to me. "I passed science. I had to go to summer school too."

Digger fidgets. "Stanford lied to us. He took us for idiots and he *lied*, pretending he got an A in Glick's class when really he got an F. If he didn't pass he wouldn't have made the A-Team."

"Wow, that would have been a bummer," says Tico.

"But he did pass," Stretch adds.

Digger is turning more and more red. "You guys are all losers," he mutters. "This is about honor and the code of the Roadrunners to always tell the truth!"

"Yeah, well, you're a liar too then," Gus tells him. "Stanford told me the only reason you got so many points off of him this summer is because you blackmailed him!"

Stretch's and Tico's jaws hang open.

"I'm out of here!" Digger shouts.

No one tries to stop him.

"I'm sorry I lied to you," I say to the guys. I really mean it.

"Why did you do it?" Tico looks hurt. "Both of you had to repeat a class?"

"Flunking's not the sort of thing you broadcast all over town," Gus mumbles.

"I can't think of anything more embarrassing," Stretch contributes to the conversation. "Except maybe sounding like some sort of old woman and being laughed at all the time."

"Well, it is pretty bad," Tico says thoughtfully. "If I ever flunked a class, I'd be so upset, I'd probably drop out of school. I'd probably have plastic surgery to change my face, and then I'd kill myself —"

"Shut. Up," Gus tells him.

"I figured if I flunked summer school, I'd be off the A-Team, and then I'd be out of the Roadrunners too," I say quietly.

Gus looks serious. "Really? You thought that? Why?"

"I dunno." I shrug. "Just something I thought."

"Wait here," he orders as he huddles with Tico and Stretch.

I wander over to the Goldfish Ping-Pong Ball Toss. I feel like the fish just swimming around in circles. What are the guys talking about? About me, I'm sure. But Gus also lied about going to summer school. What are they saying?

Finally they break and come toward me. I meet them halfway. No one is smiling. Gus begins, "We've decided that even though you still are on the A-Team, we're going to kick you out of the Roadrunners."

"But why?" I plead.

"Because you let Digger beat you at basketball," Stretch says.

"Because you never really worked for your dad," Gus adds. "At least I really did mow lawns."

Tico steps up. "And because we are all tired of purple," he says, looking grim. "It's not good for our hair. I'm getting split ends."

"Aw man. . . ." I kick the ground really hard.

"Got you!" Gus shouts. Tico and Stretch break out laughing. "We got you good!" Gus sings. "Of course you're still a Roadrunner. You're such an idiot, you fell for it!"

"You jerks!" I yell. I am soooo relieved. "You are all so lame." I jump on Gus and try to choke him. "You're all wusses!" It is so great to be a Roadrunner. Suddenly I remember something important. "I gotta go. Emily's waiting."

"Emily's Stanford's *girlfriend*," Stretch informs the guys.

They all start snickering. "Go!" orders Gus. "Go before she gets smart and dumps you!"

As I run away I can hear the guys shouting, "Emily! Oooooooh, Emily, Emily, *Emily* . . ."

6:27 P.M.

Emily looks thrilled to see me, and the feeling is mutual. With Millicent tagging along, we circle the games for a while, stopping at the B-Ball Bushel Throw. The man hands me a basketball, but I tell him, "I brought my own."

I get off to a slow start before sinking eight in a row and winning a prize.

"Hey, Emily, do you want this?" I hold up a stuffed orange elephant wearing a blue bow.

"Do you want me to have it?" Emily asks.

"I want you to have it, if you want to have it," I tell her.

"Well," Emily says, "if you really want me to —"

"Just take the stupid elephant!" Millicent yells. She grabs the elephant out of my hands and practically whacks Emily over the head with it.

Emily gives the elephant a hug. "Thank you, Stanford," she says softly.

Life doesn't get much better than this.

The three of us walk toward the exit, where Millicent's parents are waiting. I slow down and so does Emily. Millie looks over at us. We are going so slowly we're practically walking in place. "I'm going to talk to my mom and dad," Millie finally says with a sigh. "Emily, meet you there."

We both smile at her as Millicent walks away shaking her head.

For a while Emily and I just stand still and stare at each other. I don't know what to say, but I don't care. I wish this night would never end.

Finally she speaks. "I've got my volleyball awards ceremony on Sunday. Not that Millie and I are going to win anything. But maybe you could come?"

"Sure!" I answer too quickly. I pace myself. "Yeah, okay. Sure, I'll check my calendar, but I can probably make it."

"I should warn you," Emily cautions, "my mom will be there, and we'll be with Millicent's family. I hope you understand if I don't sit with you."

"I totally understand," I assure her. "I mean, if we are ever talking and one of my parents shows up, I probably won't introduce you. Not that I am ashamed of you, because I'm not, I swear! But because my parents would probably do something to totally embarrass both of us."

"I know *exactly* what you're talking about," Emily says, nodding.

Right on cue, Mr. and Mrs. Min start waltzing in public. "Come on, Emily!" Millicent shouts in a panic. "Hurry!"

"Coming!" Emily shouts back. "Call me, okay, Stanford?" she says as she runs toward Millicent. Then she turns around and yells, "And this time, don't hang up!"

Like there's any way I'd ever do that again.

SEPTEMBER 1, 10:10 A.M.

Now that summer school is ancient history, I have the whole day free. I head to the park. Stretch meets me halfway. "Hey, Mr. A-Team!" he calls out. I will never get used to his voice. He makes the rest of us sound like Minnie Mouse.

We walk a while, then he asks, "What's it like being so good at basketball?"

Do I tell him about my green jade pendant? Finally I say, "It feels pretty great. But you're not so bad at basketball yourself."

"No, I'm just tall." He doesn't sound too happy about this.

We walk some more and then I ask, "What's it like being so tall? I mean, you've got to know that you don't look like a regular kid, right?"

Stretch stops and looks all serious. "It's weird. Remember how short I was?" I nod. "Then one day it's like I wake up and I'm some sort of giant freak. I can't even do things without my arms or legs getting in the way."

"It'll all work out," I assure him. Before I have a chance to explain that any of the guys would cut off their noses to look like him, Gus comes barreling toward us.

"Stanford's got a girlfriend, Stanford's got a girlfriend!"

"I do not," I answer proudly.

"What's her story?" Gus asks.

"She's a new girl," I tell them. They nod. New kids are always more interesting than old ones, especially new girls. New girls haven't had the chance to hear how horrible we are.

"Hey, dudes!" someone yells from across the park. It's Tico. "Where's Digger?" he asks.

That's what I've been wondering. Digger will probably beat me up the next time he sees me.

"He's probably constipated." Gus laughs.

"Digger's too embarrassed to show up here," Stretch declares. Huh?

"Yeah, Stanford really showed him who's boss," Tico chimes in. "Digger was set on humiliating that girl, but what did she ever do to him?"

I don't say anything. These guys didn't see Millicent foam Digger when they were little. Not that he didn't deserve it.

"If you guys were so concerned about her, then why did you encourage him?" I ask.

"Digger just bet us he could dance a whole dance with a girl, that's all," says Gus.

"Besides, she's sort of cute," Tico adds.

I start to explain to Tico that she's not cute, she's Millicent, but then Digger shows up. We all stop talking at once. Without even acknowledging the other guys, Digger launches straight into his speech.

"Stanford, a long time ago when you were a nobody, I offered you a spot on the Roadrunners. Now, I'm taking it back. What do you think of that?"

I don't know what to say. I'm not a Roadrunner anymore?

Stretch speaks up. "If Stanford's not a Roadrunner, then neither am I."

There's a lump in my throat.

"Me too," says Tico.

My lump's getting bigger.

We all look at Gus. He plants himself right in front of Digger. "Heck, I shoulda quit a long time ago!"

Oh man, I hope I don't start bawling.

Digger's face is twitching and he's breathing hard but doesn't say anything as we all stare at him. "Fine!" he yells. "I don't need any of you guys. I'll start a new Roadrunners team. Who needs you creeps?"

As Digger storms off, Gus yells after him, "Hey! You owe us ten dollars. You never did finish dancing with that girl!"

I turn to the guys. "Thanks," I say. I want to say so much more. Instead I tell them, "Guess that means no more Lakers games."

"Or RV rides," Tico says.

"Or Roadrunners jerseys," adds Stretch.

"Or Digger to have to put up with," Gus reminds us.

Stretch tosses the ball to me. "Let's play!"

I wonder if I should tell the guys that Millicent was my tutor. I decide not to. Not yet. There's been too much confessing going on lately. Today the world is back the way it should be, just me and my friends shooting hoops in the park. Even though we may no longer be Roadrunners, we're still on the same team.

2 P.M.

The volleyball awards ceremony is two hours away. I've got to look good for Emily. I put so much gel in my hair that my head looks like a big giant slimeball. Now I have to wash it out and start all over again.

To be safe, I use deodorant (three times) and think about shaving. Not that I need to shave, but at least I think about it. Stretch says that he shaves and hates it. I look at my skin. No sign of whiskers anywhere, although I do have a small group of pimples on my forehead. When I examined them in Sarah's magnifying mirror they looked like mountains. I try to mask the zits with Sarah's tinted pimple cream, only it looks like I am wearing makeup, so I wash it off. I could wear a baseball cap, only that would hide my hair and I have finally gotten it to look just right. The little swoop in the front looks great, just like Alan Scott's hairstyle, only purple.

Before I leave the bathroom, I brush my teeth and gargle with mouthwash twice. I breathe into my hand to make sure I don't have bad breath. Smells good to me.

I change clothes several times. I want to look nice, but not look like I planned what to wear. It takes me forty-five minutes to try on every T-shirt I own, ending up with the Alan Scott shirt Stretch gave me. As I switch from jeans to shorts, I notice that my kneecaps look funny. Is it just me, or do everyone's kneecaps look like that? I change back to jeans and then go into the bathroom to redo my hair.

I get to Emily's gym early and sit high in the bleachers so I can see her when she arrives. There's a big banner that reads

I reposition myself several times, trying to look casual. Finally I lean forward with my elbows on my knees and my chin resting on one hand. Oh yeah, that looks cool.

I keep looking around for Emily. Then I spot Maddie, which must mean Millie is here, and if Millie is here, then Emily is too. There she is! I sit up and wave frantically at Emily. Millicent and her parents wave back. Emily turns red and smiles at me.

A woman in the stands calls out to Emily. That must be her mother. She looks like a nice woman, a regular mom-ish kind of woman.

The awards ceremony is boring until Emily wins the Team Spirit award. Emily's mom starts crying at the same time I stand up and whistle and applaud. A bunch of girls look at me, so I quickly sit down. Some of them whisper to each other, then wave to me. I wave back. Why do girls always whisper when I am around?

After blah, blah, blah, the coach goes on and on, and Millicent wins the Most Improved Player award. She starts bawling and then her father starts crying. Guess I'm not the only one with weird parents.

After the ceremony Mr. Min yells, "Group hug!" They all glom together in what looks like a big football huddle, except for Millie, who eventually gets pulled in by Emily.

Just as I am about to take off, I hear Maddie call out, "Stanford Wong, is that you?"

She doesn't act surprised that I am here. Instead she grabs my hand and says, "Well, I'm off to London. I've been by to visit Yin-Yin. Tell her that I will give my regards to the queen for her."

Before she leaves, Maddie turns my hand over. She studies my palm, then notes, "I see good things in your future." I want to ask her what they are, but she's already back talking to Millie.

Emily breaks away. "Oh, Stanford, you're here! Did you see? Millie won an award and so did I! Neither one of us has ever won anything for sports before, so this is kind of like a miracle."

I am tempted to tell her that I have lots of basketball trophies, but instead I just listen.

"This is a great day and a sad day because Maddie is leaving," she explains in a rush. "Have you ever been happy and sad at the same time? You look nice. Well, I'd better get back before someone notices I'm gone."

I love talking to Emily Ebers.

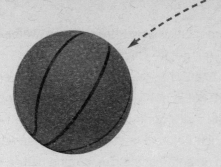

SEPTEMBER 2, 9:45 A.M.

Last night I called Millicent and asked her to meet me in front of the library. She's already there by the time I arrive. Millie's all sad about Maddie moving to London. I know how she feels. Even though Yin-Yin is only at Vacation Village, sometimes it seems like she is on the other side of the world.

To cheer Millie up, I do my best monkey imitation. It does not make Millicent smile. In fact, it makes things worse. Then I remember why we are here. My mom says I owe it to Millie to give her a proper thank-you for helping me with English.

"I have something for you."

For a moment Millicent looks curious. I take out a copy of my book report. It's laminated. "You can keep it," I assure her.

HOLES, a Book Report by Stanford A. Wong

HOLES is a book written by an author named Louis Sachar. The *protegonist* is named Stanley and he gets in big trouble for steeling shoes and gets sent to a crummy camp called Camp

GreenLake where there is no water. Ha-ha, no water, get it? This is called *irony*.

Stanly has to dig holes over and over again and he does not like this except he loses weight and that's good for him because he weighed too much before. He changes in other ways too and so do some of the kids around him.

Stanley meets a boy named Zero (more *irony*) and they run away. Well, Zero runs away and Stanley goes to find him even though everyone else says he is dead. The other boys just keep digging and digging and digging because that's what they are told to do. But Stanley starts "digging" for the truth.

Stanly finds his friend and learns that Zero really stole the shoes, but he is not a bad guy.

Stanley fears there is a curse on his family and because of the curse he is doomed for life. But he learns that he can change the way his life is going. He also learns that true friends and an interesting beverage can be *MORE POWERFUL* than a curse.

As the story goes on, Stanley learns a lot of lessons. This book has a story within a story. One story is about Stanley and another story is told through *flashbacks.* The *flashbacks* end up being about Stanley and Zero's families.

Meanwhile, Stanley's family *NEVER* stops believing in him. They hire a good lawyer. In the end Standley learns that he is a good person and that even at a dentation camp you can find good if you look hard enough. And it ends happily when Zero, who has no family, becomes part of Stanley's family.

I think this was a very good book. It was funny and serious and had much suspense. Stanley, the *protangonist*, had a bad time but it turned out great in the end because he never gave up.

Interesting fact: *Stanley* spelled backwards is *Yelnats*. *Stanford* spelled backwards is *Drofnats*. *Glick* spelled backwards is *Kcilg*.

B+

Congratulations, Stanford.
A job well done!!!!!

Millie looks up from the report and says, "Good work!" She tucks it away in her briefcase for safekeeping.

"See, I'm not a complete idiot."

"No, no, you're pretty bright," Millicent agrees, adding, "for a boy."

After the library, I make my way to Vacation Village. On my way there I stop by Salon Ferrante and say hello to Mimi. I give her $3.47 in change and a mint for the desk lady.

Mimi rushes over to me, leaving someone under the dryer. "You look happy, Stanford," she says as she rearranges my hair.

"I am," I tell her. "Did I mention that I passed my summer-school English class and will be on the basketball A-Team?"

"No, I don't think you did," she says. "It makes sense that you're a jock. You look athletic. Plus, you've always got that basketball with you. You must be very proud of yourself."

"Yeah," I tell Mimi, "I guess passing that class did feel pretty great."

"No, I mean making the basketball team."

"Oh!" I say. "That's totally cool too."

"Say, how's that girlfriend of yours?" I show her a picture of Emily and me that we took at the mall photo booth. My eyes are closed in the picture, but Emily looks great. "She's a real cutie," Mimi notes, adding, "but then, so are you. You're a lucky boy, Stanford Wong."

10:51 A.M.

This morning I got up early to be with Dad. I could have slept in, but I wanted to see him. I even made him a toast-and-Pop-Tart sandwich and coffee, though the coffee had grinds floating all over the top.

"Thanks, Stanford, but I don't have time for breakfast. I'll grab something at the office."

"I thought we could talk, you know, just sort of catch up with each other."

"No time. Gotta go! Be good."

"But Dad —"

"Later, Stanford!"

As always, Mr. Thistlewaite is in Yin-Yin's room. "Stanford, my man!" Mr. Thistlewaite bellows. "I was just about to go get this lovely young lady some tapioca pudding! Would you like some? Of course you would! Ramon makes the best pudding!"

As Mr. Thistlewaite goes in search of pudding, I ask Yin-Yin something that has been on my mind for a long time. "Why does he hate me?"

"Mr. Thistlewaite?"

"No, my dad."

Yin-Yin looks wounded. "Stanford, your father does not hate you." She stares at the tree outside her window. Someone has hung her birdhouses on the branches and the birds are flying in and out of them.

"I have a secret, Stanford," Yin-Yin whispers, bringing her finger to her lips. "Would you like to hear it?"

I nod slowly. But do I really want to hear this? I wonder.

"Even as a little boy, your father was always seeking approval from his father," my grandmother says. "Your grandfather never went to college. He barely graduated from high school. Your dad went to Stanford University on a scholarship and graduated with honors. He was expecting his father to tell him how proud he was. Instead, your grandfather said, 'So now you think you are better than me?'"

"Are you trying to tell me that my grandfather was rotten?"

"Stanford, your grandfather loved his family in his own way. He thought that working hard and providing for us was enough. He wasn't one to show emotions. Sometimes your father is very much like him."

"Then why did Mom marry him?"

"Before your father got his big serious job, he was a little more relaxed. But, as time has gone on, I have seen him retreat from the family and get buried under his work. It's what he knows."

"He knows Sarah," I mutter.

"Yes, well, your sister gets great grades and your father admires that. But you, my boy, you probably scare him."

"Me?"

My grandmother speaks slowly. "While Sarah is gifted in academics, you are gifted in sports. Your father used to be made fun of on the playground. He was never much of an athlete."

"Why didn't you give him a green jade pendant, like mine?"

Yin-Yin looks at me curiously. "Do you still have that?" I take it out from under my shirt and show her. "I bought that in Chinatown," she says. "It was on sale. I got a good deal."

"You told me you got it in China," I stammer. "You said that a mystic priest gave it to you!"

She looks right at me. "I made up that story because you were so sad. It seemed to cheer you up. I like to tell stories to make people happy."

"So you were lying to me about the powers?"

"Did you play better when you were wearing it?"

"Well, yes, but —"

"Then it did have powers. It had the power to make you believe in yourself. Now that you've proved yourself on the basketball court, you no longer need the pendant."

Oh man, my head is spinning.

Yin-Yin looks out at the birds. "Stanford, you have always had the ability to play basketball. What you lacked was the confidence. The same with passing English. You had it in you, but it took someone like Millicent Min to help get it out of you. As for your father, he truly does love you. He just doesn't know how to tell you that. Stanford, he could really use your help."

Just then the door bursts open. "Pudding! I've got pudding!" Mr. Thistlewaite yells. "Tapioca or chocolate, take your pick!!!"

"Pudding!" Yin-Yin looks delighted. "I love pudding."

My dad could use my help?

SEPTEMBER 3, 3:57 P.M.

The big Hee-Haw Game is tonight. It's going to be my debut on the Rancho Rosetta Middle School A-Team. The game's not until seven P.M., but Coach wants us there at six P.M., which means I have to eat at five P.M. and be suited up by five-thirty P.M.

I am knitting like mad. Suddenly a bomb goes off. I jump. Oh, it's just the phone.

"Yeah," I say.

"Hi, Stanford! It's Emily." She called me, she called me!

I sit up straight. "Hi, Emily!"

"What are you doing?"

"Just, uh, lifting weights to get ready for the Hee-Haw Game tonight. Are you going to go?"

"Of course, silly! Hey, do you have time to get an ice-cream cone?"

"Sure!" I say. I hope I can eat really fast and get home in time to get ready. "I always eat a big bowl of spaghetti before games," I tell her. "But ice cream and spaghetti is even better. Should I meet you and Millie there?"

"It's just me this time," Emily says.

Oh man!

Even though I run all the way, Emily's at the ice-cream parlor before me. We discuss the different flavors, and when it comes time to pay I joke, "This one's on me, only I have to pay cash since I don't have a credit card."

All of a sudden, Emily bursts out crying. I don't know what to do, so I hand her the napkin dispenser. She shakes her head and runs outside. The ice-cream lady is holding our cones.

"Um, I'll come back for those."

Emily has stopped crying but is doing that gulping-for-air thing.

"Anything wrong?" I ask.

"My dad took away my credit card," she sobs.

"That's okay," I assure her. "I have money, look." I pull a ten-dollar bill from my pocket.

"It's not that," Emily gasps. "It's just that the credit card meant something. It was something that he gave me and it was important because it was from him. My parents are divorced," she says softly. "It's horrible when your parents don't get along. Oh, Stanford, you have no idea."

"I think I do," I mumble.

She starts crying again and hiccupping at the same time. People keep walking by and staring. Some give me evil looks, like I am the one who is making Emily cry. I've got to get her to stop. If she keeps on going like this, I am bound to fall apart too.

"Emily, my grandmother gave me something I'd like to show you." I pull my green jade pendant out.

"It's beautiful," she sniffs.

"It brought me good luck for many years," I tell her as I unclasp it. "Now I want you to have it."

Instantly Emily's tears stop. She blinks several times and her eyes get big. "Really? Oh, Stanford, you would give that to me?"

I put it around her neck. It feels really weird to be that close to her. Her hair smells like watermelon.

Emily touches the pendant. "Now I have two beautiful necklaces from my two best friends," she says, showing me the necklace Millicent gave her and mine. She looks at them for a moment, and then her eyes meet mine.

"Stanford?" Emily says shyly. "Does this mean that you are asking me to be your girlfriend?"

I panic. This might be one of those trick questions, like on Mr. Glick's tests. What is the correct answer?

"Um, uh, do you want to be my girlfriend?"

"I want to, if you want me to be." Emily looks unsure of herself.

I can't breathe. "Then I guess that means yes," I hear myself say.

Emily breaks into a huge grin. She's looking at me like she expects me to do something. I freeze, then reach toward her. She's startled as I take her hand and shake it vigorously.

Then Emily does something I will never forget. She pulls me toward her and gives me a kiss on the cheek.

I could stand here forever. Emily blushes as we smile at each other. Then she punches me in the arm and says, "You'd better go, or your spaghetti will get cold. See you at the game tonight. I'll be the one cheering the loudest for you."

I mumble something that neither of us can understand, turn

around, and walk straight into the wall. As I make my way down the street, I can hear Emily laughing, but I don't care. I was kissed by Emily, Emily Ebers. Emily, my girlfriend.

When I get home, I realize that we forgot to get ice cream.

7 P.M.

Every year the Rancho Rosetta Middle School Basketball A-Team plays in a fund-raising game against the teachers and we all ride donkeys. Yes, donkeys! The Hee-Haw Basketball Game is huge at our school and it even gets on the news.

When my name is called and I run out and jump on my donkey, the crowd cheers, especially the seventh graders. Mr. Glick is on a brown donkey, and Coach Martin rides a gray one. Mine is named Peppy, which is funny because he does not move very fast. I try to steer Peppy out onto the court. He ignores me and wanders near the drinking fountain. Everyone howls.

I met Emily and Millie before the game. Emily was nervous because she is new to the school. Millicent was nervous because she was afraid Digger might show up. I was nervous, well, because of many things.

When Millie went in search of paper towels to wipe off the bleachers, I told Emily, "Don't worry about school. You'll be with me. I'll show you around and make sure you're not alone."

"Oh, Stanford," Emily said, smiling. "You are so great. Look! I'm wearing the necklace. I'm never going to take it off." I felt myself turning red and getting light-headed. I must have been more nervous about the game than I realized.

"And they're off," the announcer cries out as the bell rings. Peppy, my donkey, just does not want to cooperate. Mr. Glick's donkey is doing even worse and makes no attempt to move.

Yin-Yin and Mr. Thistlewaite wave at me. Mom is with them. I can see Millie and Emily in the bleachers. Tico, Stretch, and Gus are there too. They are all rooting for me. I scan the crowd and suddenly Digger comes into focus. He's with Joey and another boy from the C-Team. They are wearing Roadrunners jackets.

Finally Peppy decides to step onto the court. Trevor tosses the ball to me and I make my first basket. The crowd roars. Then Coach has the ball. He throws it to Mr. Glick and it hits him on the shoulder. Mr. Glick may be a great English teacher, but he is a lousy basketball player.

I get the ball a few more times. I don't want to look like a hog, so I pass it to my fellow A-Team players. They are having as many problems with their donkeys as I am. One donkey poops right on the court. Gus looks like he is going to explode, and Tico is practically on the floor laughing. Stretch keeps yelling, "Stan-ford, Stan-ford, Stan-ford!"

It feels great to be on the A-Team, even if I am sitting on a donkey.

I look toward Mom. I don't believe what I see. My father is here? My father is here! My father came to watch me play!

Gimme the ball, gimme the ball, gimme the ball!!! Someone reads my mind and instantly the ball is in my hands. Peppy won't budge, so I take a deep breath and get ready. As Mr. Glick and Coach Martin plod toward me, I execute the most spectacular cross-court shot anyone sitting on a donkey has ever done. *Whoosh!* The crowd goes wild! I did it, and I wasn't even wearing my good-luck charm.

I turn to see Dad's reaction, but he has disappeared. Was he really here, or did I just imagine it?

Game's over. The A-Team beat the teachers. It wasn't even close, but the teachers are good sports and are going to treat us to pizza. I am talking to Emily when my mother, Yin-Yin, and Mr. Thistlewaite suddenly appear. Millicent says hello to all of them and introduces herself to Mr. Thistlewaite.

Emily just stands there, and so do I. It is extremely awkward. Finally Millie says, "Everyone, this is my best friend, Emily Ebers."

"Emily?" my mother says. She gawks at my jade pendant around Emily's neck.

"Emily," Yin-Yin says as if testing out the name. "Emily!"

"Glad to meet you, Emily Ebers!" Mr. Thistlewaite yells. He pats her on the head.

I am dying. Only Millie notices.

"Emily and I have to go now," Millicent informs the grown-ups. "It was wonderful talking with you."

Thank you, thank you, Millie.

"Yes, well, see you around, Stanford," Emily says. She sends me one of her smiles as Mr. Thistlewaite fixes his hair. It was on backward.

As the girls leave, Mr. Thistlewaite bellows, "That Emily of yours is a real cutie and the Millicent girl has impeccable manners!" I am sure the whole gym can hear him.

"Emily," Yin-Yin says softly, so that only I can hear. "A love match." She winks at me. When did she learn to wink? "Don't forget our bet, Stanford!"

"See you at home," Mom says. "Enjoy the pizza."

As Mr. Thistlewaite and Yin-Yin totter toward the exit I ask Mom, "Was Dad here?"

"Yes," she says, smiling. "He had to get back to the office, but that was him. It was no ghost you saw." Mom musses up my hair and gives me a kiss before she leaves. *Awwww, not here!* I hope Emily didn't see that. I spot her and Millie rushing out the back door, and then I see why. Digger and his new Roadrunners are hanging out near the drinking fountain. Emily says that Millie's scared Digger will try to embarrass her again.

"Digger!" I call as I walk toward him. "A minute alone?"

"I'll be right back," he says to the guys. "Then we'll go to Burger Barn. Tonight's on me." He steps over to me, fists clenched.

"Hey," I tell him. "I don't want any trouble. I just want to make a deal with you."

His eyes narrow. "What kind of deal?"

"You leave Millicent Min alone and I won't tell your friends that those times you beat me at basketball were all a setup. It wouldn't look good for it to get around that you had to resort to that, would it?"

Digger looks over at his new crew. Joey waves and calls out, "Great game, Stanford!"

"Thanks, Joey!" I lower my voice as I say to Digger, "I guarantee you Gus, Tico, and Stretch won't tell either."

"What's in this for you? Your fat girlfriend put you up to it? Or maybe Miss Brain is going to help you get through the seventh grade now?"

In a flash I make a fist and swing my arm back.

"Go ahead, hit me," Digger sneers. "I dare you!"

Wouldn't Digger love for me to get in a fight and get suspended from the A-Team? I am still steaming as I slowly unclench my fist. My jaw remains tight.

"No," I spit. "I'm not stupid enough to hit you. You're not worth it."

We stare each other down.

"Digger, let's go!" Joey calls out.

Finally Digger says, "Fine. Okay, Stanford. Deal."

He starts to walk away, but I stop him. "Hey, Digger, one more thing." He faces me. "Remember when we were little and you asked me to join the Roadrunners?" Digger nods. "Well, we're even now. I don't owe you anymore."

Digger struts back toward me. I flex my fingers. He looks over his shoulder. "Listen, Stanford," he says. He looks down as he speaks. I can barely hear him. "My old man was pretty unhappy when you made the A-Team and I didn't. I know the team's already picked for this year and everything. But still, will you put in a good word for me with Coach?" His eyes meet mine. "Coach likes you. Maybe I can be a midseason replacement or something."

I wait for the punch line, but it never comes. For a moment Digger doesn't look so tough. He reminds me of someone. He reminds me of me when I was a nobody.

"Yeah, okay, Digger. Sure, I can do that."

"Thanks, Stanford."

As I head toward the guys I see Marley sitting alone on a top bleacher scribbling something. He notices me and puts down his logbook. Normally I flee whenever Marley is around. But not this time; this time I meet his gaze. Slowly I raise my fist, then open it to give him the Vulcan salute. Marley hesitates before breaking into a smile. He raises his hand and returns my greeting. Before I can say anything to him, my friends mob me.

"Why were you talking to Digger?" Tico asks. "Was he selling Girl Scout cookies or something?"

"Yeah, he's scum," Gus adds.

"We were making a deal," I tell them.

"What kind of deal?" Tico wants to know. "Are you getting an RV?"

"I promised that none of us would mention the blackmail if he'll leave Millicent Min alone. She's the girl who helped me with English. Millie's Emily's best friend, and if it weren't for her I probably wouldn't have passed Glick's class and made it onto the court tonight."

I don't tell them about the other deal I made with Digger. I'll mention him to Coach, but I doubt Digger will be asked to play on the A-Team. Coach says he looks for team players.

"Millicent Min? Isn't she a genius or something?" Stretch says. "Wasn't she on *Jeopardy!* when she was little?"

"I like smart girls," Tico says. "Dumb ones are boring."

"Tico's in love!" shouts Gus.

Tico smacks him on the side of his head. "Take it back! Take it back!" he yells.

As they fight, I tell them, "Gotta go, see you tomorrow."

Stretch gives me five. "Great game," he says.

Tico and Gus both manage to wave good-bye even though Tico is in a headlock.

When I check the bleachers, Marley has disappeared. He's

left his captain's logbook. I pick it up. I'll give it to him next time I see him.

I catch up to Trevor and the other A-Team players in the parking lot. All the guys are in the eighth grade, but they don't hold it against me. Coach Martin tells us that if we can play that well riding donkeys, then we are sure to win the championship once the animals clear the court.

Mr. Glick shows us how to fold a pizza to get more in your mouth at once. He sure is different outside the classroom. But then, he seems so different from when I first met him in English. It's amazing how much a person can change in just one summer.

Hee-haw.

9:58 P.M.

Mom's waiting at home for me. Dad is too.

"You were quite impressive," my father says.

"Thank you," I reply. My heart feels like it's going to burst.

"What's it like to have a whole gym cheering for you?"

"It's the best," I tell him. What I really want to say is, "But it's not half as good as having you be there." Only I don't want to get all mushy. It might scare him.

"I'm sorry I couldn't stay for the whole game," my father says. "But I had to get back to the office and finish up some last-minute things. Tomorrow we find out who gets the promotion."

"Good luck," I tell him. "I'll be cheering for you."

"Thanks," he says, adding, "oh, and here. This is for you. Good night, son."

I wait until I am in my room to open the package. I don't believe it! It's a pair of BK620s!!! I slip them on. They fit perfectly. I jump up and down. It's true! They are the most amazing shoes in the world. They make me feel like I can do anything! I am never, ever going to take them off.

As I am jumping on my bed, there's a knock on the door, then it opens. I freeze with my arms out to the side. My father is standing there. I expect to get reamed out. Instead he tells me, "Stanford, I just wanted to tell you that when I saw you on the court tonight, you made me so proud."

I don't know what to say.

"Well then," he finally comments, sounding awkward. "You can go back to whatever you were doing."

SEPTEMBER 4, 9:45 P.M.

I'm not even tired. Mom wanders in as I'm watching a rerun of *Top Cop.*

"How does Top Cop manage to catch all those criminals by himself?" my mother asks as she sits next to me. I put my head on her shoulder. I have to lean over because I am taller than her. I can remember when my mother used to be able to carry me.

"Top Cop's the best," I explain. "But he's the first to say that he can't do it alone."

Mom turns to me. "Stanny, shouldn't you be getting ready for bed?" She hasn't called me Stanny since I was little. "Seventh grade starts tomorrow, and you have a big day ahead of you."

"When's Dad coming home?"

"I don't know. They are announcing the promotion tonight at some fancy dinner." I nod. "But you, sir," she says, giving me a peck on the cheek. "Off to bed, you!"

Before heading to my room, I stop by the refrigerator and stare at the F on my *Holes* paper. Then I take it down, crumple it up, and score a nice clean shot into the trash can. In the empty spot on the fridge I put up my new *Holes* book report, the one with the B-plus on it.

Instead of going to sleep, I watch the black spider busy in her web. Is it too late to call Emily? I take a chance.

"Emily Ebers, please," I tell her mother.

"May I ask who's calling?"

"Stanford Wong."

"Just a moment." I hear Mrs. Ebers call out, "Emily, phone! It's a boy. Stanford Wong?"

"Mommmm." It sounds like Emily's covering up the mouthpiece. "May I please have some privacy?!!!"

"Okay, but only talk for ten minutes; then you have to get to bed."

"Hi, Stanford!" Emily squeals.

It's so good to talk to her. The minutes fly by. Before we have to hang up, I remember there was something I wanted to ask her. "Hey, Emmie, why do you put money in parking meters?"

"You know about that?"

"I saw you."

"Oh."

Silence.

"It's okay, never mind."

"No, it's all right. I'll tell you. My dad used to get lots of parking tickets. So every now and then I put money in parking meters to help people out. I know it sounds so weird. *Please* don't tell anyone."

It doesn't sound weird. It sounds Emily. The next time I see her I will give her a bag of quarters.

"I won't tell," I promise.

"Emily, it's been way past ten minutes!" I hear her mother say.

"Good night, Stanford."

"Good night, Emily. See you tomorrow."

I wait up until I hear the garage door open and close. I can hear my parents talking. No one is yelling, but voices are raised and lowered.

There is a soft knock on the door. "Come in," I say, expecting my mom.

It is my dad. "Stanford," he says, standing in the doorway so I can only see his silhouette. "Your mom and I have a few things to say to you. Would you mind coming into the living room?"

I jump out of bed. Mom's waiting for us. Her eyes are all red and she is clutching a tissue. My heart stops. This is it. It's divorce after all. I brace myself for the bad news.

"I got the promotion," my father informs me. Hey, this is not so bad. "More money, more prestige —"

"More work," I joke. I am sooooo relieved.

He nods and is silent for a moment. "It also includes a paid relocation to New York."

All of a sudden I can't breathe. New York? We can't move to New York. I just made the A-Team. Mom loves her job. New York? What about Emily? What about Yin-Yin?

"Stanford," my father says. He looks sad. "I turned down the promotion."

What?

"It's career suicide, of course. But your mother and I have been having a lot of talks lately. I had no idea how far away I was getting from the two of you. But when you ran away I realized it didn't matter how well I was doing at work when I was doing a lousy job at home. I also had a nice long talk with Mr. Glick."

Mr. Glick?

"I assured him that I was always telling you to do better in school. And do you know what he told me?" I shake my head. "Mr. Glick said that sometimes the best way to communicate is to listen. Stanford, I'm going to try my best to do less talking and more listening."

I'm speechless.

"Since I won't be working every weekend, maybe we can spend more time together and get to know each other, talk more. And since I turned down the promotion, I'll probably be on the fast track to nowhere, so I'll have a lot of free time and —"

"Rick," my mother stops him.

I'm still trying to sort everything out. "Okay, so then what you are saying is that you turned down the promotion and you're not getting a divorce, right?"

Dad looks at Mom and says, "A divorce is the last thing I'd want."

My mother bursts out crying.

Dad looks helpless. I go up to him and whisper in his ear.

"Are you sure?" he asks.

"Trust me," I tell him.

I turn on the stereo. As I walk to my room, I hear my father ask, "Kristen, may I have this dance?"

11:59 P.M.

I am alone. I can hear my parents in the living room laughing, a sound that I am not used to. I lie in bed and stick my legs in the air so I can admire my BK620s. My brain is on total overload.

I reach for the radio. Lavender is on. I catch her just as she coos, "This one is for Mrs. Wong at Vacation Village from a Mr. Thistlewaite. He wants me to tell her, 'Madame, you have won my heart.'"

Then Lavender plays a song called "Fly Me to the Moon."

I sit up, not believing what I have just heard. I hope my grandmother is listening to Lavender.

As Lavender talks into the night, I slide the blue box out from beneath my bed. I have finally figured out what to do. Slowly at first, then faster and faster, I begin to unravel my Stress Mess. There's the red section from when I first got my F, there's the green when Millicent started tutoring me, and there's the yellow when Digger found out . . .

By the time I am done there is a huge mountain of yarn in the middle of my room. It looks like a disaster, but I can untangle it. Instead of throwing the yarn away, I plan to reuse it. Only this time I'll make something other than a Stress Mess. I'll ask Yin-Yin to show me how to make something I will be proud of.

As I wind the yarn into a ball, I think about my summer and how Dad was so busy working, he probably doesn't know half the stuff that went on. But I'll fill him in. We have a lot to talk about, my father and me.

I will tell him that he was right about Digger, that Digger's not a true friend. I will tell him that Stretch found his voice. I will tell him that Yin-Yin found a boyfriend and that I have a girlfriend and her name is Emily. I will tell him that Millicent Min is not a total geek and that Mr. Glick says I am a smart kid. And then I will tell my father that I love him.

"Dad," I will say. "I know you're bummed out about your job, but you've got me on your team, and Mom and Sarah and Yin-Yin too. Coach says that teammates never let each other down. I just want you to know that I'm here for you."

I have so much to tell my dad.

THIS BOOK WAS EDITED BY CHERYL KLEIN AND ARTHUR LEVINE

AND DESIGNED BY ELIZABETH B. PARISI.

THE TEXT WAS SET IN CENTAUR,

A TYPEFACE DESIGNED BY BRUCE ROGERS IN 1914.

THE DISPLAY TYPE WAS SET IN GOSHEN,

DESIGNED BY CHANK DIESEL IN 1999.

AFTER WORDS™

LISA YEE'S
Stanford Wong Flunks Big-Time

CONTENTS

About the Author

Lisa Yee won the 2004 Sid Fleischman Humor Award for *Millicent Min, Girl Genius*, which was also selected for the IRA/CBC Children's Choice list and nominated for several state prizes. Lisa's daughter Kate inspired her to write about Millicent's nemesis, Stanford Wong: "At the age of eleven, Kate was convinced that all boys were stupid and smelly and had no redeeming qualities," Lisa says. "I wrote this book to show her the other side of the story." Lisa's most recent novel, *So Totally Emily Ebers*, continues the story from a third point of view, that of Emily Ebers. Lisa Yee and her family live in South Pasadena, California.

Visit Lisa Yee's Web sites at http://www.lisayee.com and http://www.myspace.com/lisayeeblog.

Q&A with Lisa Yee

Q: Stanford Wong Flunks Big-Time *retells many of the events from* Millicent Min, Girl Genius, *this time from Stanford's perspective. What inspired you to take this approach?*

A: I really loved Stanford, yet I wasn't interested in writing a sequel. So I thought, hmmmmm . . . I know that people often have VERY different opinions about the same event. I wondered, what if I wrote about the same summer as Millicent Min's story, only from Stanford's point of view? The minute that idea popped into my head, I just knew I had to do it.

Q: *Were you nervous about writing a boy character? What was your process for digging into Stanford's mind?*

A: Strangely, I wasn't nervous at all about writing about Stanford. I was exhilarated. I felt like I knew him, or at least a little about him already. But as I began to round out his character, the depth of his emotions and the loyalty toward his friends and family really surprised me.

It did take some work to make sure his dialogue sounded real. In an early draft, I had all the boys talking like girls, telling each other how they felt — things like that. So I plopped down in the South Pasadena Public Library and watched and listened to the boys as they pretended to study. I took notes. I also observed the boys at my daughter's middle school, at the mall, at friend's houses, etc. It was quite educational!

As for how Stanford felt about his life, that was intuitive. Feelings of insecurity, sadness, elation, and pride, those are universal and everyone can relate to them no matter what age, race, or sex.

Q: *One of your books has focused on volleyball, now one on basketball. Do you have a background in athletics?*
A: Hee hee, hahahaha . . . oops. Sorry. Uh, no. I was on the fencing team in college, and I took a bowling class, and I like to run, but I was never part of any organized sports. (I was on the debate team, does that count?)

I made Stanford a basketball star because I wanted him to be the opposite of Millicent, who abhorred volleyball. Plus, my dad was a basketball star when he was in high school, and he still plays basketball every day.

Part of what makes Stanford who he is, is basketball. He is a team player and someone whose identity is wrapped up in his sport. In order to write about basketball, I went to the basketball courts and watched the guys play. I also read books about basketball to make sure I got everything right. When I wrote the basketball scenes, I closed my eyes and pretended I was playing and then wrote about how it felt to make a basket, or to have people cheer for you.

Q: *Did your parents have high expectations for you growing up? If so, how did you handle them?*
A: Both my parents were teachers, but they never put any pressure on me grade-wise. I did enough of that to myself. I was a classic overachiever, and if I got anything less than an A, I would

freak out. Yes, I was a total geek. Some of my friends had parents who bribed them to get good grades. One time, I asked my mom and dad if they would give me money if I did well in school. They just laughed and said, "We don't need to do that."

Q: *You've said that Mr. Glick's character is based on a real teacher of yours named Mr. Glick. Can you tell us more about him? How did he respond to the homage?*

A: Mr. Glick was my seventh-grade science teacher, and he scared the heebie-jeebies out of me and every student who

Lisa Yee and the real Mr. Glick

ever sat in his class. At the beginning of the year, I just knew he was going to torture us all to death. And at the end of the year, I was sorry to leave. He was, and still is, a dynamic personality. He challenges his students, motivates them, and inspires them. I've spoken to several of Mr. Glick's classes since I became an author, and we've become friends. Imagine that, friends with a teacher! Mr. Glick is thrilled to be featured in the novel, and his wife told me that it capped off his career. (He retired the year *Stanford* came out.) Writing about Mr. Glick is my way of honoring him and the other magnificent teachers I have been lucky enough to have had. When I speak at schools, I always tell students, "Ask your parents if there was one teacher who really stood out when they were kids. I bet there is one, and they can tell you all about him/her."

Q: *What was your biggest challenge in writing* Stanford Wong Flunks Big-Time? *The biggest joy?*
A: Well, I had to make sure the overlapping scenes with Millicent's story were correct. Getting all those dates and times to line up meant I had a giant calendar that I would refer to. But more than that, it was hard for me to write some of Stanford's difficult scenes because I loved him so much. I would sit and type and cry, "I'm sorry to have to do this to you, Stanford!"

The biggest joy was to see Stanford develop as a character. After my daughter read the book, having read *Millicent Min, Girl Genius* first, she said, "Wow, he's not a bad guy after all!"

Q: *How was writing your second novel different from writing your first?*
A: It was so much easier and more enjoyable. Although there were times when I felt a lot of pressure. *Millicent Min, Girl Genius* was very well received and I worried that people might not like *Stanford Wong Flunks Big-Time* as much. Then my mom read the book and said, "It's even better than the first one!" But then, she's my mom and they say stuff like that. I hear from lots of readers and it's pretty much split down the middle with half the kids saying Millicent's story is their favorite, and half saying Stanford's. I wonder what the vote will be when Emily Ebers's book comes out?

Q: *Now that you've completed* So Totally Emily Ebers, *what's your next project?*

A: *So Totally Emily Ebers* rounds out the Millicent–Stanford–Emily trilogy. Up next is something with brand-new characters and settings. It's a novel called *Charm School Dropout*, about a tomboy trapped in a world of beauty queens. Her mother runs a charm school in Florida where girls learn how to be pageant contestants. Feeling like a total outcast, the girl runs away to Hollywood to find her famous father, who doesn't even know she's alive.

To hear more from Lisa Yee, visit her Web sites at http://www.lisayee.com and http://www.myspace.com/lisayeeblog.

Got Game?: Variations on Basketball

Stanford and the Roadrunners play a game called Silent Slam Ball, where all the players sit in a circle and try to pass the ball hard enough to knock the receiving player over. Here are some other fun basketball activities for two or more people.

H-O-R-S-E

Player 1 takes a shot from anywhere on the court. If he makes it, Player 2 must try to make a shot from the same place on the court. If Player 2 makes this shot, then Player 1 gets to take another shot for Player 2 to match; but if Player 2 misses the shot, then Player 2 receives a letter in the word *H-O-R-S-E* (starting with H), and Player 1 takes another shot for Player 2 to match. If Player 1 misses his shot, then the ball passes to Player 2, who can take a shot from anywhere on the court for Player 1 to match. No spot on the court can be used twice. Play continues until one player accumulates all the letters in *H-O-R-S-E*, at which point the player with the fewest letters wins. H-O-R-S-E can be played with any word of the players' choice; common variations are P-I-G for shorter games and D-O-N-K-E-Y for longer games.

Knock-out (or Lightning)

This game requires two basketballs. All the players line up single file at the free-throw line or the three-point line. The first player takes a shot; as soon as the ball leaves his hands, the player behind him can try to make a shot as well. If the first player misses, he rebounds his ball and shoots again until he scores, but if the second player scores before the first player makes his basket, the first player is knocked out. As soon as a player makes his shot, he passes his ball to the next person in line and returns to the end of the line; the next person in line then tries to knock out the player in front of him. The game continues until only one player is left standing and all the others have been knocked out.

21

The goal of 21 is to be the first player to reach 21 points. The shooter takes the ball onto the court; all other players aim to block her shot or steal the ball. If the shooter misses her field goal, she can rebound her shot and shoot again, or any other player can rebound the shot and take it back beyond the three-point line to clear the ball and become the new shooter. If the shooter scores a field goal, then she gets two points and immediately goes to the free-throw line and shoots free throws until she misses. All free throws are worth one point. If the shooter misses a free throw, she is not allowed to rebound the ball, but any other player can rebound it and take it back behind the three-point line to clear the ball and become the shooter. The game ends when any of the players reaches 21 points.

Yin-Yin's Won Tons

Yin-Yin is famous for her fabulous won tons. Here's the recipe she passes on to Ramon (provided to us by Lisa Yee).

Warning: *Hot oil is highly flammable and can spit hot droplets if you're not careful, so be sure to have an adult nearby when you're cooking the vegetables, meat, and won tons.*

Ingredients

1¹/₂ tablespoon minced garlic

4 stalks green onions, finely chopped

1¹/₂ lbs ground pork (you can substitute ground beef or diced chicken)

3¹/₂ tablespoons soy sauce

1¹/₂ tablespoons sugar or honey

1 12-oz. package premade won ton skins

1 egg, beaten

3 cups cooking oil

Instructions

1. Heat a tablespoon of the cooking oil in a large skillet. Add garlic and cook until browned.

2. Add green onions and sauté.

3. Add ground meat and cook until the meat is browned. Drain the oil.

4. In a separate container, mix the soy sauce and the sugar or honey. Pour over the meat and cook. When the meat is done, turn off the burner and set the skillet aside.

5. Lay out the won ton skins in rows.

6. Place one tablespoon of meat in the center of each won ton skin.

7. Dip a pastry brush or the back of a spoon into the beaten egg, then "paint" two adjoining edges of the won ton skins.

8. Fold the skin in half diagonally so it forms a triangle, and press the edges together to be sure they are sealed.

9. Heat the remaining cooking oil in a large pot.

10. Drop won tons into the heated oil and cook until golden brown. Be sure to turn them while they're cooking so they don't get overdone.

11. Drain and let cool.

12. Eat!

Stanford's Reading List

Stanford reads four books and one scary short story in the summer chronicled in *Stanford Wong Flunks Big-Time*. Here's a little more information about these literary works if you'd like to check them out for yourself.

From the Mixed-Up Files of Mrs. Basil E. Frankweiler
by E. L. Konigsburg

What It's About: Tired of her boring suburban life, eleven-year-old Claudia Kincaid runs away to the Metropolitan Museum of Art in New York City, along with her younger brother Jamie (who has money). When she sees a marble angel statue that just might have been carved by Michelangelo, Claudia knows she can't go home until she knows the truth about it.

The First Line: "Claudia knew that she could never pull off the old-fashioned kind of running away."

Stanford Says: "I couldn't even read the title without getting confused. And what's the big deal about a statue? Museums are full of them. Now, if it was a mystery about a NBA basketball that every All-Star signed, THAT would be a classic!"

If you like this, you might also like: The View from Saturday and Jennifer, Hecate, Macbeth, William McKinley, and Me, Elizabeth by E. L. Konigsburg; Chasing Vermeer and The Wright 3 by Blue Balliett

"The Lottery" (short story) by Shirley Jackson

What It's About: A perfectly normal village gathers — and gathers stones — for a mysterious yearly ritual.

The First Line: "The morning of June 27th was clear and sunny, with the fresh warmth of a full-summer day; the flowers were blossoming profusely and the grass was richly green."

Stanford Says: "Remind me never to move to that town."

If you like this, you might also like: "An Occurrence at Owl Creek Bridge" (short story) by Ambrose Bierce; *We Have Always Lived in the Castle* by Shirley Jackson; *Lord of the Flies* by William Golding; *The Giver* by Lois Lowry

Number the Stars by Lois Lowry

What It's About: In 1943, Annemarie Johansen must uncover new levels of bravery within herself to save her best friend from the Nazis, who want to round up all of Denmark's Jews.

The First Line: "I'll race you to the corner, Ellen!"

Stanford Says: "I was sure that maybe parts of this book were fake. But Mr. Glick said that even though the book is fiction, the Nazis really did all those things. It was so wrong."

If you like this, you might also like: When Hitler Stole Pink Rabbit by Judith Kerr; *Hitler Youth* by Susan Campbell Bartoletti; *My Guardian Angel* by Sylvie Weil; *Yellow Star* by Jennifer Roy

Holes by Louis Sachar

What It's About: Unjustly convicted of a crime he didn't commit, overweight thirteen-year-old Stanley Yelnats is sent to "reform" at Camp Green Lake, which is actually a vast desert. The boys at Camp Green Lake have to dig a hole a day — five feet across and five feet deep — under the cold eye of the Warden and her horrible henchmen. But what are they digging for? (Check out Stanford's book report on p. 273.)

The First Line: "There is no lake at Camp Green Lake."

Stanford Says: "At first I thought, 'How stupid. A book about holes? Boring!' But it wasn't just about holes. It was actually exciting and even made me thirsty. Plus, the boys had cool nicknames like Armpit and Squid."

If you like this, you might also like: Small Steps (a companion book) by Louis Sachar; *Danny the Champion of the World* by Roald Dahl; *Harry Potter and the Sorcerer's Stone* by J. K. Rowling

The Outsiders by S. E. Hinton

What It's About: There are two types of people in Ponyboy's small town: "socs," or "socials," who have money and can get away with anything, and "greasers," who live on the wrong side of the tracks and get blamed for everything. Ponyboy has always been proud to be a greaser, along with his fierce friends and his two older brothers. But when his friend Johnny accidentally kills a soc, he must determine where his greatest loyalties lie.

The First Line: "When I stepped out into the bright sunlight from the darkness of the movie house, I had only two things on my mind: Paul Newman and a ride home."

Stanford Says: "Oh man, this is the BEST book. It was so good I read it twice. And I hardly ever even read books once."

If you like this, you might also like: That Was Then, This Is Now by S. E. Hinton; *Fighting Ruben Wolfe* and *Getting the Girl* by Markus Zusak; *Beacon Hill Boys* by Ken Mochizuki

A Sneak Peek at
So Totally Emily Ebers

July 13

Hi Daddy,

Loved the postcard from Cozy Bear Cottages in Bangor, Maine. I showed it to Alice and she just smiled, turned around, and headed to the bathroom. For a while her 2 p.m. crying sessions really bothered me, but I'm getting used to them. It's like when I broke my foot ice-skating. At first it hurt all the time, and then after a while it only hurt when I thought about it.

Hey, here's an idea. Maybe you could send me a letter sometime. It's hard to say much on a postcard. Oh! But don't get me wrong. I love the postcard! The brown bear mascot on the postcard is soooo cute, he reminds me of TB! I showed it to Millie and she thought he looked more like a grizzly bear than a stuffed animal. Shows you how much she knows!

Really, Millicent does have so much to learn. Today at the mall I whispered, "Millie, alert! Nine at two o'clock!"

"It's not two o'clock, it's four fifty-seven p.m."

"Noooo, there's a *nine* at *two o'clock*!"

"Nine what?"

"Millie, don't you know how to rate guys? This home-schooling business has really put a cramp on your social life."

Millicent looked pained and said, "Tell me something I don't know."

"Okay, how about nine stands for how a boy is rated, ten being the best, one, the worst. Two o'clock means that if we were standing in the middle of a giant clock facing the twelve, the boy would be standing on the number two."

"Is this a mathematical word problem?"

"Duh, nooooo. It's a highly sophisticated code for rating boys. You try it. What do you rate the one at nine o'clock?"

Millie examined him for a long time as if he were a science experiment. "A three?" she finally said.

"No, he's definitely a seven, or above. Try the two boys at eleven o'clock."

Millie locked her eyes on them. "A two for the one with brown hair, and a three for the one with the baseball cap."

"No way! I'd give the baseball cap an eight, and the buzz cut is a definite nine!"

After half an hour, Millie still had not rated anyone over a three. As we were scoping out the high school boys at four o'clock, I thought I saw the boy from the drugstore. "Hey! Is that him?"

"Him who?"

"You know."

"No, I don't."

"Yes, you do."

The boy turned and walked past us. Darn! It wasn't him.

"I thought it was the boy from the drugstore," I said. "How would you rate him?"

Millie made a face like something was smelly. "He doesn't even rate at all."

"Millicent! Really, what do you have against him? I'd give him a ten."

"Stanford Wong, a ten?" she croaked.

"Oops, not a ten," I corrected myself. "A twelve!"

"You're nuts," she yelled as she shoved me.

"You're nuts," I laughed as I shoved her back. "Stanford Wong? So he has a name after all! You held out on me! I give Stanford Wong a twelve-plus."

"Plus what? A dreaded disease? A lifetime of bad luck? A wretched odor serious enough to wipe out all humans, their pets, and most of the world's rodents?"

I interrupted Millie's rant. "So how do you know him? What can you tell me about him? Is he in our grade?"

"He's just Maddie's friend's grandson. That's all I know, okay?"

"Stanford Wong is hot! Stanford Wong is off the charts! Stanford Wong is better than the Surfers of Solana Beach! Stanford Wong is —"

"Stop already!" Millie shouted, covering my mouth. "Enough of Stanford Wong! I'm sick of Stanford Wong!"

By the time we made it back to Millie's house, dinner was on the table — spaghetti with homemade sauce. After a game of "Minopoly," Maddie said, "Come along, Emily. Even though you and Millie slaughtered us, I'll still give you a ride home."

"How's your mom doing?" Maddie put on her blinker and made a slow turn around the corner. "The last time you and Millie were over, you said Alice was acting strange."

"She still is. I dunno, she dresses in weird tie-dye clothes and just works on the computer all the time. Alice says she wants to 'go with the flow,' then she gets upset if her files are out of order. She'll act all happy one minute and then sad or angry the next. If it weren't for her mood ring, I'd never know how she feels."

"Sounds like she doesn't know either," Maddie mused. "What about your father? Is he still on the road with the Tacky Boys?"

"The Talky Boys. Yep, he won't come back until after school starts."

"You miss him," she said matter-of-factly.

I was glad it was dark and Maddie couldn't see me. I'm trying so hard not to be a baby, but sometimes it feels like my heart is broken in two, and you and Alice each have one half.

By now this letter journal is pretty long. I can't wait until you read it. It's really weird, but now that we're far apart, I can tell you much more than when we were together. Millie says there's power in the written word. I wish I had the power to make you be here right now.

Love,
Emily